ADRIENNE'S AWAKENING

THE MIND DUOLOGY

BOOK ONE

© 2020 Mindy Schoeneman

Adrienne's Awakening: Book One of The Mind Duology

First edition, March 2020

Sincerely, Me

Sincerely Me LLC
Saint Clair, Missouri
mindyschoeneman.com

Editing: Shayla Raquel, shaylaraquel.com
Cover Design: Annie Hurst, offcenterdesign.co
Cover Photo and Author Photo: Kelly Hayes, joelmarionphoto.com
Cover Model: Dr. Lacey Miller
Interior Formatting: Melinda Martin, melindamartin.me

Copies of the book may be purchased by contacting your local independent bookseller or by contacting info@mindyschoeneman.com.

ISBN (softcover): 978-1-952130-00-7
ISBN (e-book): 978-1-952130-01-4

ADRIENNE'S AWAKENING

THE MIND DUOLOGY

BOOK ONE

MINDY SCHOENEMAN

For you, Mom.

CHAPTER 1

ADRIENNE

"No, I can't get out of it," I say into the phone. "There's no one else to cover. And besides that, I don't want to. This is an opportunity for me to earn a little extra." My phone makes a beeping sound in my ear. I pull it away to see the low-battery indicator. Calvin, my boyfriend of three years, takes advantage of my pause to loudly let me know how he feels about the situation.

I had called to tell him that I'm unexpectedly working until close tonight. One of the cashiers never came back from lunch. *Not that I blame her*, I think as I look across the break room. Working as a cashier at a big-box home improvement store is a less-than-ideal career path. I knew before I called I was in for an argument.

A cough across the room reminds me Parker Holtman is sitting at the table in the center of the break room. He's one of my best friends. He's also the biggest pain in the butt to deal with most days. But I've known him for years, and he's managed to be a good friend. I glance his way, and he rolls his eyes at me and takes another bite of his lunch. Calvin is still talking, his words terse. I raise an eyebrow and return Parker's stare.

Parker's the one who suggested I apply here. Big-box retail wasn't my first choice, but it pays better than many other businesses. The result of getting hired here is that I have a love-hate relationship with my job. As in, I love when my paycheck hits my bank account and I hate every second of every shift. *If only I could make money reading books and mostly ignoring the outside world*, I think with a heavy sigh. But my retail job pays the bills and fits with my class schedule, which counts for something since the schedule changes every single semester. *At least this is my last semester at community college.*

I put the phone back to my ear and listen as Calvin continues to complain because I'm canceling our plans for the second time this week. I can picture him running his hand over his neatly trimmed goatee like he does when he's upset.

"Ever since you moved in with Megan, this is how it's been," he says, obviously agitated. Megan—my tall, willowy goddess of a best friend—needed a roommate, and I jumped at the chance. She's like the sister I never had.

"Do you really want to have another argument about where I live?" He's right, but my canceling has nothing to do with Megan.

"Yes—no!" he says, backpedaling. "My point is that lately, there is always something more important to you than me. I needed you to be there *tonight*," he continues, his voice raising a little.

I was supposed to go to dinner with Calvin, his boss, and the boss's wife tonight. That isn't happening now. Calvin had been talking about it for weeks, making sure I knew this dinner was important to his career. He had even written down a few talking points for me. When he handed me the index card with the talking points, I had laughed and refused to take the card. He couldn't understand what I could possibly find funny about that. I still can't believe he was serious. I had told him I might need to work instead. Today's cashier is not the first to walk out or stop showing up recently. I heard our regional manager nicknamed spring in Missouri the "hundred days of hell" because the number of customers we see in a shift doubles and we sell four times as much seasonal inventory—stuff such as plants and mulch and topsoil and patio furniture and whatever.

"Calvin, if I'm going to go to anything other than community college next fall, I need the hours—"

Click. I pull the phone away from my ear to see the call has ended. Staring at the phone for a moment, I try to let my anger cool before I do something stupid like hurl my phone across the room. I hate being hung up on, and Calvin knows it.

Parker lets out a snort, and I jump. I forgot he was there.

"He hung up on you again," he says, shaking his head. His dark-blond hair is longer than usual and sticking up.

I give Parker my best evil stare, hoping he gets the message that I don't want to talk about it. *How does he know this isn't the first time Calvin's hung up on me?* My evil look seems to backfire because instead of looking apologetic, Parker smirks at me.

I turn off my phone to conserve the remainder of the battery, and sigh. This means I can't read my newest e-book I downloaded to my phone last night. I turn away to put my phone back in my locker, pulling out my lunch while I'm in there.

"He's such a dou—"

"Parker, stop," I say, turning my head to look at him as I close my locker door with a little more force than needed. "I know how you feel about Calvin already." *And I agree with your opinion more often than I'd like to,* I think, recalling again Calvin's adamant protests to my moving in with Megan. Once he realized I was going through with the move despite his objections, he had called my mom in the middle of our next date to try to get her to convince me that it was a bad idea and that Megan is a bad influence. He was so confident she would agree, he had put her on speakerphone. My mom, much to my delight, asked him how he got her number and told him he had better talk to me about it and reminded him I'm a grown-up.

I need to dump him. My stomach feels queasy at the thought. I've never broken up with someone before, but I can't imagine it's a pleasant thing to do. My inner coward is already quaking in her boots at the thought. But I've already put it off for more than a year. I keep thinking he'll break up with me and save me the agony of breaking up with him.

Parker raises an eyebrow while still smirking. "I heard you're having a party next week," he says after a pause.

"It's not really a party," I say quickly. "I prefer to call it a housewarming event." I wonder where he heard that and then decide Megan must have invited him. She probably went through my entire friends list on all my social media profiles and invited everyone who wasn't old or married. Not that I have that many people on my friends list. Not that that will stop her from inviting a bunch of people I don't know.

I plop down in one of the folding chairs at the lunch table, ignoring Parker completely. It's been a long day already, and I have a much longer shift ahead of me. He clears his throat.

"What, Parker?" I ask, not bothering to look at him. I know he still wants to say something more about Calvin. He hasn't liked Calvin since day one.

And he hasn't been shy about letting me know it, either.

I pull a sandwich out of my lunch bag, unwrap it, and take a bite. Parker still hasn't answered me. I glance up at the sound of his chair scraping the concrete floor. He comes around to my side of the table, pulling out the chair next to mine before flipping it around and sitting with the back of the chair in front of him, facing me. He casually rests his arms on it before he noisily scoots it closer until he's near enough that I could poke him in the eye without extending my arm. He scoots one more time, and his left knee bumps into my chair.

"You should blow off the party," Parker says, staring at me, hunched over with his chin in his hand, his elbow resting on the back of the chair as he faces me. At six-foot-three, he looks a bit how I'd imagine a middle schooler would look in a kindergartener's chair—all arms and legs folded up and sprawled out. He's never been one to miss a party. After a lengthy silence and no explanation, I take another bite of my sandwich. "You should come with me instead," he says slowly. He's smirking at me again as if he knows something I don't.

"Megan's throwing the party as a sort of celebration that we're roommates. So it'd be rude to skip it. Besides, it's not really a *party* party." Another bite. More chewing. "Hey, since when do you want to skip a party that's sure to have lots of girls?"

"Lame," he says, smirk gone, eye contact never wavering.

I will not look away first. I will not look away first. I keep his steady gaze, bringing my sandwich up to take another bite. After a few moments, he stands up and backs away swiftly, grinning. He turns his back to me and heads toward the door.

"You'll wish you had come with me instead," he says over his shoulder with a laugh. The door slowly closes behind him.

I'm afraid he might be right.

CHAPTER 2

ADRIENNE

I wipe the steam off the bathroom mirror after my shower. I run my fingers through my blond hair, unknotting the ends. I towel dry and scrunch my hair, one section at a time, encouraging natural waves. Not like I can stop my hair from being wavy, anyway. It does what it wants.

Hair not a hot mess—check.

Next, I should decide whether to keep lingering or hurry up since people are already arriving before my shower. With a deep breath, I dress in my favorite pair of jeans and a long-sleeve, black shirt. Simple, comfortable, and me. I grab my phone from the vanity and check my messages. Calvin messaged me, telling me to have a great night. *That will be all I hear from him tonight*, I think. His texts are usually sporadic when he's out of town for work. I'm sure this trip will be no different, which is okay with me.

My thumb hovers over the screen as I think about replying. I close my eyes and think about our last argument. We rarely seem to be on the same page about anything. I often wonder if this is what loving someone is supposed to be like. I'm not sure since I've never been in love with anyone else. Not that I'm sure I'm *in love* with Calvin, either. I never thought we'd still be together after high school.

I step out of the bathroom and the thump of music permeates the condo. Thankfully, the party seems contained to the lower level. There's no one in the hall, and Megan's bedroom appears empty when I pass by it. When I open my bedroom door, I stop in my tracks as I realize my room is already occupied by someone I don't know. I don't, do I? He kind of looks familiar. He has almost-black, silky-looking hair and light skin. Not a freckle or blemish in sight. He's tall too, his shoulders broad and clearly muscled. Surely I would have remembered meeting him before.

"Uh . . ." I nervously clear my throat. "What are you doing in here?" I ask. "Are you one of Megan's friends?"

"I need to talk to you privately," the stranger says with an easy smile, revealing bright-white teeth. "Your grandma Effie wanted me to deliver a message. This was my best idea. Although, I'm rethinking it."

"Wh-What?" I splutter before my brain can catch up. Now that he's fully facing me, he does look familiar, but I can't place his name or when or where I might have met him. "Who are you?"

"I'm sorry. I should have started with that," he says with a shake of his head. "I'm Sawyer." He sticks out a hand for me to shake. I don't take his hand. He blinks and lets his hand drop after a moment. "Your grandmother would have talked to you herself, but she can't manage the stairs tonight. She's says it's going to rain later." He smiles again.

"Where is she? Is she downstairs? I'll just come down to her." I take a step back.

"Adrienne?" Calvin's voice echoes down the hall. I jerk my head in the direction of his voice.

"I've timed this poorly too," Sawyer says, rubbing the back of his neck.

"Adrienne," Calvin calls, his voice closer this time.

"Timed what?" I ask, shaking my head. "I still don't understand."

"Your grandma's message was meant to be delivered before . . ." He's blushing now. "But it looks like we're out of time." I stare at him, even more confused now. His eyes dart nervously to the doorway.

"Adrienne," Calvin says, nearer to me, but I can't seem to stop staring at Sawyer. "Hey, there you are." He's striding toward me. "Come on downstairs."

I finally look at him. "Calvin, what are you doing here? And actually, I just need a minute to—"

"Come on, we don't have a minute. I have a surprise for you," Calvin says, tugging on my hand to follow him. I glance at Sawyer again, standing in my room just out of Calvin's view. Sawyer shrugs. Calvin tugs on my hand again. "Let's go downstairs so I can show you your surprise."

I reluctantly let Calvin pull me down the hall and to the stairs, stealing a look over my shoulder to see if Sawyer is following us down. But I don't see him.

"Hey." I slow my steps as we reach the top of the stairs. "I thought you were leaving this morning to go meet a potential new client in New York," I say, wondering what he's doing here.

"That's what I wanted you to think," he says with a wide smile. The music that wafts up the stairs toward us is different than it was earlier. It's much quieter and it sounds like something my parents would enjoy. *Sinatra?* I shake my head slowly.

"Why would you want me to think you're out of town when you're not?"

"Just come on," he says, his smile slipping. I blankly stare at him for a moment. His complexion is ruddy, sweat beading on his forehead. He holds out his hand for mine, and I hesitate before placing my fingers in his palm.

Calvin and I descend the stairs. I stare at the party below and watch Megan, who is directing people and funneling them to stand opposite the staircase and down the hall toward the kitchen.

I squint, staring harder as I realize that most of those people are older. Actually, they're my family. My mom and my dad are standing in the doorway to the living room. And my grandma is in the foyer, walking slowly, tightly gripping her cane. Calvin's aunt is standing in the hall, and his Uncle Bob is near the bottom of the stairs. *What is going on?*

Scanning the crowd, I pick out face after face I recognize—coworkers, old friends, and Parker. He isn't hard to spot. No, he's sticking out like a sore thumb all alone in the middle of the couch, gangly arms stretched out along the back. He's the only one sitting down. Everyone else is standing. His expression is hard to make out from here, but I know my friend well enough to see he's tense. A knot forms in my stomach. I wish he'd look up, but he doesn't.

My feet aren't moving any longer. I didn't tell them to stop, but all my concentration is focused on the strange turn of events. What the heck is happening here?

"Adrienne," Calvin says with a squeeze to my hand. I meet his eyes. He's a step below me on the landing, and instead of continuing down, he's stopped too and he's facing me. I'm a couple of inches taller than him from this step, and I feel tall looking at him. He reaches out for both of my hands, and my confusion slowly turns to panic as he kneels down on one knee.

My throat freezes up. No air goes in or out of my lungs. *Get up! Do not do this!* I scream inside my head.

I can't take my eyes off Calvin in front me. I'm silently hoping someone will do something to stop him. Surely I'm not the only one who knows this shouldn't be happening.

The knot in my stomach transforms. It's a writhing, living thing, and it's thrashing its way up the back of my throat. I manage to gulp air and push it down as Calvin releases my hand. My hands are so sweaty. He reaches for something in his pocket, his fingers fumbling as he pulls out a little box. It's black and velvety and a perfect little cube.

Put it back, put it back.

He opens up the velvety box, and I'm mesmerized by the light dancing off the enormous diamond in the center. My heart is hammering in my chest. I want to kneel down and urge Calvin to stand back up, but I can't move.

"Adrienne," he begins, "the day I met you was the best day of my life."

Do not vomit, I command myself, covering my mouth with my hand, my very sweaty, hot hand. A rushing sound whooshes loudly in my ears, and little black spots appear in my vision. *Oh no, I'm going to pass out.* I look down at the crowd again, working hard to focus on the faces below. I don't want to say yes. But I can't humiliate him in front of these people. Or can I? Should I? A strangled breath escapes me, and there's something intense behind it, pushing to get out. Tears sting my eyes.

"We are still young and just starting out in life," he says, and I nod vigorously in agreement, "but I know without a doubt that you and I are meant to be together."

I'm tasting bile again. Calvin looks like he isn't doing much better than I am. He's sweating more now than ever, and his cheeks are brigh-red circles.

"Adrienne, will you marry me?"

The room is silent. Someone shut off the music. I can feel every eye on me as they wait for a response. A flash from someone's phone goes off, shining in my face from below. My hands drop to my sides.

No, I say in my mind. My vision is blurred through unshed tears. My cheeks are hot, and I can feel my neck beginning to flush as well. The swirl of people below me is still waiting for my answer. Another flash.

"Yes," I breathlessly blurt out.

Adrienne

Calvin sweeps me up into a big hug that would have been a big kiss, but I slap my hand back over my mouth as soon as the word *yes* has left my lips. Everyone claps and cheers, and I fight the urge to push the heel of my hand against my chest. There's a pressure there behind my sternum that's building. With each new shouted cheer of congratulations, the pressure in my chest balloons larger, making it feel as if my ribs are being stretched to accommodate a giant ball.

Calvin releases me, and we walk side by side the rest of the way down the steps. I feel numb. One person after another invades my space, each wishing us well and giving Calvin a congratulatory clap on the back.

I study Calvin as another person stops him to shake his hand and offer us both congratulations. *How can you want this?* I think as I stare at the back of his head while he hugs his aunt.

He's twenty-one. He already earned his business degree and he's very proud of his job in sales. Maybe he's figured his life out. I know I haven't, though. Do I want this?

As his aunt wipes tears from her eyes and hugs me, my mind drifts to Calvin's family and I grimace. When we went to have dinner with his parents last month, they were awful to him. They talked about his brothers the entire time. His father flaunted Calvin's accomplishments, instead reminding everyone sitting at the table of what Calvin's brothers had been able to achieve while being husbands and fathers. It was painful to witness. I can't imagine being in Calvin's shoes. I look around and realize his parents aren't here tonight.

Am I an accomplishment for you? Am I on the checklist of things you're marking off to make your parents proud? I watch him smile at another person whose name I can't recall. I look down at our joined hands. The giant diamond ring is digging into my finger.

We reach my parents. My mom's shoulder-length blond hair is impeccable, not a hair out of place, but her eyes are red-rimmed. She delicately swipes at her nose.

"Congratulations, Adrienne, Calvin," Dad says. I open my mouth to speak, but Calvin steps in closer, shaking Dad's hand and leaning in to give my mom a hug.

"Mom, you're about to have another son," he says with his arms around her.

"I'm sorry. I need to use the restroom," she says with a smile as soon as he releases her. She turns and heads toward the bathroom.

Dad gives me a hug, squeezing tighter than usual. "Hey, kid," he says into my hair. I squeeze him back. He holds me out at arm's length, then lets his arms drop to his sides. "Go on, go talk to the rest of these people. I'll still be here later."

"I'd much rather stay right here." I give him a half-hearted smile and move along toward Calvin, who is talking to someone I don't know.

Megan catches my eye with her unmistakably tall, willowy frame as she moves away from me and down the hall. Calvin couldn't have chosen anyone better to help him with this. She is in her element, hustling about. She disappears into the kitchen, reappearing with someone who is holding a beautiful cake. After the cake is settled on a table I hadn't noticed in the living room, she turns and scans the crowd, smiling and waving when she spots me.

"There's plenty of cake," I overhear Megan say. "Help yourself!"

My attention snaps back to Calvin. He's saying something to his uncle, but I haven't been listening until I hear my name.

"—Adrienne will move with me," I hear him say. I turn toward him, brows furrowed, certain I hadn't heard him right.

"What did you just say?" I ask, stepping closer. His uncle looks startled at my question. Calvin gives a short laugh and then shakes his head.

"When will you be leaving?" Uncle Bob asks.

"I need to go as soon as possible to find us a place. It won't be long after that." Calvin ignores me.

What is he talking about? I don't remember anything about moving to Boston. I'm sure I would have remembered *that* conversation.

"Will you excuse us for just a moment?" I smile at Calvin's uncle. He opens his mouth to speak, but I pull Calvin away a few steps. "What are you talking about? You've never mentioned moving to Boston," I say, leaning in so only he can hear me.

He smiles and waves as someone across the room holds up a glass and gives a congratulatory nod.

"If you had gone to the dinner with me and my boss last week, you would know all about Boston," he says with a tight smile that doesn't reach his eyes.

"The promotion is in Boston, and I have to leave immediately."

"And when were you going to tell me about it?"

"I'm telling you now." He leans down so he is eye level with me. "Hey, come on, be excited. This is what we've wanted." He reaches out, placing a hand on both of my shoulders. "This is what I've been working so hard for. All my hard work is finally paying off." He smiles and cups my cheek in his right hand. His hand is soft and smooth and damp. "And it will pay off for both of us. We can start somewhere new together."

Before I can respond, Megan's voice silences the crowd. It looks like Uncle Bob has been recruited to make a toast. I heave a sigh and shake my head as I stop myself from saying anything else to Calvin. *This is what we've wanted,* Calvin had just said. I need everyone to leave.

Someone pushes us forward while someone else holds out a glass to me. I notice it's a champagne flute, and it's filled with a bubbling amber liquid. I take a sniff, relieved it smells like sparkling cider.

"I couldn't be prouder of Calvin than if he were my own son," Uncle Bob begins.

My stomach churns. *I can't do this.* I tune out the toast completely. *I cannot move to Boston—with no notice—and become someone's wife. I can't do this.* I edge away from Calvin, but he turns to me and clinks his glass against mine. *The toast has ended. I'm supposed to take a sip now.* I bring the glass to my lips and force my mouth open enough to take the tiniest of sips. I know I'm supposed to smile and appear happy too, but I don't think I'm doing a good job of that.

"Now come here and get a picture with me and your aunt," Bob continues, motioning Calvin to come stand by him. I slowly step back, hoping to put more distance between us.

"Hey," Megan says from behind me. "I have been dying to put this in your hair since Calvin asked me to make it." A white filmy material touches my arms.

"Whoa, what are you doing?" I ask, knowing it is a veil in her hand. I don't want anything to do with it.

"I thought this would be perfect for photos," she says a little dreamily. I don't have words for that. At least none I can say without possibly hurting Megan's feelings. I take a deep breath and try anyway.

"Megan," I feel a hairpin as she pushes it in, finding my scalp, "I appreciate your thoughtfulness, but I don't want to wear this right now." Her fingers stop tugging on my hair.

"Okay," she says, her brow creased. "Let me pull the pins back out then. Are you feeling okay?"

I don't trust myself to answer her. I'm screaming inside, silently begging for someone—anyone—to make this all stop immediately. I wish she could read my mind. The size of the crowd around me makes the whole condo feel small and closed in, despite the cathedral-height ceilings. I try to control my rapidly increasing breathing, as it feels like the crowd is growing larger and larger with every passing moment.

"Here," Megan says, putting the veil in my hands. I look at the thin, flimsy material, feeling it between my fingers. It's scratchy and rough. "You just let me know when you're ready for it."

Parker, whom I haven't seen since I was rooted in place on the stairs, grabs the veil from my grasp as he steps between Megan and me, his back to me.

"Hey, they need you in the living room," he says and gently pushes Megan on her way, letting the veil fall to the floor as she walks off. I could hug him. But he just keeps standing there, his back to me, his spine straight.

"Thanks," I say quietly.

"Now's your chance to sneak away," he says over his shoulder.

"I shouldn't. I don't want to be rude."

"You should quit waiting for someone else to make it all stop. Go. At least take a minute for yourself."

I press my hand to his shoulder blade. "Thank you, Parker."

Furtively, I look at Calvin around Parker—Calvin is in his own world, talking to another relative, basking in the congratulations—then flee toward the kitchen. I make it there without anyone stopping me, and I silently rejoice that the way is clear to the back door. I take the opportunity to slip out the door onto the deck and down into the yard.

CHAPTER 3

EFFIE

I move as quickly as my old legs will carry me. As soon as *yes* slipped out of Adrienne's mouth, I knew I needed to get out of there. Adrienne and her now-fiancé have just made it down the stairs, and I'm glad to see she hasn't spotted me yet. I can't imagine a scenario in which I don't end up speaking the truth. My Adrienne and I know each other too well for her not to see that I'm hoping for an immediate breakup, not a wedding. And in the midst of this crowd is hardly the place for such a conversation.

Sawyer lopes down the stairs and joins me just as I make it to the door. "I'm sorry," he says with a shake of his head. "He interrupted before I could warn her." He shuts the door behind us.

"That's all right, my boy." I give him a pat. "This isn't over yet. Help me around to the back."

Sawyer sticks out an elbow, and I link my arm through his. He's a sweet boy. I begin to pick my way through the grass and head toward the side of the building.

"I could drive you around instead," he says. His slow and sturdy steps punctuate how frail and feeble my steps are this evening. I don't much like the juxtaposition, so I let go of him and straighten my spine.

"I'm just having a bad day, but I can manage the short distance just fine." I focus on my next step and the one after that while keeping my face as close as I can to looking like every other step doesn't hurt. "Besides, it will be a minute or two before Adrienne makes her escape."

"What makes you so sure she will?"

"Come now, you saw it too. The poor child." I twist my ring, fidgeting. "How everyone else didn't see it is beyond me. As Calvin went down on one knee, Adrienne looked like she had smelled something rotten." I stifle a laugh, remembering the moment I thought for sure my Adrienne was going to get sick all over that arrogant, controlling boy trying to claim her.

"She did look uncomfortable," Sawyer says.

"I have never seen a more closed-off, unobservant, ignorant group of people in my life. All those looky-loos staring at what should have been a private moment between two people in love." I humph and take a moment to breathe. I can feel my blood pressure rising the more I talk about it. Sawyer just gives me his famous look. The one I know is usually followed by the words *Calm down, Effie*. So I try to focus on something else. Anything else. Except everything comes back to my Adrienne. That thought gives me a smile. Everything always has circled back to my darling, hasn't it?

"She's too polite for her own good, but she'll bolt as soon as she can."

We finally make it around to the back of the house. I stop while we're still in the shadows to wait and watch. The yard is short, and just before the grass ends at the alleyway, there is a small concrete bench to the left. We don't have to wait long before Adrienne comes out the back door and into the yard, heading straight for the bench. She plops down, heaves a big sigh, and covers her face with her hands.

I touch Sawyer's arm. He gives me a nod and stays right where he is. I step forward quietly, listening.

Maybe if I sit here long enough, they'll all just go away. That's what my girl is sitting there thinking on what should have been a happy occasion. If he wasn't the wrong boy, it would be. I want to tell her that, but she needs to be ready to hear it first. And I'm not sure she is.

"Not likely, my darling." She starts at my words, her phone and her hands dropping to her lap. "Someone will come looking for you sooner rather than later."

How does she do that? Adrienne is wondering now. She is staring at me, and I can see her thoughts as clearly as a sunrise.

"How do you always do that?" she asks with one of her sweet smiles. "How do you always know what I'm thinking?" I move closer and sit beside her on the little concrete bench.

"Do you remember that time you tried to run away when you were . . . how old were you then?"

"Seven," she says quietly. "I was seven."

"You were so determined you could go out on your own and be just fine," I say, a grin on my face.

"Yes, and you were waiting for me at the bottom of our driveway," she says with a sigh. "You ruined my big plans. How did you know I was going to run away?"

"I knew because you've always been so much like me," I tell the half-truth without hesitation. Little does she know I couldn't have been prouder of her the moment I saw her striding down her driveway, backpack strapped to her, full of purpose and angst. It was exactly what I would have done in her situation.

I was there when she and her mother had butted heads, again, earlier that day. I had watched as Thea did what she always does: ignore what's right in front of her. I didn't need to be a mind reader to figure out what Adrienne was thinking that day. But hearing her thoughts loud and clear didn't hurt, either.

"Watching you grow up has been like watching myself in a mirror." I laugh quietly. "When I think about how I was at the age you are now . . ." I let my sentence trail off as I scan the night sky, remembering. "What sticks out the most to me now as I think back is a feeling of excitement. I was excited about life and where I was going and what I was going to do." Breathing deeply, I savor the night air. It's feeling thicker and it tastes like rain.

"Did you know your grandfather was not the first young man in my life?" I say after a minute. Her eyebrows shoot up. "Before your grandpa, I had a fiancé of sorts." I lean in closer and so does Adrienne. "He was everything I was supposed to want," I whisper to her. "But when I thought about being tied to him for the rest of my life." I shake my head. "I wasn't so excited about life anymore. I could see it the moment he asked, my future all laid out for me." I pause and take another deep breath. "If I had chosen him, I surely would have suffocated."

"What about Grandpa Hank? How did you know you weren't making a mistake when you married him?"

"I didn't. Your grandfather was a good man, but he was sort of a mess when we got together. He had a lot of baggage to work through, and I wasn't so sure he'd be able to. But I had a feeling. A good feeling. So I leaped."

Adrienne picks at her cuticles and chews on the inside of her lip in the silence. I lay my hand on hers, and she stills her fingers. She clears her throat.

"What do you think I should do?" She turns her hands, palms up, in mine.

"I can't answer that one for you. But I do know this: You will find your spot in life, Adrienne." I pat her wrist. "You'll find the thing you were meant to know or be or do, and then you'll discover every other decision will be a little easier to make." She lowers her head, and I think I might see a single tear trail down her cheek. "But you must be patient with yourself. That piece of the puzzle is coming, but it isn't here yet."

She looks more confused now than when she first came out here. I reach out, crooking my index finger under her chin. I kiss her forehead before dropping my finger. "Grandma," she says, and I smile to myself as I hear her question before she even asks it, "did you send someone here to talk to me before the proposal?"

I nod and laugh.

"Why?"

"Because I wanted to warn you before Calvin proposed, to give you a chance to prepare yourself."

"Why didn't you just call me or come see me yourself?"

"Where is the fun in that?" I smile and glance over my shoulder. "Sawyer, come on out here, please." Sawyer steps out of the shadows and walks toward us.

"How do you know him?" Adrienne leans in and asks as Sawyer walks casually our way. He smiles and offers a nod to Adrienne. She doesn't smile back.

"He helps me from time to time," I say as I reach out to pat Sawyer's arm. *Lucky Grandma*, I hear her think. "Like he gets the newspaper off the porch and drives you places and goes grocery shopping for you . . . or what?" Adrienne asks, her tone implying she doesn't believe he does any of that.

"Don't you worry about it, my darling," I tell her with a wink. "Sawyer is a smart and capable young man. He helps me on my own little missions." If she only knew how close to the truth that really is.

"How did you know ahead of time that Calvin was going to propose? Did he tell everyone?"

"He invited us all here a couple of weeks ago, and it was the only logical conclusion," I reply as I smooth an imaginary wrinkle in my pants. I hate lying to her all the time. But soon. Soon I won't have to.

Sawyer steps forward and holds out his arm to me. Adrienne takes a deep breath. My darling girl, I wish I could keep her wrapped in a bubble and safe from everything that might be on its way.

"It's also important you know Sawyer is a good boy," I continue, "and I trust him with my life. You should too. No matter what."

Her eyes widen, and she lets out a nervous laugh. "Okay, Grandma," she finally says with a polite smile. "You're starting to make me worry."

"We'll talk soon." I return her smile. Sawyer's gaze is settled on Adrienne. She stares back, raising her chin ever so slightly, and he shrugs before extending his arm to me once again.

"It was nice to officially meet you, Adrienne," he says. She gives him a stiff nod and briefly shakes his hand. "Oh, one more thing . . ." He reaches into his pocket, then plops her keys into her hand. "I thought you might want to miss the crowd." I want to give him one of those fist-bump things I see the kids do for a job well done.

"Oh," she says with a smile and an almost laugh, "thank you. You couldn't be more right about that. Sawyer"—she reaches out a hand and quickly retracts it—"have we . . . have we met?"

"No." He gives her one of his beautiful grins. "We haven't met before tonight."

"Let's go home, my boy," I say before there are any more questions. "Good night, my darling girl." With one last squeeze-tight hug for Adrienne, I take my leave.

"We're here," Sawyer says as he pulls into the garage attached to my house.

"Sweet boy, did you hear anything else from you-know-who?"

Instead of answering, he hops out and comes around to my side of the car. He opens my door and holds out a hand. I take it.

"Well?" I ask after an old-lady grunt escapes my lips as I haul my decrepit body up and out of the car. It's a shame my body doesn't match my mind. My mind is still young and strong.

"I did," Sawyer says as we walk into the house.

"Am I going to have to peel you apart layer by layer? Spit it out."

"There has been nothing new. We're at a dead end."

I let out a not-so-old-lady curse. Sawyer flips on a light and stops, turning to face me.

"Before you say it," he says, "I'm not doing it."

I give him my best smile. "All right."

"Did you hear me, Effie?" He crosses his arms over his chest. He looks adorable when he's frustrated. It's a shame Adrienne hasn't found someone like Sawyer. If I were his age, I would look twice, that's for sure.

"Hmm?" I say innocently.

"I am not, under any circumstances, helping you kill yourself."

"You should know by now that if you won't help me, I'll do it anyway all on my own." I give him my best smile once again. He doesn't look pleased one bit with me. "Oh, stop it," I say as I swat at his arm. "I'll be fine. What's the point in living if you never take any risks?"

"You know the chances of your plan working without causing you permanent brain damage are none. That's more than a risk. It's a certainty!"

I sigh heavily and take a shuffling step forward. "That may be true, but we're fresh out of 'safe' options. Do you have any better ideas?"

"You could wait patiently. He will show himself again, and this time we'll be ready."

"Maybe by the time you get to him, it will be too late. Don't you think I've been waiting patiently for years already?" I frown at him. I've been searching, watching for an opportunity to end this for almost as long as Sawyer's been alive.

"Why don't you ask Thea to help you at least? You and I both know she is uniquely qualified—"

His face is red, but I wave him off as soon as he says Thea.

"No." I interrupt. "We've been over this, Sawyer. Thea has her head buried in the sand. She wants nothing to do with any of it."

"And you're above begging, I can see." Now I smile. Just a small smile. His resolve must be slipping if he's making jokes about the situation. He knows my ego is entirely too large for such a thing as begging my own daughter for her help.

"Absolutely. It's part of the reason you find me to be so endearing," I reply.

"I'll be sure to say so at your funeral."

"You haven't learned yet, have you? I'm unstoppable. Brain damage or not, I'm not going anywhere."

CHAPTER 4

ADRIENNE

I absentmindedly run a nail over my thumb. My usually chewed-on jagged nails are trimmed short with smooth, perfect, crescent-shaped tips. My nails and fingers are thicker, and my palms are calloused. It takes me a moment to realize these fingers and palms match the very masculine hands to which they are attached. These aren't my hands at all.

Is that knuckle hair?

I had a hard time falling asleep. Calvin had called to ask where I went. He didn't like my answer, told me I was rude to our guests. I didn't like that he had already put photos of the proposal all over social media by the time I made it to my parents' house, either. But at least he apologized for not telling me about Boston sooner.

A small shadow quickly crosses my path, and I tense, feeling a spike of fear in my chest. I back farther away from the shaft of light in front of me. Or really, I should say *dream-me* backs away because real-life me isn't the one in control of this body. I'm only an observer, watching everything this man does from his perspective.

This is a thing that happens to me often in my dreams. I become someone else entirely. Or maybe *become* isn't quite the right word, either, since I feel no sense of control over the bodies I end up in or the situations each person is in. And so far, this dream feels like every other dream I've had.

It's cool and dark out in this dream. The night breeze gusts, and goosebumps pop up on my arms and legs. Why can't I ever dream about being on a warm, sandy beach? Once the wind putters out, the scent of earth and grass surround me as the man I've hitched a dream ride with crouches in the shadows.

The man swivels his head around, and I admire the night sky sparkling with stars. It's a pleasant enough scene with crickets, frogs, and a whipporwill chattering. But this body feels jittery.

Dream-me turns a little more, and a dusk-to-dawn light catches my eye, its hum ordinary and reassuring. A bat flies around the light, trying to catch dinner.

Looks like I—*we* might be more appropriate—am crouched next to an outbuilding. The building's exterior is rough with weather-worn timber covered in faded red paint that is chipped and flaking. I'm pretty sure it's the side of a barn.

Cautiously, my body edges closer to the shaft of light peeking around the corner of the barn. His chest—my chest—fills with a deep breath as we creep forward again toward a gravel drive in front of the entrance to the barn. Once we reach the end of the barn's wall, we don't hesitate. We keep going. But I can feel my pulse racing and sweat dripping down my back. I already want to take a shower as soon as I wake up from this dream.

My body stays low as we now hurry from the barn toward an old, rusty truck about fifty yards away. Our chest is heaving as we take quick, rasping breaths. This body is definitely not in the best of shape. My thighs ache as we keep low, a muscle knotting in my neck from tension.

Reaching the truck, we open the driver's-side door softly, quietly. The light automatically turns on in the cab, and we let out a whisper of a curse. We get in, shutting the door just well enough for the dome light to go off. We begin looking around the cab for something—the keys, I assume—rifling through the glove compartment and flipping down the visor. I can feel the rising panic of this body, this person, as our hands continue to come up empty.

We stop searching and grip the wheel tightly. After a few deep breaths, we slowly open the door and climb back out. We only manage to take a couple steps away from the truck when something hits us in the back. Pain explodes throughout this body—throughout my mind. I'm falling, muscles cramping and jerking. It's sweet relief when our muscles finally go lax. I can feel the effort he's making to lift an arm, a leg, anything. But he's failing—we're failing.

"Come on," a voice a few feet away says, "we don't have all night."

I turn my head toward the voice, the effort eliciting a groan as every muscle in my neck and shoulders protests, spittle gathering on my lips from the effort required to breathe. A pair of boots is all I see before another burst of pain hits the side of my head and everything goes black.

I try speaking, but nothing comes out. There's nothing but blackness.

Bang!

I jump and open my eyes. I extract my hands from my tangled sheet and stare at them for a moment, relieved to see I'm me again.

"Adrienne, wake up," Mom says as she flips on the light. I can't see her face because her head is wreathed in brightness from the overhead light. "Get up, Adrienne," she says, her voice brusque. I squint at her, but it takes my eyes a moment to focus well enough for me to make out her features.

"Whatswrong?" I say, my voice slurred, the words running together as I wipe the sleep out of my eyes. Her usual flowing, graceful movements have been replaced with jerky, efficient bursts of action as she moves around my room. She yanks open my closet and throws clothes on my bed, ignoring my question completely, before digging in the bottom of my closet and coming out with a pair of flip-flops.

I clear my throat and try again. "What is going on, Mom?" I sit up, following her movements, wide-eyed.

She stops pulling clothes from my closet. Her shoulders slump, and she heaves a shaky sigh as she turns to look at me. "Grandma Effie has been taken to the hospital."

That statement clears my foggy brain immediately.

"Where is she?" I ask while hopping off my bed to grab at the clothes. Without paying much attention, I grab a pair of jogging pants and put them on before snatching up a hoodie.

"She's been taken to Memorial Hospital by ambulance." Mom stops, closes her eyes.

I reach over to my nightstand to grab my phone and keys. *I'm so glad I came home tonight*, I think as I slip the hoodie over the tank top I wore to bed. "Come on, Mom. I'll drive."

Mom says nothing as I accelerate through a yellow light.

Breathe, Adrienne, I silently command myself as I draw in a deep breath while loosening my grip on the steering wheel. My knuckles are white, and the tips of my fingers are beginning to go all tingly from lack of blood flow. My mind has been conjuring up all the terrible things that could be wrong with Grandma Effie, most of them ending in death, and now I'm fixated on the fact that I just saw her a few hours ago and she was fine. She was fine.

"We don't know anything yet," Mom says now, giving me a pat. It's the first thing she's said since we got in the car.

Mom's phone rings. She scrambles to pull it out of her purse and answer it. "Hello?" she says breathlessly. "Then, please, go get him," she says after listening for a few moments.

I listen more closely, but I don't know whose voice that is on the other end of the call.

"I'll wait until he comes to the phone," Mom says. I barely make it through another yellow light and look around to make sure there are no police cars in the area before I nudge the gas pedal again. "Tom, it's my mom. Something's happened, and she's been taken to the hospital by ambulance. We're on our way now."

Another long pause ensues, and I wonder what Dad was doing at his lab so late.

"Yes, Memorial Hospital. We'll be fine until you get there." Mom wraps her free hand around her robe in her lap. "Please bring him, though." With that, she drops her phone back into her lap and lets out a heavy breath.

She puts her hands to her temples, eyes tightly closed. As I slow the car to a stop at a red light, I wonder what she's doing or if she has a headache or if she's having a stroke too. Not that Grandma had a stroke, but maybe she did. *Get a grip*, I tell myself before my thoughts spiral.

I'm not sure what to do. Grandma is my grandma—well, obviously—but how much worse must this be for my mom? I reach over and touch her arm. She jumps, startled. I start to pull my hand back, but she puts her hand on mine, giving it a squeeze.

She lifts her head and looks at me. Tears are streaming down her face. A horn blares behind me, and I realize the stoplight has turned green. I pull my hand back and drive on.

Not knowing is painful. The worry and suspense congealed in my chest about the time the information desk sent us to the intensive care floor. And that was about three hours ago. Now it's an ever-present lump just beneath my ribs that's pulsing and growing, fed by every passing moment we sit here with no new information. Who brought Grandma in? Was it Sawyer? What happened? Will she be okay?

I try to distract myself. The lady across from us has been weeping occasionally since we got here. I wonder who she's here for. The guy two seats over from her keeps drifting off to sleep. His teenage daughter—I assume she's his daughter because her face is shaped exactly like his and they both have the same shade of dark-brown skin—is asleep with her head on his shoulder now. They were playing a card game of some sort when we first arrived. I wish I had brought something to keep my hands busy at least.

"Mom," I say hesitantly. I wonder if I look as tired as she does, as tired as the man and his daughter. "Did they tell you what happened or who called the ambulance?" I've already asked her this twice, but I can't stop the words as they tumble out again.

Mom shakes her head and opens her mouth to speak, but instead of speaking, she brushes past me. I turn to see where she's going. A doctor in scrubs and a surgeon's cap is striding purposefully toward the waiting area, and Mom is moving to intersect his path.

"Greathouse?" he says loudly, striding into the waiting room with a nurse trailing behind. Mom meets him at the transition between the linoleum of the hall and the industrial-grade carpet of the waiting room. She quietly responds to him, and I move to join them.

"I'm Dr. Allen," he says. "Let's find a space a little more private to talk about Mrs. Greathouse's condition." He leads us out into the hall and then to the left toward a small room that contains a few chairs. We go in and sit down. The room is devoid of color or decoration save a small wooden cross on the wall. It must be a holdout from when this place was a Catholic hospital a few years ago. The nurse joins us, standing in the corner with a clipboard and pen. Dr. Allen shuts the door and takes a seat across from my mom.

"Can we see her? Is she awake?" Mom crosses and uncrosses her arms. The air unit along the window kicks on. Its grate rattles. Surely it's supposed to be spitting out warm air, but the cool gush from its blower raises goose bumps across my arms.

"We're getting her settled in right now," he says with a pleasant smile. "She hasn't responded to us since she was brought in by ambulance. We're not sure why she isn't waking up, but we're still working on figuring that out." He pauses as my mom places her hand over her mouth, looking pale.

"While we don't know what's wrong yet," he continues, now expressionless, "we have been able to eliminate several possibilities. There are no signs of a brain bleed, and there isn't a single tumor or lesion according to the scans we've run. There have been some abnormalities in her EEG, but we can't attribute her current condition to the abnormalities."

There's a long pause. I look to Mom, expecting her to say something, but she sits there staring at the floor.

"What's an EEG?" I ask, feeling out of my depth.

"It's a test we run to check the electrical patterns of the brain. We use it to help us look for problems such as seizures or brain injuries."

"Why can't you figure out what happened? Isn't that unusual? What are the abnormalities?" I ask one question after the other, my brows furrowed.

"It's still early in the process. While there's been no indication that she is suffering from any neurological damage based on our diagnostics, we will be checking other body systems such as her heart."

"And the abnormalities in the EEG?" I push. "What are the abnormalities exactly?"

"We use an EEG to see what's happening in the brain, as I've said. In an adult who is unresponsive to all stimuli, we would expect to see alpha, theta, or alpha-theta brain waves. In Mrs. Greathouse, however, we're seeing beta waves. That's what we expect to see in an adult who is awake and responsive and talking."

Mom fixes her gaze on the doctor as he says this. "What does it mean?"

"I wish I could say, but it isn't something I've ever seen. I've consulted with the neurologist we have here on staff, and he's never seen anything like it, either. It's like she's faking, playing as if she were asleep, except it's clear she isn't."

"What do we do now?" Mom says.

"We'll keep an eye on her brain activity, and I'll take a closer look at her heart and kidneys just to make sure we cover our bases. There isn't much we can do other than wait to see if she wakes up. The young man who called the ambulance was smart to call right away. We'll take care of her."

My mind goes immediately to Sawyer. *It had to be him.*

The doctor rises and sticks out his hand. Mom takes it as if in slow motion, and he shakes her hand firmly. "The nurse here needs to have you sign a few forms. We'll let you know if anything changes. Once she's settled in her room, a nurse will come out to get you so you can go see her." He smiles kindly. I nod and try to return his smile, but my face feels too stiff for a real smile.

As soon as the doctor is out of sight, my mom puts her face in her hands. Her shoulders begin to shake.

CHAPTER 5

ADRIENNE

"Lynnette," my younger brother Toby says as another nurse comes through the double doors marked AUTHORIZED PERSONNEL ONLY. This isn't the first nurse we've seen walk through those doors. In fact, I stopped counting after the first dozen, and I've lost track of how many hours ago that was. The sun came up around the same time Toby and I started trying to distract ourselves by guessing the names of each person who walks through those double doors. While I've managed to get several right, he has failed every time. The worst part has been watching him try to read their name tags without being obvious about it.

"No, she looks like a Donna," I reply. My heart picks up its pace, as this nurse also looks like she might be coming our way. We still haven't been back to see Grandma Effie. This one really is walking straight toward us, and I'm not the only one who has noticed.

Mom holds tightly to Dad's hand, pulling his arm up with her as she stands. He gets to his feet and puts an arm around Mom protectively, as if he can shield her from whatever the nurse is about to say.

Dad picked up Toby from his dorm at Missouri S&T's campus in Rolla, and I'm glad they're both here.

"Are you Mrs. Greathouse's family?" We all nod. "I'm her nurse, Donna." Toby nudges me. "She still hasn't woken up, but you can come see her now," she says with a kind smile. Toby and I rise as well. "We can only take two of you at a time." The nurse casts an apologetic look to Toby and me.

"We'll go in first," Dad says, turning to us. "And then I'll come out, and one of you can go in."

"Right this way," the nurse says and starts walking back toward the double doors. Mom follows slowly behind Dad and Donna. I wonder if she's dreading seeing Grandma a little too. The thought of her in a hospital bed, unconscious and vulnerable, while we wait to see if she ever wakes up, makes me want to rub my chest where the rest of my worry sits.

"How can they not know what's going on with her?" I ask, turning to Toby.

Toby looks disheveled with a wrinkled T-shirt and jeans that have seen better days. He's wearing flip-flops too, which he hardly does because he hasn't ever figured out how to walk properly in them, so they fall off his feet randomly when he walks. It's also a bad idea to wear them this time of year in Missouri. Wearing flip-flops in the spring is a risky bet because the weather often quickly changes from pleasant to chilly and storming to burning hot and back again, depending on which way the wind blows.

Toby scrubs his face with his hands. He looks at me, leans, and bumps my shoulder with his.

"They don't know what to make of her because she's the most stubborn, most infuriating person they've ever met who refuses their help even while unconscious," he says with a grin. "You know she wouldn't let them near her if she was awake." He runs his hands through his light-brown hair again as he keeps talking. I'm positive he's already done this about a dozen times, and each time it reminds me of how badly I want to take a shower.

"Hello, Earth to Adrienne." He snaps his fingers in my face. My shoulders slump. "Did you hear me? Grandma wouldn't want any of this fuss."

"You're right." Grandma Effie hates doctors. And she has expressed her extreme distrust of the entire medical community enough I could quote her usual rant. *Those doctors know how to write a prescription, and that's it,* she would say.

So she does what every other doctor-phobic old lady would do: She takes a concoction of her own making every day just to avoid them. Something with hawthorn berries, flaxseed, thistle tea, and a bunch of other things I would never willingly eat, drink, or otherwise ingest.

"It helps me keep my blood pressure down," she had told me when I had asked about some nasty-smelling tea she was brewing. "It also keeps my mind sharp, which is especially important for people like us."

"And what kind of people are we, Grandma?" I had said with a laugh. She only smiled back at me in response.

"So, when is the wedding?" Toby pulls my attention back to the present. I look at him, startled by the question.

My right hand goes to where my engagement ring should be on my left hand, but my finger is bare. I must have left it beside my bed at Mom and Dad's. "I guess Dad told you about the proposal?" I smooth the hem of my shirt.

"Yeah, on the way here. At least now I know why he wanted me to come to your place in the middle of the week. Sorry I wasn't there. I didn't think it would be important and I have my early class in the morning," he says, his leg bouncing as he absentmindedly fidgets. "You know, you don't have to marry the guy," Toby says with a lopsided grin. "You could dump him on his self-important butt."

I don't respond to him. It was so easy to let it happen—to let Calvin slide the ring on my finger. I never really thought I've been one to cave to peer pressure or to be a people pleaser, but with everyone standing there watching and waiting, I couldn't say no. And now, mere hours later, I know it will be much harder to fix this than it would have been to say no in the moment.

"Hey, I shouldn't have brought it up," he says, looking genuinely apologetic as he drops a hand on my arm.

I sigh and meet his eyes. "I don't think a butt can actually be self-important since it can't think or feel emotions," I reply with a raised eyebrow and a smirk.

Toby shakes his head and smiles. "I fully support you in whatever you do."

"But?"

"But? But nothing. I'm just saying, if you need a getaway driver at the wedding before you say, 'I do,' I'm down for that. Or if you marry the jerk and I have to learn not to want to punch him every time he speaks, then I'll work on that too." He laughs. "But if I get to choose for you, dump him now before things reach the planning stage." He winks.

I roll my eyes. "Didn't you say you shouldn't have brought up the engagement?" Not waiting for a reply, I stand up. "I'm going to get coffee. Do you want any?"

Toby shakes his head. "You know you don't have to always do that."

"Do what? Get coffee?" I say, my expression blank. I cross my arms and wait for him to answer.

"You don't always have to handle everything all by yourself, locked away in that brain of yours," Toby says, exasperation creeping into every word. He looks tired. "You have a family who loves you, who would be there for you . . . if you'd let them. It's kind of the point of me saying I'd support you even if you make an idiotic decision."

"I'm fine, Toby," I say, simultaneously touched that he cares enough to say it and annoyed that he's sticking his pesky little brother nose into things. "Let's just worry about Grandma." He opens his mouth to say something else, but I cut him off before he can. "So do you want coffee or not?"

Toby rolls his eyes before responding. "You know what, I'll go get the coffee. I could use a walk."

He abruptly leaves, his right flip-flop falling off ten steps away. I smile and hold back a laugh. I feel the urge to go after him and walk with him. But I don't.

Toby disappears from view as the door to the stairwell closes behind him. As it does, the elevator doors across the hall from me opens. I glance up at the sound, and Sawyer steps off the elevator. I tentatively raise my hand and wave to him, and he nods in response and takes a step my way.

"What are you doing here?" a voice behind me asks roughly, startling me. I glance over my shoulder as the figure moves closer. The voice is coming from Mom, but she sounds completely alien to me, her voice deep and intense. Sawyer's head swivels in my mom's direction. He stands frozen in the doorway of the elevator.

She sounds angry, I finally realize. She sounds angrier than I've ever heard her sound, including that one time at age fifteen when Toby wanted to use the garage to work on a school project so he moved her car without her permission and scraped up the side of it while backing it out.

Sawyer takes another step forward and the elevator closes behind him. He stands there, looking from me to my mom and back again.

"I came to check on Effie," he says with an even tone as he slowly moves closer, bringing his hands up, palms out. I look to Mom as she takes a step toward him, her whole body tense. I didn't notice him before, but Dad walks forward until he's next to Mom. He puts an arm around her shoulders. She shrugs it off, and he lets his hands fall to his sides as he looks on.

"The doctors and nurses here don't know how to treat her," Mom says forcefully as she moves closer to me. "How could they?" she says with a short, bitter laugh. "You should leave. Now."

I turn to face Mom. "Why? What's going on?" I ask, louder than I intended. My parents don't answer. Mom's fists are clenched at her side. "What is happening with Grandma? And how do you know Sawyer, Mom?"

My mother's stare flicks to me for a moment, her expression tight. She closes her eyes.

"Stay out of it," she spits out, her eyes still closed. My expression is blank. My mind is blank. She has never spoken to me like that before.

"I, uh . . ." I stutter.

"You need to go *now*, Sawyer," she says, her voice hard as she stares him down.

"Mom, what is your problem?" I say with a huff.

"I'll go, but . . ." he says, letting the sentence fall off. I turn my head to look at him. He's looking at me as he stands there, waiting for something, but I can't imagine what. He hesitates a moment longer, then backs away toward the elevator that has just opened up. "Please let me know how she's doing and if anything changes."

I stand there helplessly. I don't understand what just happened.

After waiting for the occupants to step out, he steps in. He turns and faces us as he waits for the doors to close, hitting a button. An unreadable expression flits across his face. In a moment, the doors shut with him in the elevator, and he's gone.

"What in the world was that?" I fling an arm toward the elevator, indicating Sawyer, and put a hand on my hip as I look at Mom. She sighs heavily and steps away, lowering herself to a chair.

"Adrienne, come sit down." Mom pats the chair next to her.

"That is not like you to be so rude." I push again, not moving to sit.

Mom's shoulders slump. "Sawyer is the least of my worries at the moment. Now sit."

Dad gives me an encouraging nod. So I reluctantly comply.

"I don't know how to tell you this, so I'll just say it." She swallows. "We think your grandmother is dying."

CHAPTER 6

ADRIENNE

Your grandmother is dying. It's been a week since Mom said those horrible words. Thankfully, nothing has changed, though. She hasn't gotten any worse, at least.

And today, I'm trying something new. I'm trying to focus on the things I actually have control over. Stuff such as showing up for work and class and turning in assignments.

Right now, though, I'm waiting for Parker to show up. He agreed to come have dinner with Megan and me. But he's nowhere to be seen. He hasn't answered my texts, either. After another quick check of my phone, I give up and go in. Megan's waving at me from the table she's seated at.

"I ordered pizza," Megan says as I plop in the seat opposite of her. "And I ordered you a ginger beer."

"This is why we're friends," I say with a smile.

Megan and I are different in so many ways. She has straight, warm-brown hair, and I have blond, wavy locks; she is outgoing, and I'm not; she is tall and willowy, and I'm more compact; she thinks Calvin's proposal was super romantic and special, and I . . . well, I didn't.

While we are so different in so many ways, there is one very important thread that binds our friendship together. That thread is pizza. Not just any pizza, though. Specifically, our love of mushroom pizza from Marquart's, the restaurant in which we're currently sitting, is something we bonded over when we met.

"It should be here any minute."

"Great. I'm starving."

"Is Parker coming?" she says in a certain tone I know is her I'm-trying-to-be-nice voice.

"Good question. I thought he was, but he isn't here, obviously." I let my breath out in a huff.

She snorts. "What a shocker," she says, rolling her eyes. Shortly after Megan and I had met, I introduced her and Parker. We met for a movie, which then turned into a late-night run to our favorite diner. Megan laughed at everything Parker said and put her hand on his arm or shoulder at every opportunity. She even flipped her hair not so casually more than once, and I had felt like the third wheel on a surprise blind date.

And Parker—never one to ignore any girl who shows interest, especially a beautiful one—was just as bad. By the end of the evening, I had the urge to throw myself between them when Megan handed him a slip of paper with her number on it. He accepted, telling her he would be texting soon. But, much to my secret relief, he never did. I was glad because I wasn't sure I could deal with the two of them together. I liked having my two best friends separate, in their own roles of my life.

Megan, who was rarely—if ever—rejected, hadn't forgotten Parker's lack of follow-through. To top it off, she also knows Parker's history of being less than reliable. My stories from high school had made that pretty clear.

"So I've been trying not to ask," Megan starts, uncharacteristically hesitant, "with your grandma's illness taking priority right now." She pauses, glancing at me sideways.

"Ask away," I urge her, glad it isn't another talk about how Parker should be a better friend.

"What's going on with you and Calvin?"

I've changed my mind because another speech about Parker would be better. "What do you mean?" I stall.

"For one thing, I haven't seen him around since the proposal," she says with a shrug.

"He's in Boston looking for a place to live and getting everything squared away for his transfer and new position," I say, regurgitating words I've already said to Mom and Dad and Toby in the last week. They were surprised Calvin hadn't been around to offer his support. I didn't tell them I had been avoiding him, so it suits me just fine. I'm not sure why I haven't told Megan, though.

Adrienne

Our pizza and my ginger beer arrive. Megan raises an eyebrow and gives me the look that I know means she isn't dropping it.

"What, Megan?" I ask with a sigh, wishing she would just say what she's thinking. I take a long drink and reach for a slice of pizza. It's too hot, and I drop it onto my plate.

"You didn't go with him. And you just . . . it seems . . ." She struggles for the words. "You haven't been wearing the ring. Do you want to marry him, Adrienne?" She leans in. "You know you don't have to, right?"

I pick at the napkin in my lap.

Megan is sitting still, watching me. She's waiting patiently for me to answer. My face and ears are impossibly hot, and I wonder if I'm bright red. I finally force myself to look up and meet her gaze.

"I'd love to answer that, but I'm not sure what to say." I pause and swallow hard. "To say, 'I'm getting married' seems bizarre. Who gets married under the age of thirty these days? It doesn't make sense to me to get married now. We're both really young." I run my hands through my hair and lean closer.

"You are young. But do you love him?" Megan takes a piece of pizza.

"I . . . I'm not sure. I mean, I'm not sure I understand love." I let out a huff. "But I would know, wouldn't I? If I was in love with him? I think I'd know it."

"Do you think he loves you?"

"Again, I'm not sure. He's said he loves me, but I don't think he understands it any better than I do. It feels . . . less? Like less intense or powerful than I expected. Hollow or empty."

"Did you have any idea he was going to propose, then?"

"No," I laugh, "not a clue."

A line has appeared between Megan's eyebrows. She opens her mouth as if to say something before closing it again.

"What?" I ask, encouraging her to say what's on her mind. If she has any wisdom right now, I am eager to hear it.

"My mom has a thing she says anytime anyone talks about love."

Megan's mom has had a rough dating life, starting with Megan's father. She has dated extensively and even been married a couple of times, but no one has ever stuck around. These days, her mom seems content with her single life. Megan and her little sister Amber seem to be enough for her.

"Well? Are you going to tell me, or am I going to have to call your mom for relationship advice?" I playfully throw my shredded-up napkin at Megan.

"She would agree with you that you would know if you really love him. But only because she thinks love is a choice we make. There are crushes, and those feelings come and go. But love is a conscious choice to deepen those feelings and learn about someone and commit to loving who they are."

"Maybe I should call your mom," I say with a smile. "What else does she say?"

"She says who you choose to love changes you. If that person is worthy of your love, then you'll be all the better for loving them."

"And if they're not?" I ask.

"Well, that was during her last divorce," Megan says with a laugh. "So there might have been a few expletives in the answer to that one, but I bet you can guess. And I think she's right. It's really important to know that you're choosing someone who will help you become the person you want to be."

I consider her words. What kind of person do I want to be? And what kind of person is Calvin?

"Great," I say to her with a shake of my head, "now I can add identity crisis to my to-do list."

"You know, if you listen to everything you just said to me, I think you'll discover you already know your answer to whether or not you love Calvin." Her expression is serious.

She's right, but it doesn't make any of this any easier.

CHAPTER 7

ADRIENNE

Oh, come on, I think, *not tonight.* I'm dreaming, and I'm not me, as usual. I want to sleep a nice, peaceful, dreamless sleep. That's obviously asking for too much. I've had a dream every night since Grandma Effie was taken to the hospital, and that was nearly two weeks ago now.

I try my best just to ignore this dream after noting that my hands are gloved in supple leather and gripping a steering wheel. It looks like I'm driving a car, but it's dark out. Not much to see, really, only the highway ahead of me.

I think about Grandma instead. When I visited yesterday, I overheard Mom arguing with a doctor in the hall. The doctor was a pretty woman who looked to be in her late forties. I had never seen her before, but she was obviously well-informed about Grandma's case. She was insistent that Grandma should be sent to some kind of rehabilitation facility. My mom wanted to take her home to care for her there, though. I stood by the door to Grandma's room, listening as surreptitiously as possible while they argued back and forth. Their conversation was a little weird, though. By the way the two of them spoke to one another, it sounded as if Mom knows the doctor—as if Mom's an old friend, not a patient.

"Cynthia, I don't care," Mom had said, her voice rising. "I don't want her there." If only I could have heard what the doctor said in response.

But Calvin, who is still in Boston, had called, making my phone ring loudly by the door. Mom and the doctor both walked farther down the hall, ending my eavesdropping and leaving me to debate whether or not I'd answer Calvin's call. I didn't.

When Calvin gets back, I'll just tell him I'm not ready. The thought brings with it a twitchy nervousness that makes my palms sweat. Except in my dream, these aren't my palms and they're definitely not sweaty.

My attention swings back to the dream as the scene around me becomes brighter. Streetlamps light up the darkness, and I see a sign ahead. U-Store-It is emblazoned in Comic sans serif across the sign. I cringe at the sight of it, and a feeling of déjà vu hits me.

Isn't U-Store-It on the other side of town, near the on-ramp for interstate fifty-five? I think. I've been here before. *Not that this is real.* But I don't usually dream about places I recognize.

Dream-me pulls up to a gate with a keypad. With my hand still encased in leather, I enter a code onto the keypad, and the motorized gate begins to slide open with a creak. I put my foot on the gas and drive slowly through the open gate. Looks like a late-night visit to a storage unit. I'm bored and ready to be back to a dreamless sleep.

I wonder if Grandma Effie is dreaming. I wonder if she can hear everything that's going on. If so, she's sick of all the fussing and Mom is driving her crazy with her hovering. The two of them have different opinions about almost everything. So if she can hear everything, I'm sure she's wishing she could argue her way out of there.

Dream-me drives down the long aisle, passing unit after unit and stopping at the second one from the end. I stuff something into the pocket of a supple black leather jacket before slipping it on. I get out of the car and walk to the overhead door. I fumble the key and then insert it into a padlock near the ground. Once it's unlocked, I remove the lock and push the overhead door up. Inside the storage unit, I pull the door shut behind me. After a few moments of complete darkness, I flip on an overhead light. The bright bulb penetrates the darkness.

It's empty. The storage unit floor is completely bare. Dream-me moves forward to the back of the unit, and I realize the unit isn't completely empty—something is covering the walls. Who would wallpaper the inside of a storage unit? Wait, that isn't wallpaper. I move closer. Are those . . . photos?

A light touch of the photo in front of me on the back wall, then I pull something out of my jacket pocket. I set the items in my hand on a little table that only reaches my knee. Squatting down, the items are easier to make out. I've just set down more photos. Dream-me goes through them, and there's something so familiar about these photos of streets and buildings. I flip through one to the next, quickly, stopping once there's a person in the photo. Flip, flip, flip. Another photo. The recurring subject of each photo I pause to examine is me. The real me. That's me last night outside the restaurant when Parker stood me up. Dream-me flips through the next several photos, setting certain images aside.

Wake up, Adrienne, I think, trying to will myself awake. As usual, I'm unable to get out of the dream.

My movements don't match the panic I'm feeling as dream-me methodically pins the photos to the wall. There is photo after photo of me waiting by Marquart's last night, and then several more as I walk to my car. And there are so many—dozens, maybe a few hundred—more photos of me all around the unit. Months of photos of my life. All clearly taken without my knowledge. I don't want to see anything else.

Dream-me steps back to inspect our work.

There's one photo that's larger than the rest that we just pinned to the wall. It takes my breath away. The photo shows real-life me looking right at the camera and smiling, carefree and happy. And I know who took that photo. I remember the exact day and why I was smiling. I was smiling because my best friend had just made me laugh.

Parker took that photo.

CHAPTER 8

ADRIENNE

I walk out of my last final of the day—Foundations of the World's Civilizations II—feeling confident as I head to my car. Until my mind drifts to last night's dream. *Nightmare* is more accurate. I chew on my lip. The image of my face plastered on a storage unit wall in my dream is there every time I close my eyes.

I pull my phone out of my pocket and bring up Mom's number to call her to check on Grandma Effie. As I'm about to touch the green button on the screen, though, there's movement in my periphery. I glance to the right to check it out. It's only someone a few paces behind me.

It's just another student. He's tall and wearing a hoodie with the sleeves pushed up and the hood hiding his face. There's something familiar about him, but I keep walking, picking up the pace. He moves more quickly too.

It's just a coincidence. Surely, it has to be. Why would anyone be following me around? This guy is like the rest of us—over with finals and ready to get off campus. Right? I can tell myself whatever I want, but I can't shake the unease that has started to build.

I reach my car and fumble with the key to unlock the door. My fumbling reminds me again of my creepy dream last night, adding to my nervousness. My hands are shaking, and I drop the key. A hand reaches out quickly, snatching up my keys.

"Whoa there!" says Parker as he holds my keys out.

I shove him.

"Oy! What's your problem?"

"You scared me," I say, restraining myself from shoving him again. I can't shake my uneasiness.

My stomach drops as the photo from the dream floats back to mind. Should I be afraid of Parker? Is that what that dream meant? I shake my head. Nonsense. *Dreams are nothing more than the brain's visual interpretation of the neurotransmitters floating around in there*, I try to reassure myself. *The result is my brain just trying to make a pattern out of the nonsensical.*

"Are you okay?" Parker asks, staring at me with a raised eyebrow. I ignore his question. "Anyway, I'm glad I caught you before you left."

"What's with the hoodie?" I ask. "You do know it's like eighty degrees out here, right?" My heart is still beating a staccato pace in my chest.

"I just felt like wearing a hoodie," he says, avoiding meeting my eyes. "Can you give me a ride?"

"What? What happened to your truck?" He drives the most beat-en-down-looking Chevy truck I've ever seen. Having rebuilt the engine with his dad when he was fifteen, he is proud of the thing—missing bumper, rusted-out wheel wells, mismatched paint on the doors, and all. "And why didn't you just text me to wait for you?"

"I can't find my phone, actually."

"Hmm."

"And I have a flat."

"There's no way you don't have a spare." I laugh, knowing him being stranded by a flat tire couldn't possibly happen.

"My spare is flat too." He shrugs. I stare at him for a long moment. "Are you going to give me a ride or what?"

"Sure," I reply, drawing the word out and squinting at him, "if you're serious."

"I'm more serious than I've ever been before," he mumbles either to himself or to me. I'm not sure which.

"What?"

"Nothing. Let's go."

Once I've turned onto Route 141 to head toward my condo, I glance at him out of the corner of my eye. He's been silent since he got in, his head swiveling around as we left campus. We pull up to a stoplight that's red, and I can't take the suspense any longer.

"What's your deal? You're acting strange."

He looks over at me, then pushes the hood back. "What do you mean?"

he asks as he stares out the window again.

"Since when are you ever unprepared for a flat tire?"

"I told you, my spare was flat," he says, briefly glancing at me.

"I don't believe you, actually." I want to take it back as soon as the words leave my mouth, but it's the truth. Am I making something out of nothing? If I am, this has to be a result of my dream leaving me uneasy—something I've never been with him.

He sighs heavily, folding his arms. "It's complicated."

"Okay," I say, carefully keeping my tone and facial features casual. He'll tell me. He always does.

I make the turn off Route 141 to head to my condo. "Hey, why haven't I seen you at work recently?"

"I quit."

"You quit? What?" The car jerks ever so slightly as I turn to look at him, my eyes wide. "And you were going to tell me that when?"

"Does it really matter? I'm telling you now."

I let out a weird sound, but no words follow. "It does matter. It matters to me that you aren't telling me these things."

"I'm sorry," he says quickly with a shake of his head. "I should have told you. Now can we please drop it?"

I sit in silence. I'm feeling hurt, but I'm not entirely sure why.

"How's Megan?" Parker continues as if everything is normal. "Does she still wish I would call? You should tell her I definitely can't now, at least not until I get a new phone." He waggles his eyebrows at me.

"What really happened to your phone?"

"I lost it."

Silence stretches between us. "First, you, the fix-it guy, can't handle a flat, and now, the guy who is never more than ten inches from his phone at all times says he's lost his phone? Just like that?" I snap my fingers.

"You can't seem to let things go sometimes," he says as he rolls his eyes at me. "You know, being so uptight is probably your least attractive quality." He flashes a grin.

I take the next right down a side street, pulling over once I'm far enough away from the intersection. I throw the car into park, then sit staring out the front window for a moment before speaking.

"Pointing out others' least attractive qualities might be yours," I say, my tone flat. He shifts in his seat. "You don't owe me any explanations, Parker." I look at him. He's staring at me, his face revealing nothing. "But it would be great if you could tell me what the hell is going on with you. Are you trying to duck someone?"

I see a flash of annoyance on his face. The muscles along his jaw stand out as he clenches and unclenches his jaw.

"Is this like the time senior year where your 'customers,'"—I say using air quotes—"figured out the fake IDs you were selling weren't fooling anyone?"

A few guys on the football team had been after him for a while after they had tried using the fake IDs at the local liquor store, not realizing the cashier is an avid local football fan and knew exactly who they were.

"Hey, it wasn't my fault they tried to buy liquor while still wearing their letterman jackets," he says. A car drives past us. The silence stretches out.

Why don't you trust me with the truth? He deflates a little, slouching more in his seat. He slowly lets out a breath.

"It's not that simple," he replies.

"What isn't that simple?"

"All of it. My life, your life—the whole human existence," he says, a slight smile at the last part. "There's seldom ever one thing or event or circumstance that a person can pinpoint as being the moment"—he snaps his fingers—"the second that changed it all."

I blink and sit silently, hoping my continued silence will encourage him to keep talking. He doesn't. He sits there with an unreadable expression.

"Fine, I'll drive. And even if you don't want to talk, I do." I put the car into drive and pull away from the curb, gripping the steering wheel tightly. Parker is no stranger to trouble. In high school, it was as if he were a magnet for it. But he always told me what was going on. He rarely shut me out. He usually only kept his thoughts to himself when it came to girls he was dating—and I'm glad, because I'm discovering I don't like knowing about his latest romantic interests.

Why are my feelings so hurt? I'm not sure. But my friend definitely doesn't seem like himself. "What you're telling me is you quit your job for no reason—at a place where you convinced me to come work—and you lost your phone and have a flat." I stop, take a deep breath. "In case you have forgotten, I'm still me, the person who has been your best friend for a lot of years," I say, falsely cheerful.

"Yep, that sounds about right." I glance at Parker, and he's wearing an infuriating smirk. I clench my teeth together, willing myself to breathe calmly. I start silently counting to ten.

"Look," he says, his smirk gone, "it's all pretty complicated, and I can't tell you because it isn't my secret to tell."

I glance at him again. He seems sincere. *What isn't your secret?*

"If I could tell you, I would."

"Can you tell me who it is you're protecting?" I ask instead.

"You should know me well enough by now to know I'm always protecting my own butt," he says, the slightest hint of a smile back on his face. "And you wouldn't believe me if I did tell you."

"Fine," I say after a long pause. "But whoever's secret you're keeping . . . they had better be worth it."

His smile broadens. "You'll just have to trust me." He turns his smile toward me. I give him a look that says I'm not sure I do.

It had better not have anything to do with a girl, I think as I make the final turn before pulling into my parking spot at the condo. He laughs and winks at me.

CHAPTER 9

EFFIE

What is that blasted beeping about? It's coming from somewhere to my left. I haven't opened my eyes to look because I know as soon as I do, my dream will become little more than vapors. I'm not sure what it was about now, but I know it was important. No, it *is* important. It's vital.

How does somebody return to a dream? The harder I try to hold onto the thoughts of my sleeping self, the more that feeling of importance floats away like vapors. It's gone. I can't return to it. Which means I can only move forward now. Whatever that looks like. I don't remember going to bed.

Why won't that incessant beeping stop?

I curse, but my throat is dry and I only manage a feeble croak. My muscles aren't cooperating either as I try to lift my head. It's as if I've slept a thousand years. Not that I would know how that feels, I suppose. A creepy-crawly sensation across my face—like there's a bug or something with entirely too many legs—is now dragging my attention away from the beeping. I try to lift my hand to brush off whatever critter is disturbing me, but my arms are so heavy. I try again, inhaling deep and holding my breath as I focus on lifting my right arm. And success! My hand clumsily lands on my face.

The good news is there doesn't seem to be a bug. Instead, it feels . . . what is that? My cheeks are wet. I follow the trail of dampness up to discover it's coming from my eyes. I'm crying. *Why am I crying?*

"Mom?" It sounds like Thea. I turn my head toward her voice, and it flops to the side. If that's a precursor to the state of my body, I'm not sure I really do want to be awake. What the heck happened to me?

"Mom! Let me get a nurse!" She moves quickly toward the door.

"Th . . ." I try saying her name. I'm about as loud as a mouse. Clearing my throat, I try again. "Thea, what happened?" That's better.

"You're at the hospital, Mom." She puts a hand on my face, which feels odd. I've always been the one to care for her, not the other way around. "You've been unconscious for a couple of weeks."

Crap. I know this means I'm in for the lecture of my life. If I've been out for two weeks, then Thea has surely figured out what I've done. And that I wasn't very successful, apparently. At least I'm alive, I suppose.

"Thea, a glass of water, dear." I try a smile. Her expression doesn't change. Her crow's-feet are more pronounced when she looks at me like this, all pinched and sour. My daughter—the woman I often still see as the little girl who used to sneak in to sleep next to me every night until she was nearly ten years old—looks every bit of her age at this moment. I wonder guiltily if I have contributed to the purplish half-moons under her eyes and the tense slant to her shoulders.

"Mom," she says with a warning in her voice as she watches me sip water, "what you did was incredibly s—"

"Stupid, I know," I interrupt.

"Selfish is what I was going to say." She leans closer. "Shortsighted, suicidal—there are a couple more words for you."

My feathers are instantly ruffled. She might be grown, but like a child, she can't see anything beyond the end of her nose sometimes. "I don't know how risking my life to put an end to all this makes me selfish. Some might even call me brave." I emphasize the last word and resist the urge to try to poke her in the belly button like I used to when she was little. Back then, she would burst into giggles. Now, I doubt that's the reaction I would get.

"You tried to *hijack* someone's mind and dig through it for information!" she whispers intensely. "No one has ever lived through that!" She is right: No one else has ever survived it.

"We both know I'm not just anyone, though, don't we?" I croak out, my voice cracking. "The odds of me surviving were decidedly in my favor—" Thea opens her mouth to interrupt. "And nothing risked means nothing gained. I'd much rather risk my life than yours or Adrienne's. Besides, I didn't exactly try to hijack anything. I merely attempted to observe from within. Hitchhiking—that's a much more apt description."

"You decided, as usual, to handle this your way without even talking to me—I am, by the way, her *mother*. Surely, you of all people would understand that this should have been my decision too. Your success or failure directly affects her and our ability to keep her safe!" Her face is turning a little bit red. My eyes settle on a vein in her forehead that is now more pronounced than usual. "I shouldn't have to tell you that since you're the one who taught me everything I know."

Now I go ahead and let that sigh out. The worst part of having a smart daughter that takes after me is that she's so often right, especially when I don't want her to be.

"It's time to tell her, Thea."

"No, it's not."

"It is, and you know it. We have been trying to piece this puzzle together for decades now. Not telling Adrienne about her abilities isn't going to keep her safer, and to continue to keep that from her will only put her at risk. We need to be teaching her how to use her abilities instead of hiding ours from her as well."

"I will not be pushed into telling her on your timeline, Mom. We've discussed this." She stops and takes a deep breath. "After what happened with James, I'm doing this my way."

She stares at me intently. I stare right back.

Finally, I break the stalemate. "You're right. I should have told you what I was going to do. I should have involved you. But you're wrong about this." I punctuate it with a cough.

"Maybe, Mom, but it's still my call, and she's not ready. It will wreck her life." Thea's voice is thick with emotion. "She'll go from her perfectly normal existence to worrying about shadows. I don't want that for her. And I especially don't want her to live the legacy of having lost her father to something sinister. How could I possibly tell her one part without the other?" Thea crosses her arms over her chest.

"You mean you don't want her living *your* life." I let my head fall back against the pillows. Why haven't I realized it before? The fight has gone right out of me.

Silence follows. Thea looks down at the floor.

"I did the best I could after your father . . ." I swallow, but I can't continue past the lump in my throat. I did do my best, didn't I?

"I'm not saying you didn't, Mom." She looks at me now, a single tear trailing down her cheek. "But living my life with a hole no one could fill, wondering what really happened to Daddy . . . That's not something I've ever wanted for her. How can I tell her about her abilities and keep the rest from her?" Her chin quivers, just like it did when she was a girl trying to hold back all her tears.

I reach out a hand for Thea, but she's too far away. She steps closer, grasps my hand, and gives it a squeeze.

"I love you, Mom. I get how hard it must have been on your own with me to take care of after losing the man of your dreams. You did what you had to. Thank you for being both my mother and my father." She leans closer, her gaze turning steely. "This, though, this is me doing what I have to. We're not telling her yet."

With only a moment of hesitation, I nod.

CHAPTER 10

ADRIENNE

I made it through an entire shift at work without once worrying about Grandma, I realize as I clock out and turn my phone on. I had signed up to work late to help prepare the store for inventory next week, and it's felt like time was standing still the last several hours as I pulled extra inventory down, marked it, and put it back up.

Now, as I walk out to my car, every muscle in my body is calling for rest and sleep. I glance at my phone. Just after one o'clock in the morning.

I get in and start up my car. I should go home and go to sleep, but I hesitate because I can't stop thinking about Grandma now. I want to go see her.

A metallic tang in my mouth. It's blood. I've been chewing on the inside of my lip, and now I've made it bleed. *Ulcers. Those are totally next*, I think as I dig around in my car for a napkin. I find one and press it to the inside of my lip. My phone vibrates in my pocket. It's a text from Mom.

Come to the hospital. Grandma is awake.

I'm standing just outside the doorway of Grandma Effie's room. I stare at the closed door, my hand outstretched and frozen. What if she isn't okay? What if she isn't herself anymore? The door opens before I can bring myself to touch it.

"Adrienne?" says my mother halfway through the doorway. I can't look at her; I stare instead at my hand that is still outstretched. I know as soon as I look at her whether Grandma is really okay or not. Mom places my outstretched hand between her own two hands and squeezes. I slowly look up, meeting her eyes. Her eyes are wet, but she's smiling. I step in and give her a hug.

Pulling back, I ask, "How is she?"

"See for yourself," she says as her smile broadens.

I let go of Mom and walk into the room.

"Are you going to stand there staring all day, or are you going to come give your grandma a hug?" Grandma Effie says, her arm outstretched and beckoning to me. I heave a sigh of relief and walk on slightly wobbly legs over to her bedside. As I feel her frail arms—arms that had hugged me tightly just a couple of weeks ago—embrace me, question after question runs through my mind. *Is she going to get stronger? Will she leave us again? Is there something the doctors have missed?*

"Don't worry so much, my dear," Grandma Effie whispers in my ear as I continue to cling to her. "Life is never a certainty, but I don't plan to leave you any time soon." She smooths my hair just like she did when I was a child.

"I've missed you so much," I speak into her cheek as I give her a kiss.

"Ah, darling girl," Grandma says, cupping my face with both hands while smiling sweetly, "I've missed you too."

Mom's phone rings. She glances down after pulling the phone out of her pocket. "It's Tom. I haven't told him the good news yet," she says with a smile aimed at Grandma. "I'll be right back." She walks toward the door, answering as she shuts it behind her. I turn back to Grandma.

"Listen up, Adrienne," Grandma says, all traces of her smile gone. "I have something to tell you, and she won't be on the phone with Tom for long." She glances toward the door, and I glance with her. Her tone is urgent; her grip on me is tight now.

"Wh-What's going on?" I stammer, my brows drawing together as I look from the door to Grandma.

"I don't have time for questions just now," she says as she sits up straighter. "So just listen carefully. You are a special person, and your life is destined for great things, my girl. You are a mind reader, or at least you will be—"

I interrupt her with a laugh, my tense body relaxing. "I'm glad to see your sense of humor is still intact," I say to Grandma with another laugh. She grabs my wrist tightly and pulls herself toward me until her face is only inches from mine.

"I am not joking," she says, her voice shaking with intensity as she squeezes my wrist. I look in her eyes, and I see nothing other than sincerity and urgency.

"What are you talking about?" *I think I would know if I could read minds.*

"No, you wouldn't because you don't know any better," Grandma says, and I look at her more closely.

How does she do that? How does she always know exactly what I'm thinking?

"Because I'm listening to your thoughts, of course." She scoffs but continues quickly. "You're not the only mind reader in the family, but your mother never wanted you to know about any of it. She thinks she can keep you safe by hiding it from everyone—including you." Grandma stops and closes her eyes for a moment, drawing in a deep breath. "She's wrong." Her smile mirthless, she stares expectantly at me. Finally, she releases my wrist.

"I think maybe we should call someone in here—"

"You are a mind reader," Grandma says, interrupting me, "or at least that's the best word to describe what you are. They used to use the word *telepathic,* but they have some more sophisticated term for it nowadays. But that's what we are. There are many more in the world like us too." I hold up a hand to stop her, but she keeps going, pulling my hand down to her lap where she holds onto it with both of hers. She takes a breath. "Your mother is a mind reader too."

I jerk my hand out of her grasp now and take a step away. "Listen, Grandma," I say, my head spinning, "you have been through something, and your mind is still recovering—"

"Listen to me!" Her voice is ringing in my mind. I gasp as I realize her lips didn't move when she said that.

"I hear you . . . in my mind?" I cover my ears in a rush of movement and gasp again as she continues to speak.

"I'm sorry you had to learn about yourself in this way, Adrienne," the voice in my mind—no, my grandmother's voice in my mind—says with a sorrowful tone. I shake my head as I back away.

"No, no, no," I say. My eyes are wide, and I can feel my pulse in my temples where my palms still rest as I continue to hold my ears. "This can't be true."

"You know it's true, if you'll allow yourself to accept the facts," she says the words aloud. "Think about it, Adrienne. You *know* there's something different about you." She pauses. I'm not sure what to say. "But now is not the time to know everything. I don't have much time before your mother returns, or before—" She stops, taking a deep, shuddering breath. "I'm not sure I'll be here to teach you everything you need to know, but I plan to do as much as I can. Starting tomorrow. Promise me you'll come back to see me tomorrow while your mother is at work."

This can't be happening.

"Adrienne," her voice is soft now. "Adrienne, it's time to accept the truth of who we are." My mind is spinning. "And please, find Sawyer and tell him I told you. Tell him it's time for him to tell you *everything*." I picture Sawyer as I last saw him, looking from my mother to me and back again before retreating to the elevator. "And keep your mother out of this. She won't approve of us talking of these things."

"But if what you're saying is true, then why not? Why wouldn't she want me to know?"

Grandma's shoulders sag. She suddenly looks so tired. "She thinks she's doing what's best for you." She shakes her head slowly. "And I can't fault her for that. But she's wrong."

"Grandma—"

"Stop," she interrupts me, holding up a hand. "It's time to think about something else; otherwise, Thea will surely know what we've been talking about. You can't think about this in front of her."

Grandma's words startle me, and I'm not sure what to do, how to act, or what to say. How can this be happening? I take a step toward her, and the door opens. My mother walks in, her face impassive. I can feel my mouth hanging open as I scramble to think about something else. Anything else.

"I know, but it will be so nice," my grandma says as if we had been having a completely different conversation. I look to her and watch as she turns her smile to Mom, reaching a hand out to motion her closer. "I was just telling Adrienne I should be able to go home in a day or two. She doesn't think it's a good idea."

Adrienne

Mom glances my way and then smiles back at Grandma. "Let's not rush it now, Mom," she says. I look around the room, trying my best not to think about anything Grandma had said. I sit down, and as soon as my back touches the chair, I stand right up. I can't stay. I need to get away to think.

"You know," I blurt out, interrupting Mom and Grandma. I force a smile on my face. "I'm going to go home and get some sleep and let you two talk." My face feels tight. I walk over to Grandma, give her a quick kiss on the cheek, and walk to the door. I take a step out and then awkwardly step back into the room. "I'll be back to see you as soon as I can, Grandma." I avoid looking at Mom completely, unsure I'll be able to keep all the questions from swirling around in my mind if I make eye contact with her.

I need sleep.

CHAPTER 11

EFFIE

As soon as the door shuts behind Thea and the nurse who had been in to check my vitals for the millionth time, I urge my weak body to move. I sit up, slowly swinging my legs around to the floor. I need to sit and think and not feel so damn helpless for a moment.

What did I do? Why did I tell Adrienne about being a mind reader? It wasn't a choice I made; it all came tumbling out as if I had no control over what I was saying. What is wrong with me?

And if Adrienne finds Sawyer—not that I'm sure she knows how to contact him, anyway—and he tells her everything . . . She will never forgive us if she learns the truth from someone else.

My dream earlier comes back to my mind, not that I can remember any of the details. It's more like my dream has given me a nagging feeling, like when I left the house a few weeks ago, unsure if I had turned the oven off. I wondered the entire time if the oven would be okay, or if I'd come home to discover my house had burned to the ground. I have the same feeling right now.

Except this time, the stakes are higher. I can feel it.

"That only leaves me with one thing left to do." I scoot closer to the edge of the bed, carefully putting more weight on my legs. They feel like they'll hold me. I grab the plastic rail on the side of the bed and start to heave myself forward. As soon as I shift my weight, though, an ear-piercing screech starts coming from my bed. I freeze, unsure what's wrong or what I should do.

"Mrs. Greathouse," says the same pesky nurse as she comes charging in, "please don't try to stand up. You've only just woken up and you're still weak. We can't have you walking around without a little help."

I've only been away for a couple hours and I already hate being in this place.

"Here, let me help you scoot back." She takes my other arm, and I scoot back until the damn screeching stops. "Why were you trying to stand up? Is there something I can get for you?"

"You can get all these tubes and wires out of me, and then I need to make a phone call."

"We can arrange that phone call easily enough," she says with a smile. She reaches over and grabs something that looks like a large phone receiver and hits a button on it. "Do you know the number you need to call?"

"I do." I tell her the number, and she dials it for me. Once she's done, she hands me the phone and continues to stand nearby. I put it up to my ear, and it's already ringing. "A little privacy, please?" I smile.

"I can't leave you while you're still sitting on the side of the bed. Those are the rules." She shrugs.

"Fine!" I drop the clunky phone receiver by the bedrail and scoot myself back as quickly as I can. I lean against the pillows and grab the phone again.

"You stay right where you are and holler as soon as you're off the phone. Just hit this button here as soon you hang up. We'll get you up and moving then." She points at another device next to me, indicating the cartoon-like image of a nurse on it, and leaves.

I bring the receiver up to my ear. It isn't ringing anymore.

"Hello?" The voice on the other end of the phone sounds sleepy. I wait for the door to click shut before I reply.

"Hello, dear, it's your favorite old lady," I say, already anticipating his surprise.

"Effie? You're awake? How is that possible?" Sawyer asks, sounding bewildered.

"You should know me well enough by now to know I'm not giving up so easily." Maybe I should fall into a coma more often. It's certainly fun surpassing everyone's expectations and waking up from it.

"Are you okay?"

"I . . ." I hesitate, not sure how to answer that. "I would say there have been some leftover effects, but I'm sure those are only temporary."

"Like what?"

I think hard on this, knowing the answer I need to tell him is in this brain of mine somewhere—it's the reason I called him, to tell him, to warn him of something.

"I can't say," I respond, my voice sounding strange to me. That isn't what I had intended to say, and I can't seem to recall what I had been thinking, either. "But listen, that isn't why I called. We need to go to plan B." That isn't true, either. What is wrong with me?

"Plan B? Effie, aren't you going to be okay?" Sawyer says after a long pause.

Plan B was something we had devised in case I didn't live through my mind-hijacking experience. After all, if I did live, I would be the first person we know of who had ever done it successfully.

"I'll be just fine, but we need to move forward now." I sound much more sure of myself than I feel.

"If you're sure," Sawyer says. He sounds hesitant. "I'll keep an eye on Marcus Griffin, then."

"Good. I'll be out of the loop for a while it seems, but I'll get out of here as soon as possible." There's something else I needed to tell him. What is it? "Oh, Sawyer, if you hear from Adrienne . . ." I can't get the words out.

"Yeah?" he prompts me, but now I've lost what I was going to say.

"Oh, never mind me. I'm not sure what I was going to say." And that's as troubling as my blurting out everything to Adrienne earlier. Thea is never going to believe I didn't mean to tell her. What has happened to me?

CHAPTER 12

ADRIENNE

"And then he said, 'I'll take one hundred!'" I hear Calvin say, and then Megan guffaw as I open the front door to the condo. I stand just inside the door, pausing to take a deep breath. I had expected Megan to be asleep, and I definitely did not expect Calvin to be here.

You have the worst timing, Calvin, I think as I drop my keys and wallet on the entryway table. I cover my face with my hands, rubbing my eyes. On the drive home, I replayed Grandma's words, trying to figure out whether or not to believe her—the whole conversation feels like a crazy dream—and contemplating how to get in touch with Sawyer. Surely he would at least be able to tell me if this is a delusion of Grandma's. I mean, it's pretty hard to dispute that there has to be some truth to what she said given that I heard her in my mind. But how can it be true? How do I ask Sawyer, who is practically a stranger, about any of this? If I were him, I'd think both my grandma and I were nuts.

The question I really want an answer to is one Sawyer can't help me with. If it's all true, how could my mom be a mind reader and never even let on that something is different about us? I suck in a breath as another thought occurs to me: *What about Dad and Toby? Are they different too?*

Although, this might explain my mom's unwillingness to ever talk about her past. I don't even know how my parents met. Every time I've asked, they give me some vague answer like they had mutual acquaintances, or they were always bumping into each other. Nothing that tells me how the two ended up together, much less on a date. And they've always changed the subject when I've pushed for more.

Another laugh from the living room, and Megan calls out a hello as I let the door fall shut. I close my eyes and wish I could sneak upstairs to think this through. If only *this* were all a dream.

"Surprise!" My eyes fly open as I jerk, startled by the nearness of Calvin's voice.

"Um . . . hi," I mumble, unsure what to say or do. He is only inches away. "What are you doing here?"

"I wanted to see you, so I flew back." He moves even closer, putting his hands on either side of my waist. He leans down to kiss me, but I turn my head to the side, putting my hands on his chest. "Hey, what's wrong?"

"I just . . . I'm tired. And I didn't expect to see you." I avoid looking at him.

"I know finals are over, and Megan says you think you did well. I thought we could celebrate. What do you say? I'm only in town until tomorrow afternoon."

I open my mouth to speak, but Calvin cuts me off.

"And I was hoping we could set a date. It's been impossible to catch you on the phone in between meetings."

"Calvin," I start without planning what I'll say next, "I don't . . . I can't . . ." I pause, hoping the right words will magically come to me. He is staring intently at me. "I'm not up to any of this. I can't set a date, either." I hold my breath, glad I said it and yet wishing I could take back every word because I don't want to have a fight with Calvin right now.

"What?" He shakes his head. "I flew in this evening to see you, to celebrate the end of finals, to set a date for the wedding." He moves a few steps away. "I've been here, waiting for hours for you to show up. This"—he gestures toward me—"isn't exactly how I was expecting our night to go."

My shoulders droop. "I know, and I'm sorry—" I stop mid-sentence as he walks away from me to the kitchen. I reluctantly follow, not sure what he's doing. Why do I always end up apologizing?

"Calvin?" He's standing by the sink, his back to me.

"I expect better from you, Adrienne," he finally says. "I deserve better. I'm trying here." He turns to face me. "And I feel like I'm the only one. What is going on with you?" He stares, his eyes revealing his annoyance.

"I get that things have not been . . . *I've* not been what you've expected since the proposal, Calvin." I watch him closely, the muscles in his jaw ticking as he clenches and unclenches. "I . . . I . . ." I stop and take a deep breath. It would be so much easier to just let things continue, to keep my hesitation to myself. But I can't. "Calvin, we've never dated anyone else. I can't . . . I can't say I am in love because I'm not sure what it means or what that would look like." My face flushes. "I have this hope, this thought, that if I'm in love, I'll know it. That I won't be able to mistake it for anything else."

Calvin paces across the kitchen, stopping to sit heavily in a chair at the kitchen table. He closes his eyes for a long moment. Finally, he looks at me. "That's okay, you'll get there. We'll figure it out together, because that's what couples do."

I cross my arms over my chest, wishing he would make this easier. "I can't marry you, Calvin, and—"

"What the hell, Adrienne?" Calvin interrupts, jumping to his feet. I stay where I am and fix my gaze on the floor. I force a shaky breath in as I look up to meet his eyes. He stares for a long moment. My insides are shaking. Since Calvin's been my only boyfriend ever, I've never had to break up with anyone before, and I'm glad. This is awful. I can feel the hurt emanating from him.

He sputters and paces, making unintelligible sounds. Then he stops and faces me. "Are you . . . are you breaking off the engagement?" His voice is quiet, his words deliberate and even.

I close my eyes, swallow the lump in my throat. "Actually, Calvin, I think we should—"

"Oh my god. You're breaking up with me, aren't you?" His face changes from hurt to amazed and settling back to angry.

"I—"

"No, I don't want to hear whatever it is you're about to say." He looks up and holds both hands up in front of him. "This . . . this is just cold feet," he says more to himself than to me. "That's all this is." He looks at me directly now and takes a step, putting his hands on my shoulders and bringing his face eye level with mine. "You're just having cold feet." I open my mouth to interrupt him, but he puts a finger to my lips and shushes me. "I've forgotten you're so much younger than I am."

"I'm only a year younger than you, Calvin."

"This is completely my oversight," he says with a smile and a choked laugh. "You need time and you don't know how to ask for it. I understand now." He reaches for me with a smile on his face as if to hug me.

I step back and shake my head, not sure what to say. He's wrong. This isn't cold feet.

"So here's what we'll do," he says, bringing his hands together. "I'll go ahead and make the move to Boston, we will set a date for a couple of years from now, and everything will go back to how it was before the engagement." He finishes his sentence with a wide smile, obviously happy with himself for solving the problem.

His response didn't include anything about how much he loves me. I wonder if he can honestly say he loves me, or if I'm just part of his plans.

"Calvin, I don't think you do understand, actually—"

"Uh, Adrienne," Megan interrupts. "Parker is here."

Of course, because I couldn't possibly just break up with Calvin like a normal twenty-year-old girl, I think, resisting the urge to stomp my foot like a child. *What do you want, Parker?* I think silently.

"I need to talk to you right now." I glance at Megan first, her eyes round. She's probably heard everything. I try not to think about that right now and make eye contact with Parker. His eyes are red-rimmed and dark crescents stand out against his light skin. He looks as if he hasn't slept in a while.

"What do you want, Parker?" Calvin says as he takes quick steps toward my best friend, his voice never betraying a hint of the anger I see in the set of his jaw. When Parker doesn't answer, he continues, "Look, buddy, it's late and we're in the middle of something. Let the adults talk and try again tomorrow at a regular time. Adrienne can talk to you then about whatever your problem is this week."

Parker doesn't even glance his way. "I need to talk to you *right now,*" Parker says, his eyes still on me, not even the flicker of a grin on his face.

"That's not going to happen, Parker," Calvin says, stepping closer. "Is that what this is about? Did Parker finally get big enough stones to tell you how he feels? What kind of guy takes advantage like that? I'm not gone—just in Boston, Parker."

I shake my head and start to speak.

"Sit down and shut up, Calvin," Parker says before I can say anything, though. He takes a menacing step toward Calvin, and Calvin pokes him in the chest. Parker shoves him back.

I scoot in between them and push, trying to separate them both. "Guys—" is all I manage to get out before Calvin takes a swing. I cringe as Parker blocks Calvin's right fist careening toward his face, but Calvin follows it up immediately with a left-handed punch and connects with Parker's jaw. I put a hand against Calvin's and Parker's chests and duck as more fists fly, barely avoiding Parker's knuckles as he swings at Calvin. "Stop!" I yell. Parker's fist connects with Calvin.

Calvin pushes into me, trying to get at Parker, but all the punching seems to have stopped finally. Parker reaches out and smacks Calvin's forehead with his open palm. "You're going to trample her, moron," Parker says.

Calvin jerks back in surprise and curses.

"Both of you, stop it." I look first at Parker, then Calvin. Calvin takes a step back.

"So now that's settled," Parker says pointedly at Calvin, "Adrienne, can we talk outside for a moment?" I hesitate, and his face goes expressionless again. "I wouldn't be here like this if it weren't incredibly important."

I let out a breath.

"Do not step out that door with him," Calvin says, his face bright red, his fists clenched.

I look in surprise at Calvin. He folds his arms over his chest.

"Adrienne, I mean it," Calvin reaffirms.

If my mind weren't already made up to hear Parker out, it would be now. I nod at Parker and walk toward the back door. "Come on, Parker."

Calvin throws his hands in the air and stalks away down the hall. I reach for the doorknob, but Parker puts a hand on my arm to stop me.

"Let me, please," he says.

"Since when are you gentlemanly?" I mumble, pulling my arm back as if it's on fire. I gesture for Parker to lead the way. We step out onto the back patio, which is nothing but indistinguishable shapes in shadows. Parker stops short, and I almost run into him.

He continues to block my path as he glances around, his back to me. I wait, but he still doesn't move out of the way. "What's up, Parker? What is so urgent that it couldn't have waited until morning?"

He finally turns to face me, but I can't see his face in the darkness of the patio area. "You're in danger, and we have to get you out of here."

"What?" I say with incredulity, taking a step around him and away from the door to trigger the motion lights so I can see his face. The lights burst to life, and he suddenly looks as if he might jump out of his skin. He shields his eyes from the light and scans the area around us. He pushes me lightly toward the corner of the porch that's still shrouded in darkness. "What are you doing? If you're worried about Calvin—"

"Move over there, would ya?" There's no smile on his face; otherwise, I would think he's messing with me.

"What the—"

"Shh," he says quietly as he puts a hand over my mouth, which is still hanging open in surprise. The neighbor's cat comes out of the shadows, and Parker drops his hand, sighing with relief. I swallow and straighten up, trying to solve the puzzle that is my best friend.

"What is going on, Parker?"

"I know you're going to have a hard time believing me, but we don't have time to go over it all right now. You'll just have to trust me." He runs his hands through his hair.

"About what, Parker?"

"There is a really scary guy after you, and we can't let him find you."

"Are you being serious?" I say, blinking up at him. There's no way he is. "Ha ha, Parker. Now can we go back inside? I'm kind of in the middle of something." A look crosses Parker's face I've never seen before. *Fear? Is he afraid?* I wonder.

I step back again, trying to gain a little distance from Parker, and I bump into the chaise lounge and stumble. My arms flail in an attempt to right myself. My fingertips brush Parker's as he steps forward and grabs my wrist. He steadies me.

Maybe everyone else is perfectly sane. Maybe I'm the one who has lost her mind, and I'm imagining all of this. Maybe I'm chemically unbalanced. That explains my dreams and everything Grandma said. It's all part of my imagination. Mind readers aren't a thing.

Parker stares at me for a long moment, indecision etched on his face. He stands a little taller and seems to come to a decision. "I really do hate to be the one to break it to you —way more than you'll ever understand—but this is all real," he says as he rubs his jaw where Calvin hit him. I open my mouth to speak, but he holds up a hand and continues. "I promise I will explain everything as soon as we get you away from here. But we have to move now. The threat is real, and we don't know if he's already lurking out there somewhere or on his way here yet or what, but I'm not interested in finding out."

This can't be happening. I don't even know what to think or believe. And how is this Parker in front of me? My Parker, who never takes anything seriously.

Pondering the situation and replaying my grandmother's words in my mind—*"you are a mind reader"*—I wonder if what she said has anything to do with what's happening right now. *Or is this about Parker?*

"Does this have anything to do with you quitting your job and our conversation about you keeping someone else's secret?"

"Not exactly." He puts a hand on my shoulder, nudging me toward the back door.

"Which part is the 'not exactly' part? And where do you want to take me? You do realize it's like . . . " I look around for a clock and realize I set my phone down on the table in the foyer, and that clearly there are no clocks on my back patio.

"A little after three in the morning," Parker supplies. "Yes, I do know what time it is, Adrienne," he says with frustration. "Come on, back inside. We need to go." He pushes me toward the door again.

"Then where is it you want to take me at three o'clock in the morning?" I obligingly move toward the kitchen entrance.

"Somewhere safe." He isn't making eye contact now. He's scanning the yard again.

"And then what? You'll keep me there indefinitely until this guy dies of old age?"

"Once you're safe, we'll come up with a way to find him. We always do."

We? Who else could he be talking about? How does he even know any of this? "Who is we, Parker? You and I?" I feel uneasy, thinking now that maybe Parker is the one who is delusional. *Is he hearing voices now?* I hold my breath while I wait for his response.

"It's closer to the truth than you know," he says cryptically. "But the answer to your question is me, you, and some others who have a lot more experience with this kind of thing. We will figure out what to do once you're safe." He lets out a huff. "Can you please pester me with these questions once we're on the road? We've got to go."

"You really expect me to believe all this? To just walk out of here on your say so like . . . like what, Parker? What do you expect? What is this about?" I plant my feet. He doesn't answer right away. He sighs heavily and steps in close, leaning down until his face is mere inches from mine. His face shows his worry in the tight lines around his mouth and eyes. I swallow but hold my ground.

"In the years you've known me, have I ever done anything that would make you doubt me right now?"

I feel his breath on my face as he waits for an answer. I stare into his eyes, trying to wrap my head around what's happening. I don't know what to think or do, and I don't know if any of this is real or imagined, or if it's something he's dragging me into. The only thing I know for sure is my friend who is standing right here in front of me is asking for my trust, his concern written in his eyes.

I hesitate, feeling the weight of what he's saying. Then I turn on my heel and take the few remaining steps to the back door and yank it open. I cross the threshold and find Megan standing in the kitchen with Calvin next to her. He still looks angry and now pitiful as he holds an ice pack to his left cheek.

"Calvin, you have to leave," I say, having made my decision before I walked back into the condo. "Megan, you need to pack faster than you've ever packed in your life."

CHAPTER 13

ADRIENNE

"Whoa, whoa, *whoa*!" Parker says in a harsh whisper after he pulls me back toward the door away from the others. "Megan is not coming with us." He shakes his head.

"Yes, she is," I say, my jaw set. "If I'm not safe here, then neither is she. What if this guy comes looking for me here and finds Megan here alone instead?"

"This guy doesn't just go around killing whoever happens to be in his way. He's much more precise and specific. Megan's not his type. We can't just bring Megan with us without authorization."

"Killing? You didn't say anything about someone being killed." I don't know what to think about that.

"What did you think I was talking about when I said this guy was after you? That he's coming by for a tea party?"

"I don't know!" I throw my hands up. "But you didn't mention he's trying to *kill* me!"

"Now I have. Will that get you to move any quicker? We have to go. Now."

"I'm not going anywhere without Megan."

He rubs his hands over his face. "Fine," Parker says. "Whatever will get you out of here quicker."

"What is going on?" Megan asks, hand on her hip.

"Come on, I'll tell you what I know once we're upstairs packing." I start toward the stairs, and Megan follows.

"Adrienne." Calvin stops me in my tracks.

"Calvin, I can't talk to you right now. I know we need to finish our conversation, but I can't right this minute."

"I don't deserve to be treated like this, Adrienne. There are a dozen girls I can think of off the top of my head who would gladly take your place in an instant. If you take one more step, I'm done. That's it. It'll be over between us."

I open my mouth, but nothing comes out.

"Way to make the choice super easy for her, man," Parker says with a scoff.

"Calvin," I say quickly, hands up, hoping to calm the situation before he takes another swing at Parker, "I don't like ultimatums. I need to go, but I'd still like to finish our conversation another time." He stares at me, jaw clenched.

"I guess the last three years together mean nothing to you." He frowns, his eyebrows drawn together. It looks like he might cry, but there isn't a tear in sight. I don't respond. "What's the point? We both know how that conversation will end." With that, he stomps out the front door, slamming it behind him as he leaves.

"Glad that's over," Parker says with a snort. "I thought I was going to have to put him in a sleeper hold so he'd shut up, and we don't have time for that."

"Come on," Megan says, and I follow her up the stairs, blinking.

"So," I take a deep breath once we're in Megan's room, "a lot has happened."

"Yeah, like you just broke off your engagement!" she says, her eyes wide. "Are you okay?"

"I . . . I'm kind of numb at the moment. There are too many other things happening."

"Yeah, so tell me what the hell is going on with Parker?"

"Here's the thing," I say as I grab her overnight bag from her closet and start dumping her makeup in. "Parker says I'm in danger and that someone is after me."

"What?" Megan says with a laugh.

"And I believe him," I say, fixing Megan with a serious look. "The same way I would believe you if it were you telling me this." I see her swallow. Her eyes are still wide. She clasps her hands together in front of her. "And if someone really is coming here to harm me, then I'm not leaving you here, either. So here." I hand her the bag I've grabbed from her closet. "Pack. And be as quick as you can."

"Wait," she says, coming to the doorway as I stop in the hall. "What if someone is after you and it's because of something Parker has gotten mixed up in?"

"What if it is?" I shrug. "We would still need to go." Megan looks torn, trying to decide for herself whether or not she should go. She finally nods.

I go to my room and shut the door behind me. I lean against it, closing my eyes. Did I just break up with my longtime boyfriend? Did my grandmother really tell me we're mind readers? And has Parker added to it all with some kind of scheme that's gone wrong? I can't think it all through right now.

After packing quicker than I've ever packed before, I drag my bag and tired body to Megan's room. She's desperately trying to zip her rolling suitcase, but it isn't working—the zipper is blocked by clothes overflowing out of her suitcase.

"I don't think that's going to work out," I say.

She yanks a piece of clothing out and then another, depositing them on her floor. She tries the zipper again, and it works this time. She grabs the handle to the rolling suitcase with one hand and the strap to her obviously full duffel bag beside it.

"What?" She bats her eyelashes. "I never agreed to go run and hide without my essentials." I suppress a laugh as she struggles with the overstuffed duffel bag and her purse.

"Essentials. Right." I smile. "Let's go."

We head for the stairs. I reach the bottom of the stairs, and I can feel Parker's impatience from where I'm standing. He moves to grab my bag. I let him.

"We have to go," he says with a crease in his forehead. I nod and take Megan's duffel bag as she struggles to the door with her suitcase.

Only the yellow glow of the porch light greets us when I open the door. Parker looks around, his back to us as Megan and I pause while she locks the door. No scary guys in sight. Parker drops something to the concrete sidewalk. It looks like a cell phone, now shattered.

"Is that . . . was that—" I stammer, pointing at the mess on the sidewalk.

"Your phone?" he finishes for me. "Yes. You could be tracked with your phone." My mouth hangs open. "Which brings me to you." Parker turns to Megan. "First things first," he says as he looks from me to Megan, "you don't need to come with us. It would be much better for you, actually, if you don't come with us."

"But—"

"He's right," I say. "You just can't stay here. You're free to go anywhere you'd like."

"As if you get to leave me behind when there is clearly something major going on," Megan says with a scoff. "Not happening." With that, she takes her phone out of her back pocket and starts to hand it to Parker. I put a hand on hers, stopping her.

"Are you sure about this?" I ask her.

"I'm sure. You know my dad. He'll be happy to buy me a new one anyway." With that, she hands it to Parker.

Cursing, he fumbles with the case it's in. Finally freeing it, he smashes it on the sidewalk.

Megan heads toward the parking lot. With a glance back at the condo, I reluctantly follow.

As we approach the parking area, one of two men waiting in a big black SUV in the middle of the parking lot gives Parker a thumbs-up signal. My steps falter when I see them.

"Don't worry about them," Parker says. "They're with us, just in case." He moves to an identical SUV, but my eyes never leave the other SUV with the serious-looking men in the front.

"Don't you usually drive a rust bucket? Seriously, what is going on?" Megan says as if reading my mind. Parker doesn't answer. He takes Megan's bag from me and gestures for me to get in. I get in the passenger front seat as Megan climbs in, settling on the row of seating behind Parker and me. Parker opens the back, throws my bag in, and loads Megan's luggage as well. He comes around and gets in the driver's seat, throwing a look my way. I see his Adam's apple bob as he swallows before turning his eyes toward the windshield.

"It's time to spill it, Parker," I say as he starts the SUV and fastens his seat belt.

"Once we're on the road and all clear, I'll tell you everything I can," he responds, his knuckles white on the steering wheel as he glances around, peering into every mirror.

Everything he can? I think. *What can't he tell us?*

"I would love to know who the guys in the SUV behind us are, and why you have a shotgun," Megan says from the back seat. I raise my eyebrows when I turn to look at her and see the shotgun on the seat next to her.

"Like I said, I'll explain soon enough," Parker says as he pulls out of the parking spot and exits the parking lot. The other SUV follows closely behind.

"I need to call my mom, Parker," I tell him, suddenly realizing I should have thought of that before he broke my phone.

"Your mom already knows what's happening. We'll see her and your grandma soon enough," he says. "They'll be meeting us at the secure location. And your Dad and Toby will also be there, but it might take a little longer to round them up."

I'm speechless. I can't imagine a scenario in which any of this would make sense. Guns and a backup team and matching SUVs and secure locations—where does Parker fit into all this? He seems so casual about it. Like it's an everyday occurrence.

After a few more turns, we're on the interstate and headed north, away from Arnold, my hometown. Parker talks to the guys behind us on a walkie-talkie, confirming that no one is following us. He turns to me when he's done, leaning close.

"Adrienne, do you want Megan to know everything? That includes the things Effie told you at the hospital," he says, his voice almost a whisper.

I swiftly look at him. He won't meet my eyes. How could he possibly know what Grandma told me in the hospital?

"Megan will know everything whether you tell her or I do," I say, my brow furrowed. "Are you telling me this has something to do with what my grandma told me?" He straightens in his seat, but he doesn't answer.

"Since we graduated," he says, his voice loud enough for Megan to hear, "I've been working for a private organization that operates under the radar of the United States government and governments worldwide." Parker moves the rearview mirror to see Megan. "A couple of weeks ago, we received information that led us to someone we've been trying to track down for a while. We followed some leads, and it led us to you, Adrienne. It seems that this person has an interest in you for some reason."

Megan and I exchange a look, neither of us sure what to think about Parker's words.

"I quit my job last week because I was offered a full-time spot on the team tracking this guy." He merges onto 270 heading northwest. "I obviously have a special interest in seeing it through now," Parker says, glancing at me. "But he has managed to get away so far. And that's really all I can tell you about that."

"But—"

"There's more I want to explain to you," he interrupts, "about why I'm working with this organization." He takes a deep breath. His face is intermittently spotlighted by the streetlights along the roadside. "The organization I work for focuses on finding and helping people like you, me, your grandma, and your mom as they grow into their ability. They offer education and training to those who don't have anyone else to teach them about who they are. And the organization is a conduit for us to build our own community." He talks quickly, glancing my way. "The organization isn't naive, either, though. They understand the need for a police force that comprehends our abilities and can keep a watch on situations and deal with criminal factions that exist among those of us with these abilities. Better us than some government agency that wants to destroy us all or dissect us."

My head is spinning. I'm not sure I understand him.

"Back up a step," says Megan. "What are you talking about here? What do you mean by 'people like you and Adrienne'?" She looks to me and then back at Parker.

I'm feeling sick to my stomach now as I think about his words. *No, no, please tell me he isn't saying what I think he's saying.* I swallow hard and wait for Parker's answer.

A look of resignation is etched on his face, making him look older and tired. "I have what's called neurodivergent telepathic abilities, which is really a fancy way of saying I'm a mind reader."

I feel my heart stutter. I stare out the window and watch the car next to us in the exit-only lane. It's a man and a woman, and I wonder what has them out so late. They leave us, slowing as they take the off-ramp for Telegraph.

Megan laughs. "Okay, Parker." She shakes her head slowly. "You're an idiot. I totally believed you all the way up until now." He smiles at her in the mirror. "Who are those guys behind us, really? Are those your buddies? Is this some elaborate practical joke? You win," she says with a nervous laugh. "Best joke ever." She laughs again. "I'll send you the bill for a new phone, though. For me *and* Adrienne. And a shotgun? That's too far." She's not laughing now.

"You know, maybe it's easier if I just show you." I hear Parker's voice, but I realize belatedly he hasn't spoken a word. Just like what Grandma did. Megan's laughter dies out immediately. She must have heard him too, inside her mind. *"I promise this isn't a joke."* Parker's voice sounds in my mind again.

"What did you mean when you said the agency helps people as they grow into their abilities?" I ask, afraid I already have an idea of the answer. I swallow, pushing down the bile that's in the back of my throat. How is this real?

"For most people, their neurodivergent telepathic ability doesn't manifest until adolescence or adulthood," Parker explains out loud. "It has something to do with the maturity of the brain."

Adolescence? Does this mean Parker has been able to hear everything I'm thinking since the day he met me? He's heard every embarrassing thought that has flitted through my mind since I was fourteen, including thoughts about him.

"Stop the car," I say quietly, putting my hand on the dash. We're about to go under the overpass for Gravois Road. The shoulder here is too narrow to pull off safely. My breath comes in short bursts. I can't take a full breath. Parker keeps driving. "Stop the car," I try again, a little louder now that we're past the overpass.

"What?" He glances at me. I can't tell if his words were in my mind or spoken that time, and I don't care. I see pinpoints of darkness floating in my vision.

I suck in a deep breath. "Stop the car!" I finally manage to yell as I yank my seat belt off, jamming the button down with my thumb to release it. He hits the brakes and pulls to the shoulder, crossing two lanes in the process. I open my door before the vehicle comes to a full stop. I stumble out, falling to my knees. I open my mouth to take a deep breath. But instead, I vomit on the side of the road.

Megan is by my side in an instant. Soon, there are footsteps to my left and to my right. I see two sets of shoes out of my periphery to the right and I realize it must be the guys from the other SUV. Parker is standing a few feet away.

"I'll get you some water," Megan says, moving back toward the SUV.

As she moves away, Parker comes closer and squats down. I don't look up to meet his gaze. I can't. I feel tears falling down my face. I hate puking. I hate crying. I hate being lied to even more.

"Adrienne," he says tentatively, quietly.

"Don't, Parker," I say and swipe my hand across my mouth. Megan hands me a water bottle, and I take a little sip of the water and swish it around in my mouth. It tastes sweet after the bitterness of the bile on my taste buds. I spit it out, then shakily take a slow sip and swallow it.

"Adrienne," Parker says again as he reaches a hand toward me.

"Do not speak to me, Parker," I say, my cheeks warming either from my mortification at learning he's heard my thoughts all these years or from the outrage that he's never told me—I'm not sure which. I stand and brush my knees off. My whole body feels shaky now. Traffic flows in a loud, steady stream beside us on the highway, the sound barrier along the highway reflecting the noise at us. A few tractor trailers rush past us, one of them honking on his way by. Parker stands too, and the lights from the vehicles dance across his body. My heart is hammering away in my chest, its beat echoed in my hands and feet.

"You're telling me that not only was my grandma telling me the truth, but *you* are one of them—a mind reader, or whatever the hell it is?" My voice started out quiet, but I'm shouting to be heard over a passing truck. It feels good to shout, to release some of my anger. "And you've known about all this"—I wave my arm around, spilling water—"and you've told me nothing—not a word to your *best friend*—about any of it?"

Parker takes a step toward me. "Adrienne—"

"Don't," I bite out at him as I take a step back. He runs his hands through his hair. I didn't think any of this could be real when my sick grandmother was talking about it. And I'm just so *angry*.

"Hold the phone," Megan says. "You're really a *mind reader*? This is a real thing?" She points to Parker. He nods. "And that's why you just . . . what *did* you do, anyway? It was like you became the new voice in my head," Megan says, wide-eyed. I stare up at the sky. I don't want to talk about it anymore.

"I shared my thoughts with you and Adrienne," Parker says. He shoves his hands into his pockets and looks back to me. "And I'm not the only one who can do that. There are thousands of us across the world, and"—he swallows hard, his Adam's apple bobbing—"Adrienne is one of those people."

"If I were, surely I would know it," I scoff.

Without looking at either of them, I turn back to the SUV and climb in. I shut my door and lean my head against the headrest. *"How could you lie like that?"* I think. *"Over and over, with every word you've ever spoken to me? You lied about who you are. How could you do that?"* Silence. He doesn't respond. *"Do you hear me, Parker?"* I think the words.

"Yeah, I hear you," Parker answers in my mind as he and Megan get in.

Silence fills the vehicle as he navigates back onto the highway, staying in the lane closest to the shoulder. There are trees to the right of us. We hurtle by them.

"Let me get this straight," Megan says from the back seat. "You can read minds and project your thoughts, and you work for an organization or agency or whatever that finds other people just like you?" She leans forward.

"Yes," Parker says. The radio is on in the background. I focus on the sound of the song as it plays. It's my attempt to keep my thoughts to myself. I have no idea if it's working. *He doesn't get to know what I'm thinking.* I cringe, realizing he probably heard that.

"And Adrienne's mom and Grandma Effie are also mind readers?" she asks. Parker nods. "But her dad and Toby aren't?"

"Correct."

"But then how does Adrienne have this ability if Toby doesn't?" We take the ninety-degree exit that takes us to I-44 westbound. She braces herself by grabbing the back of my seat.

Parker doesn't answer her. I peek at him, and he appears to be lost in his own thoughts.

"Parker? How does Adrienne have this ability if Toby doesn't?"

"Luck, since Adrienne's dad—"

"Stop talking as if I'm not here," I interject, my tone flat. Parker clears his throat and shifts in his seat.

"Right. Since Tom, your dad"—he holds his hand out toward me before returning it to the steering wheel—"isn't a mind reader, then the chances are . . . well, I don't know of any other person who has the ability whose parents don't both have it as well."

"What about your family, Parker?" Megan asks. "Can all of you read minds, then? I feel silly even saying it. It doesn't seem real," Megan says incredulously.

I can feel Parker looking at me. I refuse to meet his gaze, keeping my eyes forward and my thoughts on the lyrics of the song playing.

"Both my parents are mind readers, as is my little sister," he says.

"Emma? But she's only thirteen," I say, unable to resist commenting. Emma and I have always been pals. Since neither of us has a sister, we treat each other as the sister we've never had. Parker has certainly been able to keep this a secret from me all these years, but I can't believe Emma never told me.

"It happened only recently," Parker says.

"Do you really call yourselves mind readers?" Megan says, her tone skeptical.

"Um, no, actually, but that's the best way to describe it," he says with a hint of a smile. If the situation was different, I might appreciate how well my two friends are getting along right now. "The official label, neurodivergent telepaths, is pretty clinical, and it sounds pretty ridiculous." He laughs. "We don't really call ourselves anything. We're people."

"Tell me, Parker," I say, cutting off Megan's next question, "how long have you known you're a mind reader or whatever you want to call yourself?"

"I—"

"And how did you know what I had discussed with my grandma?" I cut him off, not waiting for the answer.

He clears his throat. "I've known about my own ability and that of my family's for as long as I can remember," he says, taking a hand off the steering wheel to wipe his palm on his jeans and then repeating the action with the other. "I didn't develop telepathy until I was about sixteen, though." He doesn't say anything else.

You knew what Grandma said because you read my mind, didn't you? I think the words, concentrating on hurling them his direction. I don't know how any of this works, but I'm hoping the louder I am with my thoughts, the more it gives him a headache or hurts his ears or something.

"Yes, but it isn't as simple as you might think," he responds in my mind. I can feel the mental sigh behind the words. A glance at Megan tells me that answer was only directed at me.

I ignore it. "What about me and my family? How long have you known about us?"

"Well, I've known about you since the first time I met you," he says quietly. He's confirmed it, then. I've had no real privacy with him over the last six years. I reach over and smack the power button for the radio, shutting it off. The silence stretches, and I can feel his guilt as distinctly as I feel the slightly warm air blowing onto my arm through the vent in the dash.

"How did you know?" Megan asks.

I glance at her. We've made it a couple of miles down I-44 to my favorite stretch of road. The area around the highway isn't dotted with convenience stores, hotels, and office buildings. It's darker and less busy. Usually, I feel peaceful here. But not this time. In the dim glow of the dash lights, Megan's eyes are wide. She offers me a reassuring smile. She knows what I'm thinking, and she doesn't have to invade my privacy to figure it out.

"I can tell whenever I meet anyone who has the ability but hasn't learned how to control it yet. Most people's thoughts are a quiet hum that I have to tune into if I want to hear." He shifts his gaze to me for a moment before turning back to the road. "Your thoughts . . . well, it's like you're speaking your thoughts into a megaphone."

It's worse than I thought: I've been screaming my thoughts at Parker for years now.

How many times have I humiliated myself? I think and then wish I hadn't, because I'm sure he heard that too. Heat rushes to my cheeks. I should have left the radio on.

"Do you read the thoughts of everyone around you all the time, Parker?" Megan asks. I glance at her again, but she looks away.

"Don't worry. Like I said, your thoughts are a low hum." He reaches over and turns the radio back on, and I want to scream at him to get out of my head. He's trying to be nice. I don't want him to be nice. "And I have a policy about staying out of people's heads as much as possible," Parker replies with a reassuring smile that doesn't reassure me at all.

I almost declare on the spot that he's a liar since he's just shown he obviously doesn't follow that policy where I'm concerned. But I don't. I keep it to myself. Or at least between him and me.

"Why don't I seem to be able to tap into these abilities I supposedly have?" I ask with narrowed eyes.

"Because you've never learned how," he says with a half-hearted shrug.

I frown at him. "Uh, explain?"

"It's like being born a natural athlete: You have the ability within you, but if you never pick up a basketball, you'll never become a basketball player." He changes lanes to pass an old car with a broken taillight and an impossibly loud exhaust system. Its muffler must be either severely damaged or missing.

"Is there a way for me to keep my thoughts private from you and others like you?" I ask when the car is nothing more than a dull roar somewhere behind us.

"Yes," Parker says immediately. "We all use a simple technique that allows us to sort of keep our thoughts in a box. It shouldn't take you too long to learn, either." He glances at me. "I would be happy to teach you."

I don't want his help.

"Or you can keep screaming at people. Totally your choice," he says with a slight grin.

None of us say anything for a while as we go up and down hills, bluffs on either side of us. Their rocky surfaces have been carved away for the spacious four-lane highway. A sign alongside the road marks our passage into Franklin County. I've never been this far down I-44.

"Where are you taking us?" I ask in a bored voice that belies my intense curiosity about our destination.

"We're going to a remote facility out in the woods outside of Saint Clair. And your family will meet us there."

"Why is someone after Adrienne specifically?" Megan asks from the back, giving me a pat on the shoulder when she asks. I raise an eyebrow at her. "I mean, I get there are probably people in the world who wouldn't want people who can read minds to exist. So there's probably people and organizations on the lookout for you all. But Adrienne doesn't even know how to use her ability. Why her?"

"I don't know," Parker says, glancing over at me, his brow furrowed. "But Marcus wants to see you when we get there. I'm sure he'll tell you more."

"Who's that?" Megan asks.

"Marcus Griffin is the director of the organization for our area."

"And what is this agency called?" I ask.

"Path Endeavors," Parker replies.

"Path Endeavors," I say with a sneer. "That sounds more like a cult than a legitimate organization." Parker doesn't reply. "Why did your organization go round up my family to bring to your facility if I'm the one this psycho is after?"

"Partially as a precautionary measure, but mostly because your mother insisted you all needed to be together," Parker says as he flips the right-turn signal on and then merges right onto the exit ramp. According to the sign for this exit, this is Saint Clair. There are fast-food joints and a couple of gas stations, a boutique hotel, and a pharmacy clustered around the highway here. I glance at the clock on the dash and see it's almost five o'clock in the morning.

"Are we officially in the middle of nowhere?" Megan asks, stifling a yawn.

"Not yet, but we will be in about twenty minutes," Parker says as he checks his mirrors.

"I have one last question for you, Parker," I say, turning in my seat. I see his hands grip the steering wheel tighter. I'm sure he already knows what I'm about to ask, that he can hear it in my mind. "When were you planning to tell me about your mind-reading ability, or about mine?"

We sit at the stoplight at the top of the exit ramp even after it turns green, his eyes meeting mine. He's silent for a long moment, letting out a breath, only the rhythmic sound of the blinker breaking the silence. My thoughts flit to the first time I met Parker at school. Homework together, movies watched, the first time he drove us anywhere—he was so excited about that stupid truck. I remember them all in as much detail as I can, hoping to project each memory to him. *You had so many chances to tell me*, I think.

"Guys, the light is green again," Megan says, "and I need to pee." Parker turns just as the light changes to yellow. I notice the other SUV follows too, despite the light.

CHAPTER 14

ADRIENNE

After driving winding roads for a while, we take a left down a narrow paved lane. It's bumpy with long-neglected potholes and crumbling pavement. Several minutes of driving later, the lane turns to gravel.

The sky is getting lighter, the sunrise just minutes away. Both sides of the single-lane gravel road is lined by big trees and forest beyond. Secure location. He really meant obscure location.

"We'll be there in just a couple of minutes," Parker says, interrupting my thoughts. "The facility is actually an old retreat that was used for summer camps. There are dormitories, a lake with a dock and boathouse, a cafeteria, a lodge, and even a little chapel. Some of it was already part of the camp, and some of it we added over the years. Like the perimeter fence. There's a perimeter fence with guards at the gate and patrols walking the grounds and fence line," he says as he glances over at me. He looks tired, but his voice is strong, confident. "So you'll be safe here."

I'm sure he means that to be reassuring, but I feel my heart rate kick up a notch as we make it to the end of the tree line, only to be greeted by a fence topped with razor wire and a gate complete with guards holding rifles. Parker leans over, reaching for the glove compartment. He opens it up, grabs what appears to be a badge, and closes it back up. He wasn't quick enough for me to miss the handgun in the glove compartment, though.

We pull up to the guards and the gate, and two men in dark clothes, boots, and bulletproof vests come up to the vehicle. Parker talks to the one at his window, showing him a badge on a lanyard. I raise an eyebrow and look to Megan. She's fidgeting in her seat, her eyes fixed on the guard near my door.

The guard by Parker scans something on the back of the badge Parker's holding out.

"Hey, Parker, how's it going today?" the guard scanning Parker's badge says.

"Henry, how are you? Hey, do you know if Dr. Thompson has been back through yet?"

"We haven't seen her yet, but she should be here soon according to the radio chatter."

"Okay. Thanks, Henry."

He nods, and then after a moment, both guards back up and wave us through as the gate opens up. We go through the gate and then start down the winding drive.

There's nothing but meadows surrounded by groves of trees. A creek winds through the property, and after a turn to the right, we come to a small bridge built for vehicles and foot traffic to go over the creek. Next to the road on either side of the bridge, there's a rock path that continues on in both directions.

The terrain starts to get rockier as Parker takes us farther down the drive, then slowly up a long, steep hill. I rub my tired eyes with the backs of my hands to clear my vision. At the top of the hill, we slow down to a crawl.

"Welcome to Camp Little Creek," Parker says, gesturing to the view in front of us.

The sun has just appeared over the rise to my left, and its brilliance has perfectly outlined the serene view below us.

From the top of the hill, the lake in the valley off to the left with a dock and another outbuilding looks small. To the right, there's the little chapel Parker mentioned. Its steeple is standing proudly atop the stone building. My eyes move to the center of the valley to what I guess is the lodge Parker referred to, but the word *lodge* doesn't line up with what's before me.

The lodge is a large stone and glass building that's an amalgamation of modern and rustic design. It's several stories high, and the whole building is lit up. It's beautiful.

Beyond the lodge are long buildings, rowed up one after another. I can only guess these are the dormitories. These buildings are the oldest-looking buildings on the grounds. Behind the chapel is another building, but I can't make out many of its details from here. There are paths and roads that lead into more wooded areas, and it looks like another large building is half hidden in the woods near the lodge.

"It seems so serene," Megan says quietly. She's leaning forward between Parker and me, peering out the windshield.

Parker speeds up a little as he drives us around the lodge to the dormitories in the back. He parks in the lot between two of the metal buildings. There are a couple dozen cars parked here. I wonder how many of those cars belong to people who can read minds. Neurodivergent whatever. I still can't believe this is real.

"Grab your stuff, Megan," Parker says as he puts the SUV in park and opens his door.

We all get out, and I stretch. My body is begging for sleep, my limbs heavy and my eyes burning a little. Parker opens the back of the SUV. He grabs a bag, and I move closer to get my own bag, but Parker grabs it before I can. I roll my eyes. He hands both bags to one of the guys from the vehicle that followed us here.

"Hey, the mom and grandmother have just arrived as well," the guy who I think was the driver says to Parker.

"Megan," Parker says, walking toward her. She's standing next to me now with her suitcase and duffel bag, looking disheveled and weary. "Mike here"—he gestures to the guy who just spoke to him—"will show you around the dormitory and get you settled. I'm going to take Adrienne up to see her mom." Megan nods and turns to me.

"I'll make sure there's a room nearby for you too," she says with a smile. I smile back.

"Thank you," I say. She gives my shoulder a squeeze and then turns her attention to Mike.

"So . . . Mike, is it? Do you read minds too? Because if you do, then you'd know the first thing I want to see is where you keep the coffee around here," I hear her say as she walks away.

"Are you ready?" Parker asks quietly. He's standing next to me now. I let out a long sigh.

"Let's go," I say as I open the passenger door to the SUV, never meeting his gaze. He walks around and climbs into the driver's seat.

"Hey," he says once he's in and has started the engine. He turns in his seat to face me. I ignore him and roll my shoulders, trying to loosen the muscles starting to ache from tension. He doesn't continue, but I know he's going to.

"I'm so tired, Parker," I say, avoiding looking at him. "Can we just go and save this discussion for another time?" I lean my head back and close my eyes. His fingers gently grasp my elbow.

"Can I show you? Please?" His voice is in my head again. I can feel his desperation. And guilt. He's feeling so guilty. I open my eyes and look at him. His posture is stiff. He's wearing an expression I can't read, but his eyes are pleading.

After a few moments, I finally relent and nod. As soon as I do, my world starts fading and a new scene materializes in my mind. It's a scene that's familiar.

It takes me a moment to realize I'm looking at the world through Parker's eyes, from his perspective. He's somehow brought me back to the day I met him. He's looking down and watching me—high-school-freshman Adrienne—pick up my books that have just been scattered across the hallway at school. I'm complaining loudly about the school, my classes, my locker, and my terrible day in general.

In that moment, I lift my head to look at him, and Parker draws in a breath. I can feel him smile as my eyes meet his. My voice continues in a whining diatribe, but my mouth doesn't move. My complaints are part of my internal chatter.

The scene flashes, and next he's looking at my mom out of the corner of his eye as she wipes the kitchen counter. Parker, my mom, and I are in the kitchen of my family home. Mom is talking to him mentally as Parker and I sit at the breakfast bar, heads bent, working on algebra homework together.

"Our situation is not like yours, Parker," she says in his mind. *"If you love her and care about what happens to her, you won't tell her or anyone else what you know about her and my family."*

"How is lying to her going to keep her safe?" he asks, sending the thought to my mom. *"It's not as if others won't realize what she is."* She doesn't answer. She throws the towel she had been using into the sink, stares at him for a moment, and then walks away.

"If you want to be my daughter's friend, you'll keep her out of your world." It's Mom's voice, but she's out of sight.

I feel his indecision and a surge of protectiveness as he glances over at me. *"Okay. I won't tell her. But you should."*

With that, the scene flashes and begins to melt in on itself, as if it's a strip of film that's been lit on fire. Another flash, and the scene fades from my mind completely.

"What did you just do?" I say, putting a hand to my head. I'm blinking, trying to understand how I could be in such a scene complete with smells and feelings one moment, and right back here in the front seat of this SUV the next.

"I shared my memories with you," Parker says.

"But it was more than your memories," I say as I shake my head to try to rid myself of the emotions I had been feeling from Parker when he took me back to the scene with my mom insisting he not tell me about our abilities.

"Oh, that," he says, his face flushing and his hands fidgeting. He faces the windshield again. "Your mom thought I was in love with you."

"What?" I ask, then I remember her words: *if you love her.*

"Forget it," he says, checking the mirrors before backing up. "When I said I was keeping someone else's secret before, I meant yours. I was keeping your secret. Because it's what I promised your mother I would do."

I look out the window and watch a rabbit as it sits unnaturally still, on alert, as we pass it along the road. Parker is driving toward a building behind the lodge I hadn't paid much attention to earlier. I try to sort through my thoughts without broadcasting them. I'm not sure I'm successfully keeping them quiet, so I give up.

"You never should have agreed to keep who you are—who I am—from me," I think.

"I'm sorry you feel like I've betrayed you," he responds, *"but I trusted your mom knew what was best for you. I made that decision because I was sure Thea was right—that somehow it was the only way to protect you from something I didn't understand."*

"That's not good enough, Parker."

He stops the car. He looks at me, his lips pinched tightly together. After a moment, his breath rushes out in a heavy sigh.

"Do you think I haven't thought about telling you a million times? It's not like it has been easy keeping this from you," he says, brows pinched. "I have played the scenario of me telling you over and over." He huffs out a mirthless laugh. "And do you know what I realized, Adrienne?" He points a finger at me. I shake my head. "There isn't a single path I could have chosen that wouldn't have led to this"—he gestures at me—"to you feeling the way you do right now. I could have told you the day we met, but would you have believed me?" He runs his fingers across his scalp. "Probably not. Why would you believe some boy you just met that he knows something your own family has been keeping from you your whole life? You would have thought I was a lunatic. And if I'd told you later, once you knew me and trusted me—even if you would have believed me then, you still would have felt like I'd been lying to you, like I'd betrayed you. We see how well *that* would have gone." He looks away. Silence fills the space.

I clear my throat and say quietly, "I guess we'll never know for sure, will we?" I get out of the SUV, slamming the door behind me.

CHAPTER 15

ADRIENNE

Parker follows closely behind me as I reach the building. I crane my neck to see to the top as I stand near the entrance. It's three stories high, and its exterior matches the lodge with stone and glass walls in the front. I open the door and enter, Parker right behind me. I don't hold the door for him.

Once I step in, I stop in my tracks, surprised at the grandeur in front of me. The lobby has cathedral ceilings, exposed wooden beams, and a second-story balcony made from rough-hewn timber. I admire the large natural stone floor and the overall effect. It feels ornate and almost extravagant in a warm and natural way. Every rock in the floor looks like it was taken from a riverbed, no two stones exactly alike. But yet, they've been put together—tans and browns and ochre—to create a flowing pattern.

A guard walks over to us from a large reception desk in the center of the lobby.

"Parker," he says with a nod, his hand out, palm up. Parker steps around me and puts his badge in the guard's hand. The guard scans it and hands it back. "Is this Adrienne?" he asks, pointing to me.

"Yeah, this is Adrienne, but she left her ID in her other pants," I say with no expression on my face. I shouldn't take out my anger with Parker on this guard standing in front of me. He doesn't deserve my snark.

"Yes, sir," Parker says. "It's her all right."

The guard smiles and shakes his head as he hands me a bright-red plastic badge with the word VISITOR in large white letters across both sides and a somewhat blurry photo of me in the bottom-right corner. A lanyard hangs off the top.

"There's no doubt you're Thea's daughter," he says, one eyebrow raised as he gives me a once-over. "They're in the infirmary."

I wonder if the guard can read my thoughts.

"You should keep that visible," Parker says as he takes the visitor's badge from my hand and puts it over my head. It settles around my neck, and I quickly take a step away from Parker and toward the long hall before me. I hear him sigh behind me.

"Come on." Parker walks around me and down the hall. I watch him as he walks. His normally easy amble is stiff and hurried.

"Where'd they get my picture? It looks like the one on my driver's license."

"I'm sure it is," he says quietly. "It would be the easiest to get." I don't know that I like that much. It makes me wonder if the organization has some government ties.

We pass door after door, each with a small placard near the doorframe. The placards are numbered—no names or titles. There are a few rooms with open doors, each containing the typical administrative office furniture—a desk, a couple of chairs, and a desktop computer.

I refocus on the hall in front of us, but there isn't much to see, really. There are double doors ahead blocking the hall. We reach the doors, and Parker puts his badge over a square gray panel mounted to the wall to the right of the door. After he holds it there a brief moment, the doors swing open and we walk through.

There's a turn ahead in the corridor leading to the left. As we approach it, some voices become louder. It sounds like two people are talking. One voice I recognize, and another I've never heard. The voice I recognize is Mom's, and she doesn't sound too happy.

"—wasn't part of the deal, Marcus," she says. "You were supposed to leave her alone completely!"

"She isn't a child anymore, Thea," a man I assume is Marcus says. His voice is calm and even as he answers. Parker stops walking and looks at me with eyebrows raised. I ignore him, move a little closer to hear better. "Would you have preferred we had left her to be killed?" At that, Parker shakes his head and starts walking again. I reach out to stop him, but it's too late. He's around the corner now, and I'm sure they've already seen him. He clears his throat, and I quickly follow him.

My mom's face is flushed, her fists clenched. Marcus looks to be around the same age as Mom with worry lines permanently across his forehead made more noticeable by his receding cool-brown hair. He fixes me with a kind smile and moves toward me, hands outstretched.

"Adrienne, I presume," he says as he takes one of my hands in both of his. His hands are strong and smooth and overly warm. "It's so nice to finally meet you."

"Thanks," I say hesitantly, looking from him to Mom and back again. "I'd love to say the same, but since I have no idea who you are . . ." I withdraw my hand from his sweaty palms and resist the urge to wipe them off on my jeans.

"Forgive me." He laughs as he looks at me more intently. "I had assumed you would be able to tell that from my thoughts." Parker stiffens beside me. "I introduced myself in my thoughts. I'm Marcus Griffin. Welcome to our facility here at Camp Little Creek. I'm the director for Path Endeavors here in Missouri, and this is our basecamp, as we like to call it."

"Why am I here?" I ask, unable to force myself to participate in chitchat when I'm dead exhausted, confused, angry, and apparently on the run from some psycho I know nothing about. Mom shifts nervously beside him.

"Ah, yes, as I was telling your mother just now, let's put a pin in that discussion until we've gotten you and your family settled and let you all get some rest."

I don't answer him, and I do my best to keep my mind blank. Mom gives me that look that I know means she wants to talk to me alone, immediately. But she holds herself back and continues to fidget.

"Okay, well, I'll let you chat with your mom and check on your grandma for now," he says after I don't respond. He moves to the other side of Parker, putting a hand on his shoulder. "Once you've had a chance to get some rest, have Parker bring you to see me." He gives Parker a pat on the back, me a wink, and my mom a wave as he turns on his heel and heads in the opposite direction down the hall. I stare after him.

"Mom, do you know who this psycho after me is?" I ask. She's staring at me, her lips pressed together into a thin line. She walks stiffly toward me, her eyes moving to Parker. When she reaches me, she wraps her arms around me in a fierce hug. I just stand there, letting her hug me, not sure I want to hug her back. I'm still pissed at her. But I can't help myself as I relax into her arms, my shoulders sagging. The weariness from everything I've learned in the last twenty-four hours—and the lack of sleep—hits me. I bring my arms up to hug her back when Parker's words remind me why I'm angry with my mom.

"Thea, either talk to us both or keep your thoughts to yourself," he says. I freeze. "I won't be helping you lie to her anymore. She already knows everything, so I don't really see the point."

I gently push against my mom. She releases me. Her face flushes once again, but this time from embarrassment at being caught.

"Adrienne, there's a lot we need to talk about," she says, reaching out for me.

"Of course there is," I say with an impatient laugh, "because you've never told me anything. So I know exactly nothing."

She puts her hands on my elbows, giving me a squeeze. "And we will talk about everything, but not yet." She looks at Parker and then back at me.

I pull my arms out of her grasp and walk away a few steps, turning my back to her as I scrub at my eyes. It just makes the slight burning sensation worse. I need sleep. Or a good cry. Or both. Does she plan to keep me in the dark even now after I know the secret she's been keeping? How is that going to help anything?

"Parker, would you please give us a minute alone?" Mom asks.

"I'll be out in the lobby waiting when you're ready to leave," Parker says, touching my shoulder. I look at him—his hair tousled, his eyes a little red, his face and shoulders showing the tension he's trying so hard to hide—and I nod reluctantly. He returns my nod before turning to go. I watch him walk away and wish everything could go back to the way it was a day ago, and that I could fall onto my bed right now, close my eyes, and sleep for days.

"Before I say another word, you have to learn to block your thoughts from others," Mom says. I whip my head around to look at her.

"Mom, I can't read minds." I shake my head at her. "I can't do the things that you and Parker can do. How do you expect me to learn how to block my thoughts?" I ask with an impatient snort.

"You're right," she says quietly as she takes rapid steps toward me. "You can't *only* read minds," she said, her voice a whisper. "You can do so much more."

My mouth falls open. I can't begin to guess what she means, and I'm in no state to try.

"Come on." She takes my hand. "I'll show you. But first, let's check on Grandma. She's here in the infirmary." I pull my hand free but give her a nod. She shakes her head and starts walking down the hall. I take a deep breath and follow.

"Better, but you must stop focusing on resisting me," Grandma Effie says as I fail once again to block her from hearing my thoughts. "This isn't about pushing someone else out. You have to hold yourself in."

"Ugh!" I groan as I open my eyes and push myself up and out of the chair next to Grandma's bed. I pace around the room, rubbing my eyes that feel heavier and heavier with every attempt to keep my mind locked down. Mom watches me from the corner of the room, leaning against the wall behind her. She's been eerily silent since we entered the room. Her silence makes me wish I really could read minds.

"Imagine you're building a room like this one around your thoughts. Your thoughts can only be opened up and examined once they're inside the room and the door is shut."

I look around the room now, staring at the walls, floor, and ceiling once again. They look like they belong in a recording studio, not a medical facility. The room is covered with something that looks most like acoustic tiles with odd pyramid-shaped protrusions on the surface.

"Why do the walls, floor, and ceiling look like a padded room and a recording studio got together and had a baby?" I ask, looking from Mom to Grandma. Grandma is sitting up in her bed looking increasingly more tired by the minute.

"Because these," Mom says, indicating the floor, ceiling, and walls, "are made with a special compound of material that limits a mind reader's ability. Only those within this room can read each other's thoughts. It's a similar concept to acoustic tiles. It redirects brain waves, though, instead of sound waves, which is what acoustic tiles do to eliminate echoes."

"So no one outside of this room can listen in on our thoughts?" I stop pacing. The comfy chair next to Grandma is tempting me to return to it.

"Almost no one, which is why we're doing this here," Grandma says and leans back against her pillows. "And also a good reason to visualize this room as the place in your mind where your thoughts live," she adds with a wink.

"Why would a group of mind readers need a room like this to block a fellow mind reader if they can all block their thoughts, anyway?" I look around the room once again.

"Sometimes our sick need a room such as this to help heal their minds," Grandma says. I stare at the tile beneath my feet. While it looks like it should be soft, it's as hard as concrete. "It works both ways, keeping thoughts in and helping to keep others' thoughts out. Now let's try again. Your last attempt was better than the one before at least. You have your thoughts down to a low hum." I cross back to her side and sit down. "Remember to build the room before letting your thoughts out."

"Fine," I say as I roll my shoulders, letting my head hang down to try to loosen the muscles in my body.

"Okay," Grandma says with a slight smile. "Ready?"

I nod, and Mom pushes off the wall and crosses the room to me. I close my eyes and concentrate. Slowly, I build a wall in my mind, one weird-looking tile at a time. Once that wall is built, I add three more, a floor, and a ceiling. My room is complete.

"Think about how angry you are with me," Mom says. I try to ignore her, focusing instead as I envision my thoughts in a box sitting in the middle of the floor of my mental room. "Really think about it. Let yourself feel it." Her voice is patient, understanding, and something else. Guilt, perhaps?

"Do you have your thoughts inside the room yet?" Grandma asks. I nod and envision myself locking the door on my mental room.

"Are you feeling angry?" Mom asks. I peek at her, meeting her look with a glare.

Of course I'm angry.

"Come on, you can do better," she says encouragingly. "I can still hear your thoughts."

"I guess I wouldn't suck at this if you and Dad had simply been honest with me. Parker says this is something everyone else learns as a kid."

"We were protecting you." Mom takes a step toward me. I clench my fists in my lap.

"Are you kidding me right now? You have lied to me for my whole life, and you recruited my best friend to do the same. And I'm not supposed to be upset by that?" I sound like a whiny little child. I let go of the box holding my thoughts.

"Yes, Adrienne," Grandma says, "you're doing it! Keep doing that. I can't define a single one of your thoughts well enough to know what it is."

I check on my mental room. I imagine my thoughts are floating around inside it just as Grandma has told me to do.

"Very good," Mom says with a sad smile and flushed cheeks. I stare at her, my blood still hot. She peers at me as she steps closer again. "It's sometimes easier to use our abilities when we're angry." She puts a hand on my shoulder. I let her. "Your walls seem solid now. You are excelling by blocking your thoughts so quickly. Really." I don't say anything. I am just so tired in every sense of the word.

I can't imagine what made my parents decide lying to me my whole life about who we are was the best choice.

"All right, enough," Grandma says. "Now that you're blocking your thoughts, we can really talk."

"Yes," Mom says, running a hand across her face. She paces across the room and back again. She pulls up a chair close to mine and sits. "You are more than a typical neurodivergent telepath," she says quietly. I lean in. "You should be able to feel what others feel, in addition to hearing their thoughts."

I push off my knees and lean back in my seat. "I *should* be able to? I don't understand." I don't. How can any of this be possible? How does it work? What makes us different?

"Just like blocking your thoughts, tapping into your abilities will take a little practice. Although, others—" Mom cuts herself off and looks at the floor. She takes a breath before continuing. "Sorry. I'm so used to keeping my abilities a secret, it's hard to switch that off. I should have said *I* was able to read and feel the emotions of those around me before I began my telepathic training. But it was as out of place as breathing to me, so it wasn't something I noticed. I thought everyone was similarly in tune with those around them.

But we don't talk about this extra ability with anyone, for any reason."

"Why? Why keep your abilities a secret? I mean, in a world where people can hear and share their thoughts, why does this stand out? A feeling is just a feeling." I shrug.

"We only know of a few other mind readers who have ever had this ability, and you and your mother are the only two alive," Grandma says, rubbing her empty ring finger on her left hand. The nurses at the hospital removed her rings as soon as she had been brought in by ambulance. Mom took them home to keep them safe, and she didn't have a chance to go home to get them before they were both whisked away to Path Endeavors. I've never seen Grandma without her wedding ring until her hospital stay.

"It gives you a huge advantage over others, including those of us who are telepathic," Mom says. "And that paints a target on our backs."

"How?" I scoff.

"For the rest of us," Grandma says with a smile, "reading minds is a lot less accurate than you'd think." She readjusts the sheet and blanket covering her legs and her lap, pulling them up higher.

"What do you mean?" The dark-blue cushioned chair beneath me creaks as I cross my ankles.

"It's like those text messages you kids are so fond of," she says with a wink. "For me, reading someone's thoughts is like reading a message on my phone: I have no sense of the tone of that thought. It's flat. Someone could easily deceive others with their thoughts as a result. But also being able to sense if their emotions line up with their thoughts helps you to know whether or not they're being honest."

"And when there is no message to read, you'll still be able to sense and feel someone's emotions," Mom further explains, fidgeting in her chair. "The only way to block someone like us from feeling your emotions is not to have any."

"You sound pretty confident that I have this ability." I put a hand on my knee to stop its bouncing. What does it mean if I can't read minds or feel other people's feelings?

"We are very confident since it's something your mother inherited from her father. It should pass on to you." As usual, Grandma softens when she mentions Grandpa. "We're also confident you have more abilities as well." She continues on. "You should be able to slip into the mind of anyone whose thoughts are unguarded. It's more than simply listening to someone's thoughts. That's an extremely rare ability. You happen to be in the room with the only two people we know of who can do such a thing."

"Like, what—control their minds or something?"

"No," Mom says with a laugh. "It's not that . . . complete. It's more like you're along for the ride. You can observe their thoughts, feelings, intent—you even experience what their senses are experiencing."

"That makes even less sense." I shake my head and squeeze my eyes closed for a moment, trying to ease the burning of my tired eyes.

"It has its limitations," Mom says. "You need to know precisely who you're targeting, and you need to be close to their location. Again, it's all about brain waves."

"But let's skip the scientific explanations for another time when you've slept, what do you say?" Grandma says as I rub my eyes with the back of my hand.

"Is that it, then? I should be able to hear others' thoughts, feel their emotions, and even stop in for a visit in their brains?" I can't keep the incredulous tone from my voice.

"Yes, with a little practice," Mom says, no hint of a smile.

"How far away from someone can you be and still do these things?"

"We'll have to see for you. It's different for everyone. But generally, you have to be within a few miles of the people whose minds you're going to be visiting. And as for feeling others' emotions, I usually need to be in the same room to tell exactly who is feeling what, but I can see waves of emotion all around us from people inside this building and a little farther beyond."

"Parker said before I'm the only mind reader he's ever heard of having a father without any abilities. What if I don't have any of these abilities?"

Mom and Grandma are staring at each other now. Mom pushes her hair behind her ear.

"Thea," Grandma says, reaching out a hand toward her. She lets it drop to the blanket as Mom sits perfectly still, her face now pale.

"Mom?" My brow is furrowed. "What is going on?"

"Your father was a mind reader too, Adrienne," Mom says, finally looking at me. "But he was murdered before you were born."

"What are you talking about?" I look wide-eyed at Grandma and Mom.

Mom stands and moves to the other side of the room, her back to me. Her shoulders sag.

I take in a ragged breath, not sure I want to hear her answer now. *Is Dad dead? Did that psycho get to him as Parker was rushing me here?*

"Tom is just fine, Adrienne. He's across campus with Toby, settling in," Grandma says as she pulls the covers back and moves her legs. Her feet now dangle off the side of the bed. She grunts with the effort of scooting to the edge. "Your mother didn't mean to imply he wasn't." I breathe a sigh of relief. "But she isn't talking about Tom."

"Then who are you talking about?" I look at Mom. "Mom? What is going on?" She doesn't move.

"Theodora," Grandma says, prompting Mom.

Mom makes a noise, something between a groan and a cry. "I . . . I . . . can't," she says, her voice choked. She whirls around and heads for the door.

"Thea, don't." Grandma's voice is as hard as flint. I've never heard her sound so stern. Mom stops at the door, handle in her hand.

"Adrienne," Grandma says to me, beckoning me with an open hand. "Adrienne, come sit."

"What the hell is going on?" I practically yell.

"Tom is not your father, Adrienne." Mom answers in a shaky voice, avoiding eye contact.

I jerk my head around to meet Grandma's steady gaze, to confirm the words my mother has just uttered. Grandma's hands are folded in her lap. She meets my stare. I'm not sure what I expected my mother to say, but that wasn't it.

"Excuse me," a woman's voice says from the doorway. "I need to check your vitals, Mrs. Greathouse."

"Can you come back later, Cynthia?" Grandma says with a sweet smile at the lady wearing a white lab coat over expensive-looking slacks and a silk top.

"No, wait," I say as I back toward the door. "You can do it now. I was—" I try to swallow, but my throat is dry. "I am leaving." My voice is breathless. I'm not sure if she heard me or not, but I don't wait around to figure it out.

I exit the room without a backward glance. With tears in my eyes, I hurry toward the lobby.

"Hey," Parker says once I've reached the lobby, his voice off to my right. I don't stop. I keep striding toward the doors.

I push through the door and step out into the sunshine, and blink. Tears stream down my face. The door behind me opens, closes. Parker stops next to me. Neither of us speaks. I focus on keeping my mental room intact, examining every wall for cracks. I don't want him to read my thoughts. I don't know how I'm feeling or what I'm thinking, but I don't want to share it with him—another person who has been lying to me.

Maybe it isn't a secret to him; maybe he already knows the man I've called Dad my whole life isn't my father.

I want to scream. I want to run far away from this place, back to yesterday before any of this. When my biggest problem was how to tell Calvin I don't want to marry him. When Parker was still my friend whom I trusted.

I start walking. I don't know where I'm going, but I have to do something.

"Hey," Parker says, his voice sounding more concerned, "what is going on?"

I don't answer him. I just move more quickly. As my feet hit the grass on the other side of the parking lot, I look around to orient myself. The lodge is in front of me, and the road that Parker took to bring us in is beyond that. I pick up the pace and head toward the lodge.

"Adrienne," Parker says, his voice sounding shaky. I glance over my shoulder and see he's jogging alongside me. I'm almost at a run. "Adrienne!" He puts a hand on my arm. I jerk it out of his grasp.

I'm almost to the back of the lodge. I'll go around it to the road on the other side. That road will take me to the gate.

But then what? I stop near the lodge wall. I can't walk all the way home. I smack my open palm against the stone wall in front of me.

"Adrienne," Parker says slowly, "are you okay?" He leans closer, his eyes searching mine.

Tears are flowing down my cheeks. My hand hurts from smacking the stone. I don't care. I don't care.

Parker puts a hand on my shoulder.

"Don't touch me," I say firmly and quietly, a white-hot feeling in the pit of my stomach.

"Okay," Parker says just as quietly, pulling his hand back. "Adrienne, what happened in there?"

I don't answer him. Parker pushes his hands through his hair. I start walking again.

"Where are you going?" he asks.

I look around. I'm not sure what for. "For a walk."

"Okay. I'll come with you."

"No."

"Why not?"

"I just want to be alone. I need to think and I can't think when you're with me because then all I can think about is how you've been lying to me for all these years." I take a deep breath. "So no, you can't come with me."

"Okay, okay," Parker says, "fine. I deserve it. But, Adrienne," he says, closer to me. I keep walking. "Would you stop and listen for one minute?" He says it quietly, putting his hand on my arm. I reluctantly stop, turning to meet his eyes, hoping he can't see the anger that's boiling up and spilling over. "We might all be liars, but it doesn't change the fact that we all care about you, does it?" I stare at him, nonplussed. "Go for your walk, punch a wall, whatever. But when you're done, get some food and some sleep. Give yourself a minute to process everything you've learned. Then you might realize we're still the same people."

I nod absentmindedly and then start walking again. How could my mom have lived this lie all these years?

"Don't take too long," he says. "Your dad and Toby are here now. They've been asking to see you."

His words trigger a new thought. What if Dad doesn't know he isn't my dad? I stop. The adrenaline and anger have worn off, dripping away with each new tear. Would Mom lie to Dad too? My muscles are begging me to find the nearest bed and sleep for days. I wipe my face with the back of my hand. My shoulders sag.

"What do you say to a walk to the dormitory instead, and you can skip straight to that sleep part of the list?" Parker asks.

"Yeah," I agree without looking at him. "Lead the way."

CHAPTER 16

EFFIE

Thea drops into the chair by my bed and puts her head in her hands as soon as Cynthia leaves the room, closing the door quietly behind her.

"That couldn't have gone any worse," Thea says.

"Just wait until we tell her we think someone's been after her since James died." I wish I could pull the words back as soon as they're out of my mouth, but I can't. She sits up and looks at me.

"I'm sorry, my dear," I say. I want to smooth away the worry line on her forehead. "But I think you couldn't have expected it to go any better. You just told the girl you've been keeping her in the dark about her father right after she's learned you also actively hid her abilities from her." She sighs. I refrain from saying I told you so. But I did tell her many times this would be the result. "Give her a little space and a good night's rest, and things will get better, you'll see."

"I hope you're right, Mom," she says, giving my hand a squeeze. "What are we going to do now?"

"First, I should tell you I had already told Adrienne she is a mind reader last night when she came to see me in the hospital. I don't know why I told her, especially since I had agreed just before she arrived that we would wait to tell her." I pause, close my eyes, take a deep breath, and think for a minute. That nagging feeling that I've forgotten something is back—except no, it's more than that. I feel out of control, like a part of my brain isn't working right or responding. "Thea, I think something's wrong with me."

"Mom, you're just healing still." She waves me off, as if that will make what I'm saying untrue.

"Thea . . ." I start, but I'm suddenly feeling so tired now. My energy has drained right out of me.

"Mom?"

"What?" My eyes are heavy. I let them slide closed. Just for a moment.

"Mom," she says more insistently this time.

I'm torn between sinking into the peacefulness I currently feel and answering Thea.

"What?" I choose Thea. The heaviness lightens just as quickly as it came over me. I meet her eyes, which are round and full of concern.

"Let me get Cynthia again."

"For what?"

"What do you mean, 'for what?'" She sounds incredulous now. "You just told me there's something wrong with you and then almost passed out. I'm getting Cynthia."

"I did? Are you sure? I feel fine as a frog's hair. I'm just tired, that's all. Quit yapping and let me sleep already." I smile at her now.

"You probably do need to sleep, but I'm getting Cynthia anyway. I'll be right back, Mom."

"Before you go, will you hand me that notepad and pen?"

"Sure." She looks at me quizzically.

Why do I want it? I've already forgotten. I need a nap. A nap. Sleep. Sleeping can bring dreams. That's what it is. I want to be able to write down anything I dream about as soon as I awake.

"In case I think of something while I dream, I want to be able to write it down when I wake." I smile, and she steps toward the door, eyeing me as if I might disappear as soon as I'm out of her sight.

"No sleeping until Dr. Cynthia comes in and checks you out."

"I can't make any promises."

CHAPTER 17

ADRIENNE

It stinks in here. Not overwhelmingly bad exactly, but it makes my nose itchy. The combination of dampness and disuse and something more earthy makes me want to open a window. I slowly open my eyes, blinking as I look around. It's mostly dark. I can't make out much. But I'm standing, and my shoulders are in agony. How did I get here? The last thing I recall is Parker showing me to my room in the dormitories I'm sharing with Megan.

My head flops back. Muscle control seems to be outside of my abilities right now. I peer in the darkness, trying to see what's around me. Above me are my arms, which are raised and pulled tightly. I close my eyes for a moment, wishing I could rub the grainy feeling away, but I can't. Opening my eyes again, I squint and stare up, following the length of my bicep and forearm until I make it to my wrists and hands. Something is definitely not right. My wrists are bound, I think. My arms don't look like my arms, either.

Whatever is wrapped around my wrists is digging into my skin. My arms are keeping me upright, taking my considerable weight. My wrists ache and my forearms burn. Just my toes touch the floor.

I must be dreaming, but this feels differently than my other dreams. I feel almost as if I'm in control of this body.

I try to flop my head forward to look down, but I don't make it all the way and my head falls back again. I try again, concentrating harder. It works! Staring, it looks like I'm on a concrete floor. There's a small drain nearby.

Black work boots, black pants, and a black T-shirt—all covering my body, a body that is obviously male and much larger than me.

A scraping sound followed by a shutting door echoes through the dark, damp room. My heart rate shoots up and my breathing increases with the echoing of heavy footsteps heading my way. I try to lift my head to see who's coming, but I can't.

Someone moves in close. I can't see the person's face, though, since it's hidden in shadows. Whoever it is looks tall, his stance and shoulders giving his silhouette a masculine appearance. He steps closer to me, reaching out a hand covered by a medical glove. He swabs my neck with a small square of something that's wet and cold. Then he jabs a needle into my neck. I flinch. But soon a warmth flows from my neck, radiating to the rest of my body. I'm tasting something like rubbing alcohol before he's finished. Heaviness settles over me quickly and my head hangs limply. My legs are no longer able to support me on tiptoe, either, and my knees buckle. As a result, the pain in my shoulders keeps the heaviness from my mind. But only for a moment. Everything goes black.

I wake up covered in sweat and gasping.

"What's through there?" Megan asks Mike while pointing to a door at the end of a hallway in the lodge. I'd say he decided to join us on our tour, but I get the feeling we aren't really allowed to go anywhere without him.

I slept most of the day yesterday and all night long. I was starving when I woke up. So we left for breakfast around six o'clock this morning. Mike was waiting for us outside the dormitory.

"Behind that door is our library," Mike says as I wander around the expansive lobby. I gaze out the windows to the east—windows that span from floor to ceiling, which in this area is three floors up. The horizon is starting to show the first signs of sunrise, painting the walls yellow two stories up. Noticing movement, I glance at the entrance in time to see Marcus push through the door, a young woman following closely behind him. She's talking quickly and keeps looking down at a planner in her hand, scribbling notes as Marcus answers her. His gaze is locked on me as he strides my way.

While Marcus is still halfway across the wide, open room, he holds up a hand and the young woman following him stops in her tracks. He crosses the room and stops in front of me.

"Adrienne," he says with a smile that's too bright for seven o'clock in the morning. "I'm glad to see you've had some rest." He stands there, letting the silence stretch on. I say nothing. His smile broadens. "Let's talk in my office. I understand you must have questions."

"Um, sure," I say. I look over my shoulder to find Megan and Mike. They're across the room near the library entrance. I raise a hand to wave Megan over.

"Mike," Marcus calls, following my line of vision. Mike and Megan head toward us. "Please, won't you and Adrienne join me in my office?" Marcus says to Megan when she and Mike reach us. Megan's eyes dart my way briefly before she moves closer and loops her arm through the crook of my arm. Her stance is relaxed and casual, but I can feel the muscles in her arm are tense. "That is, if it's all right with you that Megan tags along?" Marcus turns his questioning stare to me. I nod.

"It's never good to be called to the principal's office," Megan says with a smile.

Marcus laughs. "That's true." Marcus's smile broadens. "Come on." He gestures to Mike as he starts moving without waiting to see if the rest of us follow.

Marcus leads us across the room and down another hall and toward an elevator. The elevator doors open, and the four of us step in. The young woman, who I assume is his assistant, quickly steps in as well.

"Marcus!" someone down the hall calls.

It's Mom. I'm not ready to see her yet. She jogs to us and steps into the elevator. I can feel my neck and shoulders tensing up already.

"Thea," Marcus says with a smile, arms spread in a welcome, "I'm so glad you could join us. We were just headed up to my office."

Mom doesn't answer him. Instead, she fixes him with a steely stare and steps closer to me. I step away from her and bump into Megan's side. I glance at Megan apologetically. She lets out a quiet laugh followed by another and then a snort. I raise an eyebrow at her.

"I'm sorry," she says, smiling, "but you and your mom look so much alike right this second."

I frown at her.

"So, Adrienne, have you started training yet?" Marcus asks, looking to me and my mother.

"I, uh—"

"You know Adrienne hasn't been trained because you know she wasn't aware of her ability until Parker picked her up and brought her here," Mom says, interrupting me.

I keep my face passive and my mind blank, trying to keep my thoughts in my imaginary room so Marcus can't hear them. I'm not sure what her beef is with him, but I don't want anything to do with either of them right now.

The elevator dings as we come to a stop on the fourth floor. The doors open to reveal a scene I wasn't expecting. From this elevation, I can see the entire compound laid out before me. The sun is just above the horizon, lighting up the fog, which meanders through the lowest portions of the terrain with the foothills surrounding it. The scene is ethereal in its peaceful beauty. It feels out of place.

Megan gives me a nudge and loops her arm through mine once again. Everyone else has already exited the elevator, and the group is following behind Marcus as he strides to his office. I follow reluctantly with Megan.

"I'm not sure . . ." I begin hesitantly. "I'm not sure how it works for you, but try to keep your mind blank while we're in here, no matter what Marcus says."

"What? Why? What's going on?" Megan asks.

"I just have a feeling that it would be better not to let everyone around us know everything we're thinking. And I'm not sure I trust Marcus," I say, adding the last part so quietly I'm not sure she heard me. But she raises an eyebrow.

A smile slowly brightens up her face.

"I'll be mentally retelling the book I just finished last week, then." She bats her eyelashes.

"The super-trashy romance novel Mrs. Selner in 2B insisted you read?" I ask with a smile of my own.

"That's the one." I laugh as she waggles her eyebrows.

"Please, come in," Marcus says. We step in, and Mike quietly shuts the door behind us before he moves to the corner of the room.

Marcus's office is picture-perfect. The expansive wooden desk to the right of the room is gleaming with polish, not a single piece of paper on its surface.

"Do you think he decorated this himself?" Megan asks quietly, looking around.

The room itself is elegant. It's large with vaulted ceilings that reveal wooden beams. Along the exterior walls, tall windows provide a view much like the one I saw when the elevator doors opened. And to my left is a small couch with a few chairs facing it and a coffee table in the center. The decor is sparse, but in a good way.

Hanging on the wall behind Marcus's desk is a tapestry that catches my eye. It's a coat of arms, embroidered in faded red and orange and shades of brown on a thick, ivory material. A roaring lion stands on one side with a sphinx on the other, separated by two shields, one of which is covered in harps and the other in torches. It looks ancient with its fraying, tattered edges.

"Please, take a seat," Marcus says, gesturing around the room. His smile is casual as he sits on the edge of his desk. I remain standing, and Mom comes to stand next to me.

"Let's get on with it, Marcus," Mom says. His smile slips for a fraction of a second.

"As you know, Adrienne, we brought you here because we were concerned for your safety." He nods to someone over my shoulder as the door clicks shut again. I start to glance back but see an image appear on the wall to Marcus's right. The blurry image of a man in a leather jacket with the hood up is being projected.

He certainly doesn't look familiar, not that I can make out any features, really.

"Someone is targeting you and your family."

"Targeting us how?" Mom says.

"How did you find out he was targeting me?" I ask at the same time, not sure I'm ready to hear the answer.

"Jillian," Marcus says. His assistant, who must be the one who just entered, steps forward and hands him a file folder.

"An unknown caller left a message on a machine that's not exactly in use anymore." Marcus takes the folder. "It's a number we gave our undercover agents decades ago that we've kept active just in case. That message was simple: It was an address and a storage unit number. We gained access to that storage unit facility just a couple of hours before Parker picked you up. In it, we found pictures. Lots of pictures."

Marcus flips open the file folder in his hand. He pauses, handing a photo to me and another to Mom.

The air rushes out of me. It's as if I've stepped back into the storage unit. It's the same storage unit I saw in my dream. And the walls are all plastered with image after image of me.

I drop the photo Marcus has handed me, releasing it from between my fingers as if it's been lit on fire. I watch it as it falls to the floor, landing faceup. I try to look away, but I can't stop staring at my own smiling eyes in the largest photo on the wall pictured. It's the photo from Parker's phone.

"After we saw that, we looked for security cameras. The only one in the vicinity didn't give us much to go on. We have an image of him as he entered the storage unit at U-Store-It. Do you know the place?" He looks to me, then Mom. My heart skips a beat before resuming at a furious pace. The place sounds familiar. "It's just off interstate fifty-five near your home in Arnold." The image of a sign flashes in my mind, the words U-Store-It written in Comic sans serif. "The rental agreement appears to have a false name on it, but we're still looking for any leads from the information on the agreement— Thea?" Marcus interrupts himself, concern obvious in his voice.

I look up then, tearing my gaze from the photo on the floor. My mom is pale.

She clears her throat, puts a hand on the back of the chair in front of her, and leans almost imperceptibly on it. "You think this is the same guy linked to all the disappearances, don't you?"

"Yes," Marcus answers her, although her tone implies she already knew the answer.

"So what's your plan, Marcus?" she says through clenched teeth.

He smiles at her. "My plan is what it's always been, Thea."

"Why don't you fill the rest of us in on it, then?" I say.

"My plan is to keep you and the rest of our people safe until we know more about this situation. Once we know more about him"—he jabs a finger at the surveillance camera image of the hooded man—"then we can plan our next move."

"And just how do you expect to learn more about him? You have zero leads." Mom's cheeks blush an angry red.

"Leave that to me," Marcus says with a reassuring smile. Mom doesn't look like she's buying it.

"Am I supposed to live here forever, locked away for my own safety?" I glance around the room, feeling like this is an obvious problem.

"No, you certainly can't, can you?" Marcus turns his smile to me. His words feel almost gleeful. His emotions are out of place, and I feel a chill as goose bumps rise on my arm. "We have a plan in place, and we are working on getting answers. In the meantime, maybe it's time you start training. I'm sure your mother can help you with that. And with that, I'm sorry, but I need to move on to my next meeting." He looks around, smiling at each of us.

"Marcus, I need to speak to you alone," Mom says, quietly moving forward.

"If you plan to talk about this"—I gesture toward the photo on the floor and the blurry image that's still being projected onto the wall—"then I deserve to be present. I'm not a child."

"Of course, Adrienne," Marcus says. "But as I said, I have a meeting I need to attend shortly. So if you and your mother would like to speak with me further, Jillian will schedule an appointment for you."

Mom steps closer to him. "If you think I'm going to sit back and let you handle everything just like you did twenty years ago"—she pokes him in the chest—"you're going to be very mistaken." She stares him down for a moment before turning on her heel and heading for the door.

"Mom," I call to her as she reaches the door. She stops and turns to look at me. Her cheeks are still flaming red. "Wait."

I move to the door, and Mike and Megan follow. We move toward the elevator.

"Now isn't the time, Adrienne," she says between gritted teeth.

"You've been lying to me about everything since I was born. When exactly is a good time?"

"Never, Adrienne!" She practically shouts at me, spinning around. I step back. She puts a hand on my arm and takes a deep breath, a tear streaking down her cheek. She exhales, her breath leaving her in a rush, her shoulders sagging. "What you see as lies—Tom has been your father in all the ways that matter." I open my mouth to speak. She holds up a hand to stop me. "You haven't suffered by not knowing the truth until now. Please trust me for now and know that I fully intend to have this conversation with you, but not here." She lowers her voice. "And not now." She wraps me in a hug before I can stop her. Her shoulders feel taut, pulled tight by an invisible force.

She lets me go. Then she scrubs all signs of her tears from her face with the back of her hand.

My mind is racing. I want to tell her I've seen that storage unit before in my dreams. Maybe she can tell me whether it's some sort of strange coincidence, or if I have yet another strange ability that isn't typical for people like her. *No,* I mentally correct myself, *people like* us. What if this *is* one of the abilities she and Grandma talked about yesterday? And what about my dream last night when I was someone tied up in a basement? Was that real too? I have to tell Mom about that storage unit and my dream.

"Mom, I—" Mom's eyes go wide. I check my mental room where my thoughts live. I can't even picture the room at the moment. I must have been broadcasting my thoughts.

"Don't," she says firmly, looking around quickly, "as I said, not here, not right now." The others are several feet away, giving us as much space and privacy as possible in this situation, but I doubt it's any use, even though Megan is talking loudly about architecture in an obvious effort to avoid eavesdropping.

She leans in closer, making direct eye contact. "Take a deep breath and picture the room with the weird tiles." I hesitate a moment, doing exactly as she said before giving her a nod. "Better," Mom says with a slight smile. "Now, let's get out of here."

CHAPTER 18

ADRIENNE

"I know what you need," Megan says, putting an arm around my shoulders as we follow my mom to the exit. "You need coffee. Do you know how I know you need coffee?"

"Because you need coffee," I say with a smirk.

"Yes, yes, a million times yes. Does anyone else need some coffee?" she says louder. "That's my next stop."

"No, thank you, Megan," Mom says. "Adrienne, are you going with me to see your grandmother?" I look to Megan.

"I'll meet you in a little bit for more coffee and breakfast," Megan says. "Go see your grandma."

"Okay. Thanks, Megan."

"Perfect." Then she calls over her shoulder, "Hey, Mike!" He approaches from a few feet away. "Can you take me to the best coffee this place has to offer?"

"Of course, but just a moment," he says and then approaches me. "Here, take this." He opens his palm and holds out something that looks like a wristwatch, except it's missing a clock face.

"What is it?" I ask, taking it from his palm.

"We call it the watch, but it's a panic button."

"The watch? That's the best you guys could do?" Megan says, eyebrow raised.

"Yeah, our tech guys aren't known for their creative naming ability." He smiles at her. "This is just in case you need help. This button here"—he indicates a slightly recessed area where the clock face should be—"will send help running if you hit it."

"But how will 'help' know where I am?" I ask, using air quotes.

"The watch transmits a signal that allows us to pinpoint your location. Well, your location down to about ten feet of your actual position."

"Okay, then," I say, not sure whether to be grateful they are taking my security seriously, or freaked out that someone will be tracking my location at all times for the foreseeable future.

"It's waterproof," Mike says. "You can shower with it on or go for a swim. You can even dive up to twenty-five meters deep before we'll lose your signal."

"Thank you, Mike," Mom says, stepping forward as I struggle to put the watch on my wrist. She reaches out to help.

"We'll do our best to give you your privacy," he adds, confirming that the concept of privacy is officially flimsy now.

I swallow the lump in my throat.

"We'll see you at second breakfast," Megan says, looping her arm through Mike's. His eyes widen. We agreed as soon as we were done with breakfast earlier that we'd need a second breakfast just to make it to lunch since we ate so early. "Now, enough with the scary stuff," she says to Mike. "I need caffeine."

"Let me know if you need anything, Adrienne." Mike gives me a warm smile before walking away with Megan.

"I think this might be more terrifying than those photos upstairs," I say with a half-hearted laugh. I glance at Mom, but she isn't smiling. It doesn't appear that she even heard me.

Mom and I walk toward the entrance. I can feel the tension between us settle in my chest.

"We can talk once we're in your grandmother's room," she says as she opens the door and we step out. "Also, Grandma isn't doing as well as we thought."

"What do you mean?"

"We're not sure, but there's something off. She's been sleeping a lot and forgetful when she's awake. She told me about telling you about your abilities at the hospital." Mom sighs. "She had just agreed to wait. I'm sorry you found out that way."

I don't respond. I want to tell her I'm glad she told me, that at least Grandma told me the truth, but I don't. It's all been done. Now it's time to move forward.

The sun is up now, and a cold wind causes my skin to prickle. Most of the fog has disappeared now, vanquished by the warm rays of the sun. I lift my head to enjoy its warmth when I spot a lone man across the lot.

"Dad," I say a little breathlessly. He's standing next to one of the two SUVs parked there. His hands are in his pockets, his thinning hair ruffled slightly from the breeze. I can't read his expression from here, but his feet are squared, pointed directly at us. He's been waiting.

"Adrienne," Mom says quietly as she covers my hand with hers, "Tom loves you as if you are his blood. Try to remember that." I look at her in surprise. It hadn't occurred to me to think any differently or even to blame him for not telling me the truth. I had blamed my mother and thought the worst. I thought he didn't know.

Why did Tom—

I stop my thoughts. I mentally shake myself. Tom? I've never called him Tom in my life. Dad. Why did Dad agree to raise me? Maybe I should be angry at him too, and I am a little. But mostly I feel grateful he chose to be my dad.

I take a reluctant step forward. Mom gives me an encouraging pat. I take another step, and she stays where she is on the sidewalk. Dad starts walking toward me as well. We meet in the middle.

"Adrienne, I . . ." His voice is scratchy, as if he hasn't spoken yet today, like his voice usually is in the mornings. When I still lived at home, we were almost always the first two up for the day. My mind flashes to those mornings when he would take the time to make eggs or pancakes with me and we'd eat together and tell terrible jokes before the sun ever came up. He clears his throat now. I hold a hand up for him to stop. He does.

I look at his face. The lines around his eyes and mouth are deeper than I had noticed before, his hair thinner than ever. His eyes are swimming in tears, and I realize I've never seen my dad cry before. I'm glad too, because his unshed tears make my own eyes fill up.

"Dad," I swallow, "you're still my dad in every way that counts." I surprise myself as I repeat the words Mom had spoken to me only minutes ago. He lets out a breath. I can't help but smile at his relief. "I'm still angry at both of you, though." I laugh softly as I say it.

He takes another step and wraps me in a bone-crushing hug.

"I take all the blame. I made your mother promise not to tell you, and she's stuck by that promise all these years for my sake."

I take in a deep breath and try to push him back so I can look at his face.

"No, let me say this all while I'm holding onto my girl; otherwise, I'm not sure I can." He sucks in a quick breath. "Your mother has always wanted to keep you out of this community to keep you safe and separate. But the real reason we've never told you about him—about your biological father—is because I couldn't stand to lose you. You've always been my little girlsince your mother let me come stay with you both in the hospital the night you were born, and I wasn't man enough to share you. Not even with a ghost. It makes me ashamed to say it, but that's the truth." His words are no louder than a whisper by the time he finishes speaking.

After I return his hug, he slowly lets me go and takes a half step back. I'm not sure what to say. I look around and let out a sigh.

"Parker tells me he can read minds, Mom acts like a mad woman, someone's trying to kill me, and you're talking about your feelings. What dimension have I ended up in?" I say without making eye contact. Dad laughs. I can't help but join him. It feels good to laugh after so much tension in the last day.

"You sound just like your brother," Dad says with a laugh, then his smile fades. I haven't asked if Toby really is my brother. I'm sure I won't like the answer.

"Dad," I say, swallowing the lump that's in my throat, "is Toby my biological brother?" I have to know. Dad sticks his hands back in his pockets as he looks away. His cheeks flush.

"He is your half brother, yes." My heart loses its rhythm for a moment. My chest feels heavy, and my throat aches as tears well up in my eyes. I blink them away. I didn't expect to feel this much relief to learn he shares half my DNA.

"Can you take me to him, Dad?"

Mom crosses the parking area to join us. "He's waiting for us with Grandma."

Dad gives Mom a second look as she reaches us. "Are you okay, Thea?"

I stare at them, trying to understand what could have made them keep such big secrets from both their children. Mom bites her lip, looks away, and nods. Dad reaches for her hand. "Hey, it'll be okay," he says quietly, and she moves closer to him, grasping his hand. I feel like I'm intruding so I turn and look across the grounds.

Dad turns back and heads to the SUV he had been standing next to when we came out. He opens the front passenger door and gestures for me to get in.

"You ride up front," he says with a smile. I raise an eyebrow but move toward the front, anyway. As I turn to get in, I realize why he wanted me up front.

"How'd you sleep?" Parker asks with a lazy smile. I stare at him for a moment, trying to decide if I'm still angry at him or not.

"Fine," I say before turning to stare out the front window.

"I hear you met with Marcus," Parker says, all traces of his smile gone, "which means you know pretty much everything we know."

"Yep." Mom and Dad shut their doors. Parker starts the SUV and puts it in reverse.

"Did Marcus show you everything they found in the storage unit?" Parker asks. I tense up immediately.

"Yes." I watch him closely for a reaction. "Have you seen it?"

"No, but I heard about the photos of you." Parker shakes his head. I try to decide if he's telling the truth, if he really doesn't know one of the photos would be very familiar to him. We drive across the campus in silence.

Parker pulls into a spot and puts the vehicle in park, and Mom and Dad hop out. I open my door, but Parker stops me with a hand on my arm.

"You don't have to worry, Adrienne," he says with a steely look. "I won't let whoever that is come within a hundred yards of you."

"Somehow that's not as reassuring as I think you'd hoped that would be, Parker." I swallow as I think about Parker in harm's way.

"Don't you worry about me, either," Parker says with his grin that always means he's about to do something stupid. "I'm good. This isn't my first bad guy."

I sit up straight in my seat as a thought crosses my mind. I quickly look to Parker and then out the front window again. My mouth has gone dry. I force myself to swallow.

"Hey, that day on campus after finals when you needed a ride," I start, then stop, trying to calm my nerves. "You said you had lost your phone."

"Yeah, I must have lost it the night before while I was at work. What about it?"

"Which work?"

"Um . . . while I was on duty for Path Endeavors."

"Did you ever find it?"

"No," Parker says, slowly drawing out the word as he stares at my face, his brows pulled together in a silent question. "Otherwise, it wouldn't be lost."

"Adrienne, are you coming?" Mom asks through Parker's open window.

"Yeah." I swallow again. "Coming."

CHAPTER 19

EFFIE

"Let me see if I understand this," Toby says, his voice steady as he paces my small room in the infirmary. My head hurts, and I find myself wishing he would hold still.

"There are communities of mind readers across the world," Toby says as if he's reading from a script. "Many of which have their own compounds just like this one, run by this agency. Someone is stalking Adrienne because . . . " He draws out the word, letting his sentence trail off. When no one supplies an answer, he pushes his hands through his hair as he paces. "Great. Either we don't know why, or neither of you is willing to tell me." He turns and points at Thea and Tom. "Oh, and you're not really her father, which means she's only my half sister. Does that cover it?"

"Yes," Tom says with a patient nod after shooting a glance to Thea. Taking his parental cues from her, as usual.

"Fantastic," Toby says with fake enthusiasm. "Now I'm starving. Who wants breakfast?"

Adrienne laughs and covers her mouth. Toby is his grandfather's boy through and through. Tom and Thea exchange another one of their cryptic looks. And my head feels worse by the moment.

"I'm starving too. Let's go." Tom gives Adrienne a hug before he walks to the door. Of course he would want to bow out of any more serious discussions. Unless we were talking about his work, that is. That man has always prioritized things much differently than I would.

"I just have one last question," Toby says, sticking his head back through the door. "Doesn't anyone think being here is overkill? Sure, it's weird someone had pictures of Adrienne plastered on the wall of a storage unit, but does that really mean we have to hide away from the entire world?"

"It's never a harmless thing when someone has spent that much time secretly taking photos of someone else," Tom says, arms crossed. "And since you, Adrienne, are a mind reader, we can't be too careful."

Finally, he's right about something. Thea shoots a sharp look my way. I must have let that thought slip through my mental barriers. Adrienne doesn't seem to have noticed.

"What does that have to do with it?" Toby asks.

"There's a long history of people like us being killed for no reason other than being different," I tell him. There have been too many of our people slaughtered over the centuries for us to possibly know the total, but the slaughter at Mount Hope comes to mind. It was the first ever community of our people in Missouri, but several people in that town were murdered because of a treacherous community member abusing his special ability to control minds. We're in just as much danger from those within our community. Maybe even more at risk of corruption within our community because of the potential for power that comes with the ability to read minds. I don't tell him that, though. "So that means we must take nothing for granted." He nods. "Now go, but make sure you come back to see me soon, and sneak some cobbler in with you. I hear there's peach cobbler today, and it's my favorite."

With another nod, he shuts the door behind him as he leaves.

"I think there's something I need to tell you both," Adrienne says, avoiding eye contact with both me and Thea. The pain in my head intensifies.

"You know the storage unit with the photos on the wall?" We both nod since Thea had already told us what Marcus showed them. "I've . . . I've sort of been there before, inside that storage unit, and I've seen those photos on the walls."

"What? When?" Thea asks, crossing the room and sitting down on the bed in front of me.

"In a dream," she says. Thea's face drains of all color. I'm not feeling well, either, as my throbbing headache becomes unbearably sharp.

"That's what you wanted to tell me earlier, isn't it?" Thea asks.

Adrienne nods.

"Why do you think it was a dream?" I ask. We need to be sure whether or not this was Adrienne's abilities manifesting or someone else's manipulation of her mind.

"It was at night, while I was sleeping." Her voice goes up at the end of the sentence as if her statements are questions. Oh, how I regret not starting to train her as soon as she was old enough.

"What I mean is, are you sure you were sleeping, my dear?" I sit up straighter, fidgeting with my hands in my lap.

"Yes. I mean, I think so." The look on Adrienne's face tells me she isn't sure of anything. "There's something else, though." She glances at Thea before returning her focus to me. "The largest photo in the storage unit—the one where I'm looking at the camera and smiling—that photo came from Parker. He took it."

"What?" Thea says. This is her worst nightmare—someone targeting Adrienne. But to her credit, she hides what she's really thinking.

"He lost his phone right around the time I had this dream, and he took that photo with his phone just a couple of weeks before, so I'm sure it was still on there." Thea looks at me. "Actually, he lost it while on duty with Path Endeavors. I don't know any details other than that, though." Adrienne shakes her head and shrugs.

Silence fills the room as Thea and I both carefully think through the implications. Would Parker, the boy who has been in love with our Adrienne since he met her, do anything to cause her harm? I can't believe that he would. I wonder, what other information was on that phone?

"What?" she asks, wiping her palms on her jeans. "I don't think Parker is in league with this guy, if that's what you're thinking. He may have lied to me about both his ability and mine, but . . . "

But so did we. Thea runs her fingers through her hair and then curses under her breath.

"We believe you, dear, and we trust Parker. Which means—" I begin.

"Your stalker has been watching Parker too," Thea finishes.

My headache is making me wish I could close my eyes and sleep until it's gone, and now my hands are feeling a little shaky. I close my eyes for a moment's reprieve, but I must have shut them for too long because both Adrienne and Thea are looking at me in concern when I open them once again.

"Grandma, why don't you get some rest?" Adrienne says, her brows pinched.

"First, I think there's something else you should know about your abilities." I will myself to sit up straight and tall. I give her a small smile. "My illness . . . well, it isn't exactly an illness. Your mother didn't want me to do it, but it was the only way for us to learn more."

"Do what? What are you talking about?"

"You described the instance when you saw the storage unit and the photos on the wall as a dream," Thea says.

Adrienne nods.

"You saw the storage unit through someone else's eyes, right?" I ask.

"Yes," Adrienne says as she crosses her arms. "I pinned more photos to the walls."

"Dear, it sounds like you were inside the mind of the person pinning those photos to the wall. That means you weren't dreaming, Adrienne. It was real. That is the ability you inherited from me that we talked about before." I smile broadly, proud of her for no reason other than carrying on my ability.

"Your ability requires your body and mind to be in a relaxed state for it to work," Thea says. "It makes sense that it would feel like a dream. But it definitely wasn't."

"How . . . why did I see the guy in the storage unit specifically, though?"

I look at Thea briefly, wondering if she's thinking the same thing I am.

"We're not really sure," I say, shrugging, unwilling to put words to the terrible thought in my head that he somehow manipulated her thoughts or her mind. It's incredibly rare, even in our rare community of neurodivergent telepaths, but I've learned to never count anything as impossible.

"He should have had his thoughts locked down, and you shouldn't be able to just sort of float to someone else's consciousness," I tell her. "That takes years of practice. It's not something your mother or I have been able to do."

"I didn't hear any of his thoughts while I was in the dream," Adrienne says. "I was just watching everything he was doing from his eyes. I could feel things too, like the gloves he was wearing while he drove. But I don't understand. What does this have to do with your illness?"

"Grandma used her ability, similarly as what you've experienced, to try to observe someone and his movements," Thea says. "She can sort of lock on to whomever she wants to observe and look at their world through their eyes as long as she's within a couple miles of their location."

"And as long as they're not shielding their thoughts like we've taught you to do. Even if they are, I can still get a sense of where they are. This time was a bit of a stretch for me." I shake my head. "I don't know how near or far away I was from the person I was trying to reach. And it's dangerous for a mind reader to try something like that without knowing the distance. My mama told me stories about those of us from my family line with the same special abilities who had tried to visit someone as I did, or even to control a person's mind. Sometimes, those people would end up going mad or dying."

"But you're okay, right?"

"Maybe." I smile. I can't bring myself to tell her I'm fairly sure I have permanent brain damage since I haven't quite been myself.

"So what happened, then? Did you go into this person's mind?"

"I only intended to sort of . . ." I shrug, looking for the words to describe a process that is simultaneously in my mind and miles away from it, shaped by feelings, guided by instinct, and yet dynamic, full of movement and change. "Knock and see if I could get in. But I don't remember what happened."

"We're telling you because we want you to be very careful while exploring your abilities," Thea says, sounding as if she's instructing a kindergartener, not her grown daughter.

"This is what I've been doing when I've been dreaming," she says quietly to no one in particular. Adrienne curses. "Could it be possible my other dreams aren't dreams, then?"

"Absolutely," Thea says, leaning in. "What other dreams have you had? They might help us figure out who's stalking you."

She tells us about her recent dreams—the man being captured after he had been trying to steal a truck and sneak away; a woman was taken out of her own home; another man awoke in a dank basement, his hands bound above his head; other dreams too, dating back over the last few years. By the time she's done, I know one thing for certain: My lovely granddaughter has an amazing gift that far surpasses my own.

"When was the dream about the man in the basement?" Thea asks.

"It was last night," Adrienne answers. "Why?"

"I overheard Jillian at breakfast this morning on the phone. She was talking to someone about another disappearance. Someone from the Ironton area. She said his name. Let me see if I can find him on social media."

Thea pokes at the screen on her phone. After a minute or two of poking and swiping, she holds her phone out to Adrienne.

"Does he look familiar?" she asks.

"No, I never saw his face," Adrienne says distractedly as she taps on the screen. "But he looks like he's the right size." She hands the phone back, her eyes wide. "What does this mean?"

It means her gifts make her vulnerable, more vulnerable than we imagined, because she's visiting the minds of those in our community who are being kidnapped.

"There have been kidnappings going on for decades," Thea explains. "While we don't understand why, Path Endeavors thinks it's one person kidnapping all these people from our community. It sounds like you're witnessing these kidnappings or the aftermath somehow."

"What do we do about it?" Adrienne asks, eyes wide.

"I think for now, the best thing you can do is try to pay attention to every detail in these dreams," I respond. "Keep a journal. Write down the date, what you see, what you hear, the smell—all of it. Maybe it will lead to a detail that can help to stop these kidnappings."

"What will she do with it?" Thea asks. "We can't hand that over to anyone, Mom. It will put her at risk." Her voice sounds strained and higher-pitched than usual.

"We should give it to Sawyer. He's been investigating the kidnappings with me for a while now."

CHAPTER 20

ADRIENNE

Purple and blue waves slowly, lazily flow closer and closer to me. The waves originate somewhere in the hall beyond the room I'm currently kneeling in. As the almost-white blue reaches me, it's cool, indifferent, brushing against my body. The purple follows closely, a gentle wave of confidence penetrating my being, mixing with the blue wave of emotion. That's what these are: waves of emotion, flowing from someone beyond this room. I try not to consider the source of these emotions too carefully; otherwise, I'll lose my hold on my concentration, but the waves are coming from the infirmary area of this hallway. Chances are I'm looking at the inner emotional workings of a nurse who is cool, calm, and confident as she goes about her duties.

Like Mom has taught me, I focus on the movement of the waves, and I practice pushing them away from me. For now, I use my hands. I need a physical movement to help guide my mental effort. Is it mental, or is it emotional? I'm not sure, and it's not like I can google the answer. Either way, the waves break against an invisible barrier and flow around me instead of into me.

Over the last week, I've been working on concentrating well enough to see the waves and figure out how to manipulate them away from me. Yesterday when I tried, I fell asleep when I was attempting to clear my mind and concentrate. My dreams that aren't dreams have increased, and I've been visiting people in my sleep, watching person after person being captured or taken to a dark, dank basement.

Today, though, is a success. Once the waves have flowed past me, I take a deep breath and open my eyes.

I'm kneeling on a cushion along the wall, on more of the strangest flooring ever. Only the floor is covered in the same weird material as Grandma's room in the infirmary. Her former room, anyway. She moved to the dormitory with us.

There's a bookcase in the corner with a large cabinet beside it. Desks are lined up in neat little rows. It would look like an ordinary classroom if it weren't for the ability-blocking tiles on the floor. The whole room is being converted to a classroom, which means it will have the tiles on the walls and ceiling soon.

This room is one of many like it. Mind-reading preteens and teens come here every summer for camp and training on using their abilities, according to Parker. I wonder how different my life would be if I had attended summer camps here. Surely it would be different. Perhaps we wouldn't be here now, hiding.

My left foot is tingling from a lack of blood flow. I rise slowly, push the cushion into the corner where it belongs, and move to the door. *Everything is in its place*, I reflect as I give the room a once-over before I close the door behind me. Everything except for me.

Not that it will always be this way. I won't cower behind a security fence and armed guards forever. I just need to figure out how to control my abilities first. Now that we know about all of my abilities.

I've been training nonstop with Mom and Grandma, each taking their turn putting me through drills and exercises and lessons. They are pushing my informational training as much as practical skills training.

My mind drifts to today's lesson on the suspected origin of those of us with telepathic abilities. While Mom and Grandma presented the information very matter-of-factly, it all sounds like the makings of a great science fiction movie to me. One small genetic deviation that survived through natural selection that led to a family known for their empathy and uncanny ability to tell when someone was lying. They were lucky they were alive after the witch trials had ended.

I round the corner in the hall and spot Mom ahead, standing in the opening to another hallway. She left just a couple of minutes before me from the training room. I groan as I realize she's stopped to talk to Marcus. Mom is still angry with him or angry again, I'm not sure which.

Grandma told me Marcus had been the one put in charge of investigating the disappearance and death of James Rutherford, my biological father. It seems he and Mom have been at odds with each other ever since. She never felt like he did enough to find James's killer, and Marcus had been too pushy about wanting to keep in touch and support her through her pregnancy and my birth.

"It's been two weeks, Marcus," she says as I come closer. "We can't all stay here indefinitely. We each have a life and a job." I stop next to her. Marcus is standing there expressionless as he scribbles something down and then hands the paper and pen back to his assistant. He gives me a slight nod when he looks up.

"You know Tom's job is secure. We practically own Synergy. And besides, he's working exclusively in our labs here for the next month," Marcus says.

What? I think. I know Dad works for Synergy Laboratories, but I didn't know the lab was affiliated with Path Endeavors in any way. Why is there a lab here in the compound?

"Look, I realize it's inconvenient, Thea," Marcus says, tapping his foot, "but we have no idea where Adrienne's stalker is. He could be anywhere. It isn't safe for any of you to leave at this point."

"Do you have a plan for figuring out who this guy is?"

Marcus smiles. "I do. Because I have something he obviously wants very badly." His eyes flick to me and back to Mom. "He'll come to us." For the briefest moment, joy hits me in the chest.

My heart races. I feel my cheeks flush. *Is he happy about this situation?* I try to keep my face neutral, but I can feel my lip curl in disgust.

"You will not be using my *daughter* as bait," Mom says and barks out an incredulous laugh.

"Um . . . excuse me," Jillian, Marcus's assistant, says as she hesitantly steps forward. "I'm so sorry to interrupt, but your next meeting begins in two minutes across campus."

Marcus looks down at his wristwatch. "We'll have to continue this discussion at a later date, Thea," he says with a tight smile. "Adrienne, it's good to see you again. First thing tomorrow morning, come see me. It's time for you to get a proper tour." He pats my shoulder.

"Uh, okay."

"What's a proper tour?" is what I want to ask. But I don't.

With that, he turns on his heel and walks rapidly away with Jillian hurrying along behind him. Mom turns toward me, her face red. She takes a deep breath.

"Come on," she says with a gentle tug on my sleeve, "we need to talk to your grandmother. She has something to tell us, apparently."

"What did he mean about owning Synergy Laboratories?" I ask her, hurrying to catch up with her as she heads toward the lobby and exit.

"Path Endeavors pays a significant amount of money to Synergy in contract work every quarter."

"Why? What does Synergy do for Path Endeavors?"

"Synergy's CEO and cofounder Hal MacMillan started a long-term research project years ago, a couple of years before you were born. Path Endeavors wants to make sure he continues that project because the results will affect all of us."

"What's the project?" We nod to the security guards as we exit the building.

"He's mapped the brain, including the brains of over a hundred of those like us. Synergy, with your father as one of the leading researchers, has also mapped the human genome to isolate the genetic expressions that result in a person with telepathic ability. And now, the project is focused on manipulating genetic factors to turn the expression of those genes on or off."

I stop in my tracks in the middle of the parking lot. Mom stops after another couple of steps, realizing I'm not by her side. She turns to me.

"What? What's wrong? Come on." She gestures for me to follow. I put one foot in front of the other and move with her to the SUV waiting for us. I get in, and Mom backs out of the parking spot, turning to head to the dormitories. But I can't stop thinking about what she said.

We head to the dormitory we're all staying in, including Grandma now.

"Why is Synergy manipulating DNA? Are they hoping to make more people who are neurodivergent?"

"The researchers are hoping to understand which genes trigger our ability because the rate of Alzheimer's disease and dementia in our population is exceptionally low."

"I don't understand," I say, blinking.

"Your dad and the researchers hope to create a gene therapy to sort of 'turn on' the expression of the genes that they think are responsible for the portion of the brain that is always on for those of us who have telepathic abilities. By turning on this portion of the brain in people who are suffering from dementia or Alzheimer's disease, they think they can end Alzheimer's and dementia." She glances at me. I'm shaking my head, hands up, brows furrowed. "They're looking for a cure for dementia and Alzheimer's with this research, Adrienne."

"But why does any of that matter to Path Endeavors?"

"I'm not sure, but I can come up with a half dozen scary ways it could hurt our community," she says, frowning. "Like if they were to use this knowledge to create more mind readers, to normalize our ability."

"Wouldn't normalization be a good thing? Wouldn't that mean no one would ever have to hide their ability again?"

"It's rarely a good thing when any entity starts manipulating the natural order of the world." She sighs. "Besides, it isn't legal in our country to just alter a human's DNA. Anything like that would eventually trigger an investigation of some sort, which means government involvement, and government involvement in our community has never gone well."

"So what is Dad's part in this?"

"He was the one who identified the genes or alleles or whatever it is responsible for our abilities. He gathered samples from the mind readers in this area. That's how he met—" She glances at me before continuing. "That's how he met James, your father."

"And now? What is he doing now?" I completely ignore the part about him knowing James. I don't know how to feel about that.

"His department keeps in contact with all the mind readers who have participated in the study. At least those still around. Some have moved on, others have since died. He helps with keeping in contact with them since he's met so many of the participants. But he's working hard on figuring out how to turn the right genes on and off. They're using some genetic manipulation tool. I don't know anything about it other than they use it to sort of cut and paste what makes us telepathic into the genes of rats. How do you know if a rat is telepathic?" Mom says with a laugh. "I don't know. That's not what they're doing, anyway. They give the rat Alzheimer's disease before they cut and paste our DNA into its genome. Or something. I am not the scientist in the family. The goal is to figure out a gene therapy that will reverse Alzheimer's in rats and then eventually in humans."

We arrive at the dormitory. Mom puts the SUV in park and shuts it off once she pulls into a spot near the door. She turns in her seat to look at me. We both sit in silence for a moment. A semi-secret organization protecting a wholly secret population with the ability to listen to thoughts—and maybe more, given what I now know about my additional abilities—is funding research that could show us how to create more people like me. Maybe. Or destroy the community completely. Or expose us to the world.

CHAPTER 21

EFFIE

After an electronic beep that signals the unlocking of the dormitory door, Adrienne and Thea walk in. The two are quietly laughing at something, and my insides clench a little tighter as I think about what this news is going to do to them both. Adrienne has purple crescents under her eyes. Those showed up shortly after her arrival, coinciding with an uptick in the number of dreams she's having each night. Not that they're really dreams, but Thea and I haven't come up with a better word for it over the years. I wonder how much more sleep she'll lose tonight.

"I was beginning to wonder about you two," I say with a smile that feels stiff. But so do my neck and shoulders. "Parker brought me dinner." I'm not sure why I mention dinner. I hadn't intended to. I resist the urge to rub my temples, trying my best to ignore the pain that's slowly been building there since I left the infirmary this morning.

"Oh?" Thea says, moving slowly to sit on the bench against the gray wall across from them, looking around the room as she does. "Thanks, Parker."

Parker sits there silently staring at his shoes; the boy has been sulking since he got here. He's been as enjoyable to be around as a wet blanket. Adrienne nudges his boot with her sandaled foot, but he looks directly at me, ignoring her completely. I raise an eyebrow at the boy. He looks away and puts an arm across the back of the empty chair next to him.

"So, what's up, Mom? Why did you want to talk to us?" Thea asks as Adrienne crosses the room and takes the seat next to me.

"Parker also brought me a visitor," I say, giving Adrienne's hand a squeeze. As if we practiced the timing of it, Sawyer walks in from the kitchenette at that moment. "Sawyer has some news for us."

"Uh, hi," Sawyer says, smiling at Adrienne by my side before looking nervously at Thea. Thea stares back expressionless.

"Path Endeavors knows who your stalker is," Parker says with a huff, not waiting for Sawyer to share his news. Parker's pouting is beginning to grate on me.

"What? We just spoke to Marcus, and he didn't seem to know anything new," Thea says, touching her throat.

"Marcus has known, or at least suspected, who it is all along," Parker says, his tone bordering on angry.

"Who is it?" Adrienne asks, looking from Parker to Sawyer.

"James Rutherford," Sawyer supplies, stepping forward and rubbing the palms of his hands across his jeans.

I can't help but study Thea. She appears frozen, not even a twitch.

"You don't mean James as in my biological father who is supposed to be dead, right?" Adrienne says with an incredulous laugh.

"That's exactly who he's talking about," Parker replies. "Path Endeavors has suspected James is behind the ongoing string of disappearances and murders that started a couple of years before we were born."

"But he's dead," Adrienne says with a shake of her head.

"Uh, I don't think he is," Sawyer says. "Or at least Marcus really doesn't think he is. He has photos of James from a couple of years after his supposed death up until a few months ago, and Marcus should know what he looks like since the two of them were friends. Here." Sawyer holds out his phone to Thea; on the screen is a picture of a man who looks to be in his forties or early fifties.

"Why would he fake his death?" Adrienne asks.

"Why does a man usually want his pregnant wife to think he's dead?" I say, surprising myself.

Thea is pale now, the fist hanging at her side now clenched. Her fingers wrapped around Sawyer's phone are turning white, and I'm afraid she might break his phone.

"Why wouldn't anyone have told us this?" Adrienne says with a shake of her head. "Do we really think he's a . . . a . . . serial killer?" She holds her hand out to Thea. Thea puts the phone in Adrienne's palm.

Those are the questions I've been asking myself too. There's another beep at the door, and it opens.

"I came to see if you all wanted to head to dinner," Tom says. I sigh. "How 'bout it?" he adds with a smile when no one answers.

Thea hands the phone back to Sawyer. All eyes are on Thea now, none of us sure what to say to Tom.

"It appears James isn't dead, and he is the one taking photos of Adrienne," Thea says, hands hanging at her side, her stance somehow loose and tense as if she's preparing for a fight. She's never been one to choose flight.

Tom swears quietly. I roll my eyes and wish he'd disappear.

"Why would he fake his death?" Tom echoes Adrienne's earlier question.

"Why would any man want his pregnant wife to think he's dead?" Thea says, making eye contact with me. Her hands still hang at her sides, her fingers absentmindedly fiddling with the hem of her powder-blue scoop-neck T-shirt. Red splotches have appeared on her throat and chest, a stark contrast to her light skin.

"But why would he come back then and follow me around?" Adrienne asks with a blink.

"Maybe he faked his death because he was in fear of his life," Sawyer supplies a guess, ignoring Thea's. "I mean, with the disappearances clearly linked to the community his father helped to save—"

Thea's gaze swings to Sawyer, the corners of her mouth downturned. He closes his mouth, deciding not to voice whatever he had been about to say.

"What are you saying?" Adrienne asks. I squeeze her hand.

"Well, I mean, all the people who have disappeared have been connected with the community James's father helped build several years prior to the first disappearance and death," Sawyer says. "We know those people had been looking to James to continue in his father's footsteps and lead them too. I can't imagine what reason he would have for murdering them. But his connection with that community means he might have known something about it."

"Or he could have been behind it all somehow," Tom says with a shake of his head.

"After all my years of digging," I say slowly with a look at Tom, "I haven't found any reason to suspect James to be responsible for the murder of our own people—"

"You didn't suspect James was alive, either, though," Tom inserts. "So how much can we trust—"

"I don't understand," Adrienne says, interrupting. "There isn't just one person kidnapping these people. Why does Path Endeavors think that's what's happening?"

I glance at Sawyer, who raises an eyebrow. Thea shakes her head. This is a big reason she never wanted Adrienne to know about her abilities or our community. The inherent risk of saying the wrong thing in the wrong crowd, of someone knowing about your ability who shouldn't. There's something risky in being different from the general populace of any area, community, nation. Adrienne is not only different from the average person in our nation, but she is also different from the typical person in the neurodivergent telepathic community. Her added abilities carry an added risk. Thea was poignantly aware of that risk at the time of Adrienne's birth, having watched James and his family fight to protect our community from the kidnappings, and fail. Then having lost James months before Adrienne's birth. Alive or not, he was still lost to her.

When Sawyer told me James was alive, the thought did cross my mind that Thea might have known he was alive but chose to keep it a secret. That the two of them had a plan or were trying to protect Adrienne, our community, or something else. Her reaction to the news doesn't support that, though. My heart hurts for her.

"How do you know it's not one person?" Tom asks. Now I want to kick him. For such a smart guy, he doesn't understand much.

"There have been one hundred seven people from a small community who settled in the southern part of Missouri murdered in the last twenty years," Parker says, glancing at Adrienne and standing up. "Some were originally from that community while others were descendants of that community. We assume they've been murdered, but it's hard to say since the only thing that appears to be wrong with them are small puncture wounds and zero drugs found in their systems." He runs his hands through his hair. "In the last year, the number of people somehow related to that community who have disappeared has hit a new high at sixty-seven people. Some bodies haven't been found yet. But keeping in mind, of course, not everyone is reporting a loved one who goes missing for a variety of reasons—like suspected runaway, because they're too private, so forth—then Adrienne's right. There's no way one person is responsible for all that."

That's why I like that boy. He understands what just happened. And he's doing what he always does—caring for Adrienne. I want to applaud him.

"Why is it only people from that community?" Adrienne asks. The throbbing in my head intensifies.

"Because that community is supposed to have a range of abilities most of our kind don't," Sawyer says.

"Like us," Adrienne says quietly.

Parker shoots her a look, shakes his head.

"No, not like you," Tom says. "He means these people who died could do more than hear the thoughts of others."

I look to Thea and silently pray Adrienne doesn't say anything else. I'm surprised Thea hasn't told Tom about our additional abilities, but I'm also relieved. I've never liked him. Adrienne pulls her hand out of mine.

"Dad, I mean the other stuff, like feeling others' emotions, the dreams . . ." She trails off, brow wrinkled.

"What are you talking about?" Tom slowly turns to Thea. "Thea?"

"Tom, let's talk about it later," Thea answers with a glance at Adrienne.

"No, we will talk about this now," he says, hands hanging at his sides, face pinched.

"There was one kidnapping in particular that was especially worrisome," I blurt out to no one specifically. What am I doing? "Adrienne, your babysitter was snatched up right under our noses. We were never sure if she was the target or if you were."

"What?" Adrienne says with a hand to her parted lips.

"Why did you really think your mother hid our community, your own heritage, your abilities from you?" I can't stop the flow of words. "Just general anxiety? Someone broke into our home and took your babysitter on an ordinary Tuesday afternoon."

"Mom!" Thea says, the weight of her tone making the word sound more like a command than a title.

"I showed up and interrupted things, but I couldn't go after her without leaving you unprotected. So I chose you. I had to watch some man in a mask drag her out of the house and to a waiting vehicle." I swallow and try to stop my words, but I can't. "He took her." I stare straight at Adrienne. "And he broadcast his thoughts to me, warning me that he'd be back for you too." I point at her. I want to snatch my hand back, to reverse the last minute and take it all back.

"Mom, that's enough," Thea says, now a mere foot away from me, hands clenched. "Adrienne, you shouldn't have to worry about something that happened twenty years ago."

"Why not? We've never stopped worrying about it," I say, a challenge in my voice. Why can't I stop talking? I'm not helping matters whatsoever.

"What is wrong with you?" Thea says. Adrienne appears frozen.

Sawyer clears his throat. "I need to go," he says. He walks to me, leans in to give me a hug.

"Take care, my boy." I give him a quick kiss on the side of his head and return his hug. "Thank you for bringing me news."

"I'll let you know if I find out anything else. And I'll be around here for a day or two." He straightens up, walks to the door, and gives an awkward wave, which no one returns. As the door clicks shut behind him, Parker walks to the door as well.

"I'm gonna go," he says with a glance over his shoulder at Adrienne. She doesn't notice, lost in her own world of thoughts. Parker hesitates a moment before he opens the door and steps through.

"Adrienne, you'd better go too. I need to talk to your father and grand-mother," Thea says, giving her a tight smile. "But please stay with Parker for now until we can talk about this and your safety some more."

Adrienne opens her mouth to speak, then closes it again.

"Go," Tom says with a reassuring nod. She stands, hugs Tom quickly, and then exits almost soundlessly.

"So, Tom," I say through gritted teeth as my head swims from the pain of my headache, "it seems we should talk."

"Actually, Euphemia, I'd like to talk to my *wife* alone." Tom scoffs. "And I think you've said plenty tonight." He shakes his head.

I open my mouth to tell Tom that Thea is my blood, that we've been through more together than his limited neurotypical brain can comprehend. Our lives, our experiences, and our anxieties aren't something he can ever fully understand because he's never had to worry someone might hunt him down and end his life because he's different. Because he's *gifted*. That his marriage to my glorious daughter doesn't give him the right to claim ownership of her. She belongs to no one, and she deserves no less than someone who has enough sense to understand why keeping her added abilities as quiet as possible is ingrained in her, in our very way of living, and it's been what's keeping her safe. Living is the key word here, because many others have died for being much more *normal*, whatever normal really means. That he should be man enough to set his fragile ego aside and realize her choice to keep this information quiet has nothing, *nothing* to do with how she feels about him.

But instead, I laugh. And laugh.

"Mom?" Thea looks startled by my laughter. She can't be any more startled by it than I am.

My laughter ramps up. I'm not stopping. I can't stop. What the *hell* is going on? "Thea," I barely manage to breathe out in the midst of my mirth, my eyes beginning to weep, "something . . . is . . . wrong."

Thea moves closer, kneeling down in front of me and taking my hand in hers.

"Mom, are you okay?"

Through the laughter and the pain that has been building, building, building in my head, there's a tickle in the back of my mind. It intensifies, becoming an itch and then a rattle. It feels like something being jiggled loose, reverberating through my brain, sending electric shocks along my synapses. Then all at once, it stops.

My jaw is slack. My pain is gone, and the noise inside my head has fallen silent.

"Mom!" Thea yells, inches from my face, her hands roving up my arms, to my face, on my neck, and back down again to my hands. "Mom, can you hear me?"

"I . . ." My voice sounds scratchy, weepy. *Swallow, Effie.* "I'm okay. Better."

"What the hell was that?" Tom says, stepping closer.

"No, don't do that," I groan at Tom.

"Do what?" he says absentmindedly.

"Do not turn on that 'I'm a scientist, and this is intriguing' part of your brain. Stop it now. I am not a guinea pig."

"And that's how I know you're okay," Thea says. But her forehead is still creased with worry.

"I'm just tired, that's all." The conviction in my voice doesn't sound as firm as I'd like it to. But I am tired suddenly. So, so tired.

"Are you sure?" Tom asks with a surprising amount of concern.

"Yes, it's been a long day."

"Then why don't you go to bed, Mom? I'm not happy with you right now, but it isn't the first time." Thea squeezes my hand. "We'll talk more in the morning about all this and what it means."

I hate to give Tom the satisfaction of leaving him alone with his *wife*, but I can feel my limbs growing heavier.

"I'll be up early. I'll come wake you." I give her a wink. She doesn't wink back.

CHAPTER 22

ADRIENNE

As the door clicks shut behind me, I hesitate. I want to listen in. Why doesn't Dad know about our extra abilities? Why would Mom keep that a secret from him of all people—the guy who knows all about our community down to the areas of genetic code that make us tick?

"Parker, do you think we can hear them from out here?" I ask. He doesn't answer. "Parker?" I say again with a look over my shoulder. He isn't there. I turn and scan the area, spotting his retreating back. "Hey, where are you going?" He doesn't stop.

I follow Parker, but he has set a rapid pace and I'm struggling to keep up. I'm definitely not gaining any ground on him. We make it past the other dormitories quickly, and I jog to get closer as he nears the tree line.

"Parker," I manage a little breathlessly, "where are you going?" He doesn't answer. I jog faster, getting closer. I'm just behind him now, so there's no way he won't hear me this time. "Hey," I say between breaths, "would you slow down?" I manage all in one breath, my annoyance clear from my tone. "You're a foot taller than me, and I'm going to have to jog to keep up."

He stops in his tracks. I run right into his back, his shoulder blade colliding painfully with my forehead. I back up, putting a hand to my head. I start to whine about his refusal to tell me what's going on, but the sound dies on my lips as he turns, and I notice his tense jaw and the bounding pulse in his neck.

"Did Sawyer really need to come in person to deliver that news?" Parker asks, feet apart, head tilted. "I mean, has the guy never heard of a phone?" He raises an eyebrow.

My face scrunches up in confusion. Surely this can't be what has Parker so upset. "Um, I don't know."

"Yeah, I think I like him about as much as I like Calvin."

"Hey," I say, putting a hand on his arm, "what is going on?" He lets out a huff. "Whatever the issue, it'll be okay. We will figure it out." My voice sounds more confident than I feel.

He moves his arm, brushing off my hand. Parker's behavior is baffling to me. He's never acted like this with me. I already feel like I've swallowed a bag of rocks, and there is the mind-bending fact that I just learned my biological father faked his own death. And the fact that someone threatened me as a baby, and that one act has changed the entire course of my life, not to mention that some poor woman who was watching me was most likely killed. I'm not sure I have the patience to hear about whatever is bothering him.

He takes a long, deep breath before briefly meeting my eyes. "Let's keep going," he says. This time, he gestures for me to take the lead. I do so gladly, pointing us in what I hope is the direction of the big lake.

After a few minutes of tense silence and walking, we clear the trees to come out onto the shore of the lake. The surface is calm, the sounds of the local wildlife in the surrounding woods reassuring.

"Come on, over here," he says, heading for the dock. I follow him.

We reach the end of the dock and he sits down, giving my pant leg a tug when I just stand there staring at him. I sit, tucking my legs up into a crisscross. He looks around again as he takes another deep breath, but it doesn't seem to relax him since every line in his body is still rigidly straight.

"Start talking, Parker. What's your problem?"

"Last week, you asked me about my lost phone—you know, the one I lost the day before I needed a ride." Parker looks out at the lake and then back at me. "I didn't think too much about it until this morning when I saw the photos from your stalker's storage unit."

I turn my face away from him so he can't see my expression.

"Why didn't you tell me there was a photo I took as the center of that terrifying masterpiece?" Parker's voice is low and hard. I can feel the hurt radiating off him in increasingly more powerful waves. I blindly stare at the water.

Why didn't I tell him? The silence between us stretches on as I struggle to find my voice, to find an answer.

"You also didn't tell me Tom isn't your biological father," he says, a hint of accusation in his tone.

I still don't answer, but now I fix my gaze on his face, wishing I could call a timeout on the whole confusing mess of all that I've learned.

"Or that you have more abilities than the average mind reader. You don't trust me." His stare is intense. I want to turn away again, but I force myself to keep looking at him.

"Parker, I . . ." I pause, shaking my head. I want to deny it. But I can't. If I really did trust him, I would have told him. Wouldn't I?

"Save it," Parker says, rolling his eyes. The hurt, sadness, guilt, and frustration from him washes over me in a rushing wave, and I suck in a breath from the intensity.

We sit in silence for a long time with him staring out at the water and me staring at him.

"I don't blame you for not trusting me," he says quietly, his shoulders sagging ever so slightly. "I have lied to you the whole time we've known each other." He looks right at me, his face an unreadable mask. "No matter what I promised your mother, I should have told you about my ability at least. I never should have agreed to keep that part of who I am from you."

His words equally soothe my guilt and compound it, a wave of remorse accompanying every syllable.

"If it helps, I didn't know my dad wasn't my father until about the same time I saw that photo you took." I offer him a hopeful smile. "So it's not like I've been keeping it from you for years."

"Unlike the lies I told you," he says. He offers me his lopsided grin. While it's much dimmer than usual, it's still good to see. "Adrienne, you don't need to explain yourself to me. It's okay not to tell me things. I'm just not used to it, or used to feeling like I'm a terrible friend."

I blink, not sure what to say. He's right, though. I don't owe him an explanation.

He holds up a hand to stall any response from me. "What we really need to talk about is what to do about Marcus Griffin."

"What do you mean?" I sit up straighter.

"You want to talk about epic lies? He's been lying to us from the start of this, and it looks like he's been lying to your mom for decades." Parker digs something out of his pocket. He holds a folded piece of paper out to me, the edges curled. "I found this when I was looking through some files in Marcus's office this afternoon." He sighs, and I take the paper from his hand.

"You were doing what?" I ask, not sure what to think about him snooping around in Marcus's office. He technically works for him. It could get him fired at the least.

"I was looking at the case file for your stalker, checking for updates. This was folded up in a file folder on James Rutherford under your case file. Just look at it."

I unfold it quickly, flattening it in my hand. I begin reading, but I'm not understanding the significance. It appears to be a letter to Marcus. The tone is of someone talking to a friend. It's signed J. Nothing scandalous in the contents of the letter.

"I've settled into a new routine, and I appreciate your help with getting here," I start over, reading it aloud. "I don't get it. What's so important about this letter?"

"Did you see the signature?" Parker asks.

I nod. "J. You think that's James Rutherford?"

"Yes." Now Parker smiles a cold smile that doesn't reach his eyes. "After all, I did find it in a file folder with his name on it."

"We already knew they used to be friends."

"Look at the date of the letter at the top."

There, at the top right, written in the same handwriting as the letter, is a date: It's a few months after my birth. That's well after James Rutherford supposedly died.

"You need to put it back," I say, shoving the letter into his chest.

"What? Why? This is evidence. We need to keep it somewhere safe."

I stand and walk away from the end of the dock and toward the shore.

"Where are you going?" The dock creaks as he stands up to follow me.

I can't help it. Tears are accumulating in my eyes, threatening to trickle down my cheeks. And I don't want to cry right now. But the possibility of James actually being alive suddenly feels real.

"Hey, wait," Parker says, and I stop, turning to face him.

"What if my grandma is right?" I say quietly.

"Right about what?"

"What if James just didn't want to be a dad?"

"What?"

I swallow the boulder in my throat and say timidly, "What if he didn't want to be *my* dad?" My sight is blurry with unshed tears, but I focus on the center of Parker's chest, unwilling to look him in the eye.

"Adrienne." He takes a step closer, joining me on the shore. "Look at me." I don't. He sighs. "If avoiding stepping up to be the father you deserve had any part in his disappearance, then he's an idiot. But if that's all it was about, think about it: There are millions of deadbeat dads out there who didn't have to fake their deaths to get away from child support. I seriously doubt someone would go to that length to avoid being a father."

I meet his eyes now, my jaw set and nostrils flaring as I keep holding back my tears. I want to believe him. "So then why would James Rutherford fake his own death?"

Parker shrugs. "I don't know."

"Maybe he is a murderer. I mean, he's obviously been following me around, taking pictures, stealing your phone."

"I think he picked it up off a bench outside in the common area at college." Parker closes his eyes for a moment. "Yeah, the day I lost it, I left it on the bench with my stuff for a minute when I got up to go harass Jacob about his failed attempt to get Megan's number." Jacob is one of Parker's friends I never really know what to think of; he's socially awkward but obviously smart. "I don't remember having it at work that night."

"So he's a murderer and a creep who has not only been following me around, but also following my friends."

"It's definitely interesting behavior if he's just a deadbeat dad." Parker nudges my arm with his elbow. "If it is him kidnapping and killing our people, wouldn't Effie have recognized him when he kidnapped your babysitter and threatened you?"

"I don't know how that works. Can you recognize someone when they talk to you telepathically?"

"Definitely. Everybody sounds a little different, just like our audible voices are different."

"So he's not the one who threatened me and took that woman from my house. I know there is more than one person doing the kidnapping, though."

"How do you know that, by the way?"

"I'm seeing the kidnappings in my dreams at night. They're not really dreams, according to Grandma and Mom, but they only happen when I'm trying to sleep."

"Have you seen who is doing the kidnapping?"

"Never their faces, but there is always more than one person there during the kidnapping."

"I wonder if Marcus is involved in this with James somehow? The letter suggests he's hiding something at least," Parker says, biting his lower lip.

"But if this letter really does incriminate Marcus somehow, why would he leave that file and this letter somewhere anyone could easily find it?"

"I don't know. There's something going on here we're not seeing." Parker paces away, hands in his hair. "And Marcus is in the middle of all of it."

"Why don't we ask him about the letter?"

"Really? It seems pretty clear we can't trust anything Marcus Griffin says." Parker's eyebrows scrunch together.

"What if this guy following me around isn't James? What if it's never been James? What if he's really the serial killer behind all the kidnappings trying to screw with us?" I don't like that idea. It feels more sinister, if that's possible.

"Then he's playing a long game," Parker says, letting his hands hang at his sides. "Sawyer said they've had James on their radar as the one responsible for all the disappearances since shortly before his supposed death. Either way—whether it's him or not—we can't just ignore this." He pokes at the paper still in my hand and swallows, his Adam's apple bobbing up and down.

"You're right."

"I think we should show it to your mom. She might be able to tell us if that's James's handwriting. While I don't doubt it's him, confirmation would be nice. I wish I could poke around in Marcus's suite of rooms. I might find something else."

"He has a suite of *rooms*, and I'm stuck on a twin-size bed in a room that's about the size of a postage stamp?" I say, eyebrows raised. "I guess there are bound to be benefits to being the one in charge. What are you doing tomorrow morning?"

"Nothing. Why?"

I pause, not sure I should suggest this. He's right, though. We need to know what Marcus knows and why he has been keeping this a secret. While we might not learn anything from his suite of rooms, it won't hurt to check.

"I'm supposed to take a tour of the camp with him first thing tomorrow morning. That will take at least an hour, right?"

"At least. And if he starts talking about the founding of this place as he likes to do whenever he has a captive audience, then probably closer to two."

"Good. I'll keep him busy while you check out his suite," I say with more confidence than I feel.

"Have I ever told you your most attractive quality is that beautiful brain of yours?" Parker is giving me his familiar lopsided grin. I roll my eyes, but I can't stop my answering smile.

"It got you through calculus."

"Yes, you did. I'm sure we can piece this all together and figure it out too." He smiles, and I feel optimistic for the first time since this all started that he might be right. We might be able to get real answers.

I stare at the woods, not really focusing on the trees as I consider the situation.

"Hey, why do you think my mom lied to Dad about our additional abilities all this time?"

"Well . . . I don't know. You should probably ask her that," Parker says, scratching the back of his neck.

"How did I not know you have been lying to me all this time? You're a terrible liar. You know something."

"It's just a rumor. A rumor about something that happened before either of us was even born." He stops and looks away.

"So tell me anyway," I say, my impatience clear.

"Okay, but like I said, it's a rumor. I have no idea if it's true or if it's the reason your mother didn't tell Tom about your abilities." He takes a deep breath. "Synergy has been mapping out our genomes, looking for what makes us different, right? When Synergy's genome project was still in its earliest stages, your dad was responsible for all the new samples that came in from the field. He checked them to make sure the sample wasn't contaminated or whatever, and then he'd run the initial analysis. These samples all came from our community, but he noticed there was some variation within the sample results. The genomes for some people were slightly different." He pauses.

"You can't stop now. What happened?"

"Supposedly, he figured out all the samples that were different came from the same medical assistant who was getting samples in the field. So he asked to go with this medical assistant and observe to make sure the samples weren't being messed with somehow. Or at least that's the story he sold to everyone."

"And? If I have to drag this story out of you, I'm going to scream," I threaten.

"He started asking questions about people in the community being able to do more than read minds. He scared a lot of people because he wasn't quiet about it, either."

"What made him think it was a possibility? I mean, if he was just looking at strands of DNA or whatever, why would he have thought it meant additional abilities?"

"Again, rumor, but the story is that someone talked. Someone told him," Parker says. He looks uncomfortable at this.

"What happened after that?" I ask.

"It wasn't too much longer before he wasn't shadowing that medical assistant collecting samples anymore. So nothing, I guess."

"So you think my mom heard these rumors too?"

"I know he met both your mom and James during his time shadowing that medical assistant. Your mom was in the right position to hear the same rumors. Most people looked to James for leadership and Thea by extension as his wife. I'm sure they talked to her about things that worried them as well, like some neurotypical science guy poking around and asking questions no one wants asked."

"You think she didn't tell him because she knew he was already fascinated? But why? It's Dad—it's not like he'd experiment on us." I laugh at the thought. He used to get panicky any time I would fall and scrape my knee. I can't imagine him trying to poke and prod me for the sake of science.

"Her reasons might not have anything to do with him. It might just be a result of what she was taught. You didn't grow up in it, but trust me, we're drilled over and over on keeping our abilities a secret from a young age. Add in additional abilities, someone threatening to come steal you away, and I can't imagine how much more that's ingrained in someone who has additional abilities."

"How has she managed to keep that from him all this time? Wait, no, that's a stupid question. She kept my own abilities from me my entire life. It was probably easy keeping this from Dad."

"Yeah." A comfortable silence follows, both of us lost in our thoughts.

My mind drifts back to James Rutherford and that letter. Strange to think of my mother married to anyone other than Dad. What must she be feeling learning he's still alive?

"It's starting to get dark," Parker says. "We should go back."

"Will you do me a favor?"

"Maybe," he says with a grin. "It depends."

"Don't show that letter to my mom just yet. I want to ask her a few questions first."

CHAPTER 23

EFFIE

I'm surrounded by blackness, nothingness. I feel as if I didn't arrive any-where, but rather like I've always been here. But the last thing I remember is closing my eyes to sleep after leaving Tom and Thea to talk. Thea told him about Adrienne's abilities and where they came from, I'm sure. That makes Tom the first regular person to know about my family's history with additional abilities. He'll be ready to swab us all for DNA by breakfast.

"Euphemia," a shapeless voice calls to me gently, softly, like a whisper along my skin beckoning me closer. I try to move, unsure which direction the voice came from, but my foot doesn't connect with anything. My body doesn't feel defined or definite, even. I'm floating in this nothingness, neither suspended nor grounded. I'm in some kind of strange in-between land.

"Euphemia," he says again. His voice is stronger this time, the timbre familiar, sorrowful. I wish I could propel myself nearer to him, to find the source, but my efforts yield no movement. I'm stuck.

"Hey!" I holler. No response. "I don't know what's going on, but I don't plan on floating here and waiting forever to find out."

"Euphemia," the man says, closer this time. "I am so sorry I haven't been there for you."

The air leaves my lungs. It can't be possible that the voice belongs to my Hank. Can it? None of this is possible or real, though. I must be dreaming.

"Effie, I am so sorry," he says again. I can hear the truth of his words, feel the emotion behind them. It's been so long since I've heard him speak.

"Hank?" I sound like I did forty years ago when I first met Hank, unsure and breathless.

He doesn't have much time with me. I don't know how I know that, but

I do. I feel it.

"It's me, Euphemia," he says, his voice urgent, more intense, nearer. "For once in your life, you have to listen to what I'm telling you to do."

I am overwhelmed by emotion. There are things I want to tell him, things I want to ask him. And more importantly, I just want to be near him, to hear him speak to me more about anything and everything. I'm frozen, unable to decide what to say. I can feel the time slipping away from us.

"Hank, I—"

"I know," he says tenderly, "you don't have to tell me a thing. I know." Tears drip from my chin, falling away into the ether.

"Why can't I see you? Where are you?" He doesn't answer, but I feel his answer; I understand the truth of it just as I know we didn't have much time together. He's here in my mind, reaching me through space, time, planes of existence, breaking so many rules we thought we knew about the universe. About our existence. He's in my mind and yet not in any definable place. His soul is tethered to mine and also tethered somewhere else. I can feel his essence can't stay here with me because it's supposed to be somewhere else, somewhere beyond my understanding. I'm afraid his presence here is costing him something, that it might tear our tether in two when he goes.

"I'll always be tied to you, and you to me," he answers my unspoken worry. "Do you remember Mount Hope? Do you remember the day we found it?"

I don't speak my answers or nod, but I know he feels my affirmation.

"You remember what we learned?" he asks. "Don't let history repeat itself."

"How? How do I stop it?" I feel him slipping away from me. I want to go with him.

"You have to stay, and you have to stop him." His words are full of strength, confidence, assurance I can do what he's asking of me.

"Where do I find him? How do I stop him?"

He doesn't speak his answer, but I feel his response that my answers can be found within my own mind. I wish I could ask him what that means, but we're out of time. He's leaving me again. I don't know if my heart can withstand it this time.

"Euphemia—"

"I know. You don't have to tell me a thing," I say, repeating his words to him, my heart full of love for him. I do my best to hide my pain, the hole his absence created. A hole that will be reopened, expanded when he leaves me again. I don't want to weigh him down with my grief. I want him to leave knowing how much I deeply care for him still, to feel my joy at having this moment with him even if it is fleeting.

"Euphemia," his voice is no louder than a caress now, "fight, live."

I will.

As if someone has snapped their fingers and awakened me, my eyes open and I find myself in my bed. The clock on the bedside table tells me I've slept later than I would normally. I sit up quickly—and groan. My joints hurt.

Was that real? Did I dream it all? Could it be dementia?

I need to pee. I'll consider my sanity in a moment.

My feet hit the floor and I stand slowly, reaching for my cane. I take a tentative step forward and wait for the usual pops and cracks to issue from my ankles, knees, hips, and back. I roll my neck, stretching, adding another pop to the mix. Gradually, I make my way to the bathroom. I flip the light on. The sink is to my left, holding my partial dentures. I'm glad Hank never had to see those, much less all these wrinkles. And saggy skin. No one talks about the amount your skin will sag as you get older. It's probably for the best. Who wants to preview their fate?

After I do my business, I glance in the mirror while washing my hands to inspect the saggy skin that is my face, but I am instead paralyzed by what I see. Staring back at me is an older man I don't recognize. I rub my eyes and look again. He's still there.

"Effie," the face says, teeth bared into a grin, "you're too late." While his face doesn't seem to be familiar, his voice certainly is. I know I've heard it before.

Startled, I jump back from the mirror and nearly trip over my own feet.

I have truly lost my grip on reality. How is this happening? There's no way that was real. Is there? I don't look in the mirror again.

I shuffle back toward my bed, grab my robe, and head for the door. I need to find Thea or Sawyer immediately. I don't make it a step before my head starts hurting, though. There's a pressure behind my eyes that's building, blurring my vision. I grip my cane tightly as the pain intensifies and my vision swirls.

Don't let history repeat itself, Hank had said. There's something about that

that I need to know, right now, but I can't think with all this pain.

The agony ratchets up another notch, and I drop to my knees. The impact sends more pain throughout my body, making me whimper from my arthritic knees hitting the hard floor. I'm clammy and nauseated, and I can feel the darkness of unconsciousness at the edges of my vision.

"Surrender, Effie, you can't win," the voice of the man in the mirror echoes inside my mind.

"No, you son of a bitch," I get out through pants, my face scrunched up in pain. I reach out, pulling myself across the floor toward my bedside table. There's a phone there. I can at least call for help.

My pills are there on the bedside table too.

I got them before I went into a coma, before I attempted to hitchhike in his brain—the mirror man. It's him all right. I recognize him as the one I felt the night Adrienne's babysitter was kidnapped. He told me then he'd be back for my Adrienne, and I've never doubted him.

Now to get to my phone and pills. I've never suffered pain this intense in my life, and overcoming it now to drag my feeble body across the floor takes all my focus. My progress is slow, but I make it. Using my fingers and the bedside table to pull me up, I manage to make it to a sitting position, propping myself up against the side of the bed. I dig in the drawer there until I find the medication I'm looking for. It's often needed when someone like me becomes feebleminded, and feeblemindedness was one possible side effect of my little experiment that put me in a coma. It's something only crazy old mind readers take to mute their abilities, but I think it also dampens the effect *others* can have on a person's mind. I've been keeping it on hand, just in case. If I wasn't in such agony, I'd pat myself on the back for asking Sawyer to bring it to me here. I thought it might be something I'd need for my own mind to heal and repair itself. I didn't anticipate ever using it for this.

I pop the lid off the bottle and dump a few into my mouth. *Focus, Euphemia*, I tell myself. After swallowing, I drop the bottle and look for my phone.

But as I reach out, something in my mind feels like it explodes and fractures synapses. I cry out and reach for the cell phone I barely know how to operate, but my arm isn't working. Neither arm is working. My hands won't even move now. I start to sway, and there's nothing I can do to stop it.

CHAPTER 24

ADRIENNE

M egan and I walk to the lodge, arriving with damp feet and ankles from
the early-morning dew still clinging to the grass. I am distracted on
the walk, unable to focus on Megan's chatter. Not able to catch Mom this
morning—she was up and gone by the time I woke up—I've been checking
my pocket over and over to make sure the letter Parker found is still safely
hidden away. I have a million questions—like why she didn't tell Dad about
our abilities, or if Marcus really has been hiding that James Rutherford is
alive—and I don't see an answer to any of those questions falling out of the
sky.

"Good morning, ladies," Marcus says with a smile firmly in place as
Megan and I enter the lodge, meeting us on the ground-floor lobby. Mike,
our ever-present shadow when Parker isn't around, is close behind.

Megan and I both nod our hello, and I quickly hit send on the text I had
already prepared to send to Parker, letting him know Marcus is with us and
nowhere near his suites.

"I wasn't expecting you, Megan, but I'm glad you could join us. Let's take
a walk," Marcus says, his smile even brighter now.

I wonder if he has his teeth professionally whitened, I think as I cringe at his
extra-bright smile. If so, there's no way he's listening to his dentist's recom-
mendations on the frequency of those treatments.

"Uh, glad to be here," she says with a shrug and a smile.

I'm glad to have Megan with me. She agreed to come with me before
enthusiastically telling me about the history of the camp Mike shared with
her yesterday. I almost told her our goal is to keep Marcus busy while Parker
searches his suite for information or evidence of anything else he might be

keeping from us. But Parker reminded me that Megan hasn't learned how not to broadcast her thoughts for any neurodivergent telepath to hear. I don't like her not knowing what's going on. I make a mental note to teach her how to block her thoughts later.

"Are we ready?" He gestures toward the door we just entered.

"Why not?" I say with a polite smile.

"We're headed to the chapel," he says after we exit the lodge.

We walk along in silence. It's strange seeing Marcus without his assistant trailing behind him. I try to think of something to say, but I know almost nothing about Marcus.

"Do you give every visitor a tour?" I ask the first question that comes to mind.

"Not every visitor, no," he says, turning his high-beam smile on me again. "It's something I enjoy, though, and you aren't just any visitor."

"If only I had known having a stalker would make a person special, I totally would have gotten one too," Megan says with a smile. "I'll settle for reaping the benefits of your stalker, Adrienne." She gives me a wink. I raise an eyebrow. "What? Too soon? Not funny? I personally think I'm hilarious." She stage-whispers the last part.

"James Rutherford," Marcus says, casting a quick glance in my direction. I blink, trying to think on my feet and anticipate where this is going. Is he about to admit that James Rutherford is my stalker? "I understand you only recently learned that James is your father."

"Yes, that's correct."

"That's what motivated me to give you a tour," Marcus says. "I thought you might like to know a little more about your father."

"I don't think I understand what a tour of the chapel has to do with James Rutherford," I say in a measured tone. I don't like Marcus knowing things about me or making assumptions about what I'd like, either.

"Your father was a good man, Adrienne." Marcus continues walking toward the chapel, with Megan and I on either side of him and Mike following along behind. "We all felt his loss keenly. I know I wouldn't be the man I am today if I hadn't met your father. You'll see once we get to the chapel."

I'm not sure what else to say to him, so we walk in silence the rest of the short distance to the chapel.

The chapel is a stone building that looks like it could hold no more than fifty people. The irregular shape of the stones makes me wonder how anyone was ever able to piece this rock jigsaw puzzle together. Above the entry, there's a smooth stone with the words NEW MOUNT HOPE CHAPEL engraved in its surface. As we reach the front of the little stone building, Marcus leads us over to the corner of the building and squats down.

"Do you see this stone here?" He puts his hand against the smooth rock face.

It's etched with a list of names arranged alphabetically. Thomas Adams is at the top. I didn't know Dad had helped with this chapel. After what Parker had to say about Dad's early involvement with the community, I'm surprised to see his name here.

I keep scanning the list of names. Marcus Griffin is a few names below Dad's near the top, and James Rutherford is etched close to the bottom. Next to the names, it says 1996.

"This chapel wasn't originally part of Camp Little Creek," Marcus explains. "It was James's idea to add it to the property. He built it with a few other volunteers after he took over the leadership here." Marcus runs his hand over the stone. "He had said we needed it as a reminder. While we do have abilities that allow us to know so many things we wouldn't otherwise know, we must always remember we're not gods." Marcus straightens up and takes a step back. Hands on his hips, he looks over the chapel. "Every name on that stone helped to build this chapel in one way or another."

"James had your job when he was here?" Megan asks.

"Yes, he did. He had experience leading another smaller community alongside his father. He was a natural choice. He had a knack for seeing things no one else did. It made him insightful. And he was charismatic, intelligent, fair . . ."

Marcus lets his words trail off. His face is relaxed, his eyes focused on some faraway point. Waves of a mixture of emotions flow from him in slow, undulating currents. I let them wash over me, filling my chest with respect, friendship, and something I can't quite put my finger on. Homesickness? Longing? He seems to notice my scrutiny and stands. He clears his throat. His phone lets out a trilling notification.

"Excuse me for a moment, I need to answer this message," Marcus says, pointing to the phone he's just extracted from his pocket.

I nod, and after he's stepped away, I lean down and run my hand over the indentations on the cornerstone that make up my dad's name. The stone is weathered, but not significantly. Next, my fingers explore the letters that spell out James Rutherford. How can this man Marcus describes be the same man who faked his death? The man who is and, because of his absence, isn't my father?

My chest is suddenly tight, tighter. Pain emanates from behind my sternum. I push against it with the heel of my palm. It doesn't help. The pressure in my chest builds, builds. My breaths are shallow bursts now as tears from the sudden pain prick my eyes. I stand up as straight and tall as I can, willing the pressure to subside, arching my back a little to stretch against it like it's a charley horse I can work out. It doesn't help. *Pain. There is so much pain.*

"Adrienne," Megan says, gripping my elbow, "what is it?"

"I . . . I don't know," I say between breaths. I'm panting from the agony. "It's like . . . the pain is in me, but it's . . . not mine."

Waves of hurt, fear—no, terror—are crashing around us, into us, but I'm the only one affected. I look around, trying to find the source. Is it Marcus? No, the pain isn't coming from him. I frantically scan around us, but I don't see anyone else. I look instead to Megan, sweat beading on my forehead. It's not coming from her, of course. I wish I could concentrate, locate the source of those emotions. But I can't. The pain and terror are overwhelming my senses.

"The pain," I say, "it's too much." Another wave, this one more intense, hits me, and I realize too late I should push it away, relieve myself of its burden. Megan's face blurs. I close my eyes and try to focus on breathing in and out, but the agony is crippling me. I fall to my knees.

"Get Vincent to my location immediately!" I hear Marcus say, his voice feeling distant even though he sounds very near.

Megan is on one side of me, knelt down. Another pair of hands comes into view. A part of my brain registers that it's Mike, and he's holding me up. I raise my hands in an effort to boost my mental efforts to push the emotions away from me, but it doesn't work. I'm feeling weaker, weaker.

A wave of pain hits me square in the chest, and I can't stop the agonized scream that builds in my belly and rips it way up through my throat and out of my mouth.

The world turns black.

"Where is she hurt?" Marcus shouts near my face, his voice panicked.

Rough hands explore my torso.

"Roll her over!" Marcus shouts again.

I don't open my eyes. Instead, I lie still, letting them roll me to my side. More rough hands on my back, my neck, my head, before I'm gently rolled again to my back.

The agony from my chest is gone. All that's left are the echoes of the terror that felt like a living, breathing thing within me, trying simultaneously to suffocate me and tear me apart. I seem to be fine, though, which doesn't seem right, either. That much pain should have at least caused a sore muscle or two. But I feel fine. So I slowly open my eyes, hoping it will stop any more examinations.

"Adrienne? Adrienne!" Dad says, but I don't see him. Where is he? "Are you okay?"

"Yeah, I'm okay," I say with a slow nod. How long was I out? How did Dad get here so quickly?

"What the hell happened here, Marcus?" Dad's voice is angry. I roll my head in his direction, and I finally spot him above me about a dozen feet away, his hands balled up into fists, his face red. Marcus holds up a hand to him as he listens intently to the walkie-talkie.

"Are you okay, really?" Megan asks me, pushing my hair from my face.

"Yeah," I say with more confidence as I grasp Mike's hand and pull myself up to a sitting position. "Just a system overload," I say, rubbing my chest and offering her a smile. "My throat is a little scratchy, I guess from screaming, but that's it."

"Somehow I don't believe you," Megan says, fixing me with a stern look. "That was—whatever it was—bad."

"Come on," I say as I heave myself forward to my knees. "I'm fine. See?"

I gesture Vanna White–style at my body. "Now help me up." I give her a smile, but I can't stop the trembling in my hands.

"Just sit here a minute, okay?" It's Mike, face pinched and pale.

Megan rolls her eyes at me. "You just sounded like you were going to die right in front of me. Be still."

The place is crawling with men. Guards with guns are everywhere, searching the grounds and the nearby buildings. Two come out of the chapel.

"Vincent," Marcus calls to one of the men nearby, "help Mike take Adrienne to the infirmary."

"No," I say, waving him off as he comes toward me. "Really, I'm fine now. Whatever it was has passed." I get to my feet before anyone can protest.

"Adrienne, maybe you should go get checked out," Dad says, lines of worry across his face. "I heard you scream from the lab."

I glance at him in surprise. "From the lab?" I ask, looking around before I remember the lab is down the hill a little, behind the chapel.

"It was the most agonized thing I've ever heard in my life," he says. "What was this, Marcus?" He turns away from me again. "Was this an attack from her stalker?" Dad is back in Marcus's face now that he's put the walkie-talkie on his belt.

"I have my men combing the surrounding areas and searching the buildings," Marcus says. "If there is anyone who shouldn't be here, we'll find them."

"Adrienne, can you tell us what happened?" Mike asks. The four of them look at me expectantly.

"I don't know, really. I just felt . . ." I hesitate, not sure I should say anything in front of Mike or Marcus. Or Megan, for that matter, since she doesn't know how to keep her thoughts private from all these mind readers. "Chest pain," I say lamely with a hand to my chest, hoping they'll be satisfied with the abbreviated version.

"Can you give us a moment?" Dad says to the others, never taking his eyes off me. Marcus nods and gestures for Mike to step away. Megan takes a few steps away as well.

"What's up, Dad?"

"What really happened?"

"I just had a pain—"I swallow—"in my chest."

"Does this have something to do with those extra-special added abilities you mentioned last night?"

I don't answer right away, but he's my dad. I don't see a reason not to tell him.

"Yes," I whisper, leaning in. "It was someone else's emotions, overwhelming me suddenly. It was fear, pain, despair—awful feelings—hitting me. And the emotions kept building, getting stronger and stronger. I've never felt any emotion that strongly before." I pause and take a deep breath, letting it out slowly. "It was intense."

Dad turns on his heel, moving toward Marcus.

"Why the hell was she here in the first place?" he demands from Marcus.

"I . . . I was giving her a tour," Marcus says, brows scrunched, his head tilted questioningly.

Does Dad think Marcus set this up? Waves of emotion are rolling off Dad and Marcus. What is that you're feeling, Marcus? I try to focus on him. Dad is standing too close, though, and I'm feeling like one giant raw nerve ending, every little emotion around me is flowing up together, amplified, overwhelming, screaming at me, making it hard to make out any single emotion.

"Who asked you to do that?" Dad asks, jabbing a finger at Marcus. "Why?"

"I thought she might want to see the chapel and some of the things her . . ." Marcus's face turns tense as he lets his sentence trail off.

"Her what? What, Marcus? Why were you here?"

"Her father," he responds, clears his throat. "I wanted to show her the chapel because, as you know, her father spearheaded its creation when he was still with us, running this place."

Dad's face gets even redder.

"Hey!" I say quickly, loudly, hoping to interrupt them and stop Dad from doing anything like punching Marcus. "Are we going to keep standing here, or does someone want to go with me to see Mom now?" I ask, looking at Mike and Megan, who are hovering at either elbow, as if waiting for me to faint, and then looking at Dad. "Dad? I want to talk to Mom and Grandma about what just happened. If anyone is going to know what I just experienced, it will be them."

"Yes, take her, Mike, Vincent," Marcus says. I roll my eyes at Vincent and

Mike, who move to either side of me. "You'll find Thea at the infirmary."

"What? Why is she there?" I ask Marcus. He opens his mouth to answer, but Dad cuts him off.

"Can you make it there without me, sweetie?" Dad asks. "I want to have a word with Marcus."

I nod slowly, hoping he won't do anything foolish.

CHAPTER 25

ADRIENNE

"What's happening?" Parker asks from behind me. "Mike sent one of the guys to get me. He said something happened to you. Are you hurt?"

"I'm fine," I say, turning from Megan to face him. He looks me over as if to verify what I've said is true. "It's Grandma."

"What's going on?"

"We don't know." I hug my body with my arms, shifting my weight from one foot to the other. "Mom found her on the floor in her room this morning." I tell him that Dr. Thompson said they're waiting for test results.

"Whoa," Parker says. "That's awful."

Movement catches my eye from the other side of the narrow windows on the double doors Dr. Thompson went through earlier. It looks like a nurse quickly walking our way. There is no waiting room, so Mom, Megan, Mike, and I have all congregated here in the hall by the doors that separate the infirmary from the rest of the facility. The nurse isn't smiling as she strides the last few steps and holds the door open. *Please, let Grandma be okay.*

"Thea? Adrienne?" the nurse asks, looking to Mom and then me.

"Yes, what's going on?" Mom says, reaching for my hand.

"Come with me," the nurse says and turns around.

Mom and I jog after her. She ushers us past the area where Grandma was before and into what looks like a typical hospital critical care unit, except every glass cubicle appears empty. All except one.

"Over here," she says and leads us to the cubicle that's bustling with activity.

Mom rushes to Grandma's side, but I freeze at the doorway. Dr. Thompson is in the corner, speaking quietly to a man in a lab coat. He's nodding, glancing occasionally at Grandma. The nurse by Grandma's head is attaching wires to little round sensors placed on her scalp while another at her side injects something into her IV tube. A third nurse is entering information into the portable terminal there next to the bed.

The man in the lab coat writes something down and then moves toward me to the door.

"Adrienne, Thea," Dr. Thompson says. She pauses, moving closer to Grandma by the head of her bed and displacing the nurse that had been there. "Euphemia has been in and out of consciousness these last few minutes." Mom clasps her hands together and brings them up to cover her mouth as a sigh of relief escapes.

"That's good, right?" she says.

I turn my attention to Grandma. Her eyes are closed, her breathing slow and even. *Is it too slow?*

"We've been examining Euphemia's initial brain scans from when she was first brought to the hospital weeks ago." She doesn't answer Mom's question. "While there didn't seem to be any significant findings from that incident, it gave us a good baseline for comparison." Dr. Thompson holds out her hand, and the nearby nurse offers her a tablet. "When we took over her care shortly after she awakened, we performed another brain scan. We repeated that scan a few hours ago." She pauses and hits a button on the tablet. She touches the screen several times before turning it around so we can see it. "When comparing the second and third scan to the first, there's evidence of significant neurological changes."

There are three images on the screen, but I'm not sure what I'm looking at.

"These areas in particular have degraded rapidly since Euphemia's first scan." Dr. Thompson points to an area on the latest scan that looks less defined than it did on the first scan. The structures surrounding this area are more irregular as well. She points out an area that's all black right in the center. It's much smaller and shaped very differently in the third image. "And we see atrophy overall."

"So can you do something about these changes then?" I ask, hopeful.

"The brain is the most delicate organ in the body. We don't have a method of treatment for changes this significant." Dr. Thompson tucks the tablet under her arm. Waves of sadness radiate from her.

"But she's been awake." Mom crosses her arms, grips her elbow.

"She's only somewhat conscious right now because of a medication we've given her. Her current state won't last long. I've never seen someone who was seemingly healthy the day before show this much neurological atrophy. That alone suggests the damage to her brain is compounding and occurring more quickly now."

"What are you saying?" I ask.

"We've done everything we can for her, but this is the end. Euphemia is dying." Mom jerks back, both hands covering her mouth. She stares silently at Dr. Thompson. "We have given her everything we can think of to slow the rate of her neurological symptoms, but it's not working. She's deteriorating rapidly." She stops, purses her lips. "Please, take this time to talk to her, to hold her hand, to sing her a song. Whatever you need to do to tell her good-bye. She may linger for minutes, hours, or a few days, but this may be your last opportunity to see her conscious."

"Will you please ask someone to go get Tom and Toby?" Mom asks, touching Dr. Thompson's arm lightly.

"Of course." The doctor clasps her hands together. "Mackenzie," she says. The nurse nods and briskly carries out an unspoken task from the computer terminal.

Mom hesitates a moment, then walks as if on wooden legs to Grandma's bedside. Her hands shake as she reaches out to her. She leans down and kisses Grandma's cheek, then rests her forehead against Grandma's. Grandma stirs, her eyes fluttering open.

"Are you sure of your assessment?" Mom asks Dr. Thompson. The doctor nods slowly, a frown on her face.

I watch, my back stiff. Mom turns to Grandma and talks to her. I can't hear what she's saying. What do you say at a time like this to someone you love? What do you say to the person who is slipping away from you right before your eyes?

Dr. Thompson stays at my side. "If you talk to her, she will hear you. Tell her you love her. Tell her about your favorite time together. Just talk," she says kindly.

Grandma's lips are moving now. Mom, cheek to cheek with Grandma, nods. The tears fall freely from Mom's face as she strokes Grandma's cheek.

"We're going to step out now and give you three some privacy," Dr. Thompson says, giving the nurses a look. They all walk out, and Dr. Thompson gently shuts the door behind her as she exits.

Grandma turns her face toward me and weakly holds out a hand, beckoning me to her side. Her arm flops to the bed after only a moment. I swallow, willing my feet, which feel completely detached from me, to move. I walk around the other side of her bed and lean in close to Grandma. I try to force a smile on my face, but my face feels frozen, unyielding and stony.

"Ad . . . Adrienne, come . . . closer," Grandma forces out with great effort, her words slurred. I bend closer, reaching for the hand that beckoned me. "I . . . can't . . ." She mumbles something I can't make out. ". . . using my mind . . . Mount Hope . . ."

I'm not sure what she's trying to say. I glance to Mom, hoping she can tell me what Grandma is saying or what I should be doing. But tears continue to fall unhindered from her chin, her hands wrapped around Grandma's. Grandma closes her eyes, and I fear this is it, that she won't open them again. With a heaving breath, she blinks and tries speaking again. I'm only momentarily relieved.

"You . . . must . . ." She utters something I can't understand again. "Stop him." She nods, appearing to be satisfied that she's said all she needs to say.

Mom buries her face in Grandma's neck.

"What?" I pause and swallow hard, trying to form the words. "What about Mount Hope, Grandma?"

She shushes me weakly. "You . . . and your Mom . . . must tell . . . no one." She swallows, the effort visible in the tight lines on her face.

"Grandma," I say quietly as she closes her eyes again, "you have to fight."

"I am fighting," she says, her voice a little clearer, her eyes still closed, a smile on her face. "And I'm . . . about to win." She takes a great shuddering breath. Her hand in mine goes limp.

"You . . . you can't give up." I hear my voice, stilted, distant, as if it's not really my own. I feel separate from this moment. "I need you." Her eyes remain closed. Tears stream down my face. I wipe my eyes so I can see her clearly. I lean closer. "Come back to us," I plead.

Her eyes open, flicking back and forth. She smiles and laughs weakly.

Adrienne

The back of my neck tingles, and goose bumps form on my arms at the eerie sound. She suddenly stiffens, a grimace on her face. Then her eyes roll back and her face relaxes. I don't believe what I'm seeing. I reach out for her, shaking her shoulder gently. Her face is slack, her whole body limp.

She doesn't respond. The air leaves her lungs. I wait, soundless and numb, silently praying, watching carefully for any sign that she's still with me. I take a shuddering breath, willing her to do the same. *Breathe, Grandma,* I silently beg.

She doesn't. Her eyes are glassy and unseeing. Her face is slack. She's gone.

Mom lets out a moan that splits the silence. I drop Grandma's hand and stumble back, my hands and feet clumsy and numb. Mom sobs, but her cries sound so far away now. I'm aware of Dr. Thompson's presence, and a nurse rushes back in, but it's like I'm watching them through an aquarium with all the action happening somewhere I'm not. Dr. Thompson moves Grandma's gown aside and puts her stethoscope to Grandma's chest to listen.

"She's gone," I say quietly, wishing they wouldn't touch her. She wouldn't like it. Dr. Thompson continues anyway, moving her stethoscope slightly.

"She's gone," I say a little louder. "She's gone." Dr. Thompson checks her wristwatch. "She's gone. She's gone!" My voice has grown progressively louder. I'm screaming it now.

Dr. Thompson's head swivels in my direction. Someone says something. I can't hear them. It sounds like the aquarium glass is all around me now, enclosing me, muddling and dampening every sound as if I'm underwater.

I back up quickly, suddenly desperate to get away. I turn and move swiftly to the door, stepping out into the hall and right into someone else. I look up to see Marcus standing there, his expression blank.

"You," I spit out.

"Adrienne?" He reaches for me, his brows knit together. I jerk back, not wanting to be touched. Not by him of all people.

So I leave and I walk the other way down the hall.

CHAPTER 26

ADRIENNE

"She should take a nap for a few hours and then be back with us," Dr. Thompson says quietly as I come to. My eyes are closed, and I keep them that way. I'm not ready to talk to anyone. I'm on my side in a hospital bed, the blankets heavy over my body.

"Thank you, Dr. Thompson," Dad says.

I hide behind my closed eyes, my motionless body, pretending I'm not conscious.

After I had ran into Marcus, I walked until I ended up back in the hallway we had stood waiting in earlier. When I saw Megan and Parker standing there, the tears finally came. It's like the aquarium glass shattered, and everything that had felt muted suddenly felt overwhelming. My sadness poured out of me in a torrent of sobs and pulsing waves of dark gray. I've never cried like that—wrenching sobs that left me breathless. Parker, concerned about my overall inability to slow the sobbing, got Dr. Thompson. She offered me a sedative. I nodded my consent, the best I could do in that moment. Parker half carried me back to a room and a bed, and then Dr. Thompson injected me with something. Sleep wasn't immediate, but there was a gradual lessening of the tide of sadness. I asked Parker to climb into the hospital bed next to me. He did, pushing my hair from my face. He lay there next to me until I finally fell asleep.

And here I am now, awake, wishing I wasn't. He's gone, but I'm not alone. It sounds like a packed room.

"Thea." I can hear Dr. Thompson's quiet inhale of breath in this too-quiet room. "We received results back from Euphemia's labs. We were looking for possible toxins and medications. We found lorusimide. As you know, lorusimide is commonly used in our elderly population as a way to suppress neurodivergent telepathic abilities to help those with dementia be more present and lucid. Do you know why she would be taking that medication?"

"No. She doesn't have dementia," Mom answers. "Didn't," she amends quietly.

"Was she having any trouble with tuning out others' thoughts, or any issues at all since her illness?" Dr. Thompson asks gently.

"She was having headaches, but you already knew that," Mom says. "As far as I know, that was it."

"Okay. I'm going to refer Euphemia's case to our genetic and rare disease committee for further study. Her illness presentation isn't something I've seen before. Hopefully the committee will have seen something similar at least."

"Will they be able to tell us what was wrong with her?" Mom asks softly.

"The committee is comprised of seven of our rare disease specialists from around the world. Any time any of us comes down with something we can't diagnose, they review the case files. I don't want to misrepresent the chances of getting a diagnosis and answers from this process, though. Most of the time, these doctors don't have the answers, either. But if there's another similar case, knowing about Euphemia will help them to start to look for the answers."

"We understand," Dad says. "Thank you, Cynthia."

"I have a few things I need you to sign, Thea. Would you mind following me out to my office?"

"I can do that. Will you stay here with her until she wakes up?" Mom asks. "I don't want her to wake up in a room alone."

"Of course," Dad answers. "Toby, why don't you go with your mom? Keep an eye on her for me."

"Yeah, I can do that," Toby answers.

The rustling of movement is followed by the click of the door shutting.

"Adrienne," Dad says, "I know you're awake."

In the silence, I listen to the sound of my breathing, in and out, slowly, calmly. It doesn't match how I'm feeling on the inside. *Grandma will never draw another breath*, I think. I feel pinpricks of heat behind my closed eyelids as the tears well up in my eyes. The chair next to my bed creaks. I'm facing away from the sound, thankfully, and I squeeze my eyes closed more tightly.

"Do you remember when we rented a houseboat that one summer in Lake of the Ozarks?" Dad says, his voice coming from the general direction of the chair. "You and your brother had so much fun being on the water all day." I don't respond. Instead, I focus on letting my tears fall silently, unnoticed. "Our last day there . . . well, that was the most terrifying day of my life. You had been begging to swim without your life vest all week long. And that day, you decided you were going to." The chair squeaks as Dad shifts his weight. "That moment when you screamed—a little burst of panic before you were quiet again—I felt it in my gut, in my heart. My heart knew what was wrong before my brain could piece it together." He sighs. "I'll never forget the sight of you spluttering as you bobbed and fought the water, trying your best to keep your head above its surface."

Another tear slips out, tracing down the side of my cheek.

"Today, when I heard you screaming," Dad continues, "it was the same shot of panic to my gut. But this time, I didn't know what was wrong. My heart couldn't tell me." He lets out a long breath. "I didn't know," he says, his voice shaky, "because you've shut me out. I don't know what's going on with the girl I love more than anything." I focus on breathing in and out, listening to the sound of each breath. "Watching you fight everything that's been happening, watching as you struggle to keep your head above water again with every new thing you learn about yourself, your biology, a past you were too young to remember—it has brought me right back to that day on the lake. And it terrifies me. I don't know whether you're going to be okay or not when this is all over." His voice is low. I get the feeling he's talking more to himself than me now. He sniffles.

Is he crying? My tears fall quicker as I lie there, pretending to be asleep.

"To save you from yourself in the lake, I had to get you to stop struggling. Do you remember? I jumped in, but I couldn't get a hold of you to get you back in the boat because you were flailing and fighting me so hard." He takes a deep breath. "It's the same here. Stop flailing, Adrienne, stop struggling. Let me help you. Let me in."

My tears are flowing unhindered now. Is he right? Have I been going at this all wrong? I think about opening my eyes, about turning my head to face him, letting him comfort me as the tears fall. I know he would hold me and let me cry just like he always has. But I don't. I can't.

I hear the rustling of more movement. A moment later, the door clicks as it's slowly, gently shut.

CHAPTER 27

ADRIENNE

I wipe my sweaty palms on my jeans. It's been a week since Grandma's funeral, and I can't spend another moment waiting for answers. I spent most of last night thinking and planning, trying to figure out what's going on. It finally occurred to me that I was missing the simplest of answers. I fell asleep for a couple of hours, confident in my decision. Now as I stand here, though, I'm already feeling nervous.

"Hey," I say as I open the door to the dorm room where Parker has been staying.

"Most people actually knock and then wait, you know," he says, throwing the towel he was just holding. I freeze. He's shirtless, barefoot, and his hair is damp and tousled. "What's up?"

"Uh, I can come back in a minute if you're busy," I say, my cheeks hot. What's wrong with me? This is Parker. There's been an awkwardness between us over the last week, though.

"Just getting dressed." His half grin in place, he seems to be enjoying my awkwardness.

"Whatever, just put a shirt on." I stand a little straighter. "We've got things to discuss. Plans to make."

"Okay. What are we planning?"

"A fishing trip, with me as the bait."

"What?"

Someone knocks on the doorframe. I turn and almost bump into Sawyer, who's standing too close, arm raised, knuckles against the trim.

"Creeping around a new hallway, Sawyer?" Parker asks with a sneer.

"Yep, you caught me," Sawyer replies, putting a hand in his pocket.

"That's why I knocked." He gives Parker a steely look before offering me a nod. "How are you doing?" He puts a hand on my shoulder for a moment before letting it fall to his side. He looks terrible, like he hasn't slept in days.

"What do you want, Sawyer?" Parker says before I can answer.

"I asked him here," I say, wondering why Parker is so hostile toward Sawyer. "We're going to need his help."

"Hmph." Parker sits on his bed, puts on his socks, and jams his shoes on his feet. "No, we won't, because we're not going to use you as bait. Ever. Not happening."

"I don't see how that's your choice," I say, instantly angry, stepping farther into the room. That's been happening a lot since Grandma's death, since her funeral a week ago. People making decisions for me. Me being angry at everything, anything.

"We're not putting you at risk," Parker says, standing.

"We aren't, you're right," I say, leaning against the wall casually, closing my eyes for a moment. "I'm taking the risk." My tone is bored. I'm doing my best to emulate Parker's usual calm, careless demeanor while I get my anger under control.

"You, out." Parker points to Sawyer, steps closer, shuts the door on him.

He turns to me slowly, carefully. He reaches toward me, toward my face, and my heart beats a little faster. He gently tugs my hand away from my mouth, inspects the raw nub where my thumbnail used to be before I chewed it off over the last few days. The nail-biting has been worse since Grandma's funeral because now I don't even realize I'm doing it. He doesn't let my hand go. I don't try to pull it away, either, and I'm not sure what to think about that so I don't. My anger vanishes. Instead, I feel every bit as exhausted as I should be since I've barely been sleeping.

"I can't just sit here and do nothing, day after day," I say. Parker should understand. He should know me well enough to know I can't keep sitting here when we think my grandmother died because of whatever is going on. "I can't sit here and hope someone else will find out what happened to her. We need more answers. We don't even know enough to be asking the right questions."

"It's a bad idea. We don't know what we're dealing with. Aside from James, who has been stalking you for an unknown reason, there's Marcus. We still don't know where he fits in to James's faked death and the other deaths and disappearances." His voice is intense, tight. "No," he says, an edge to his voice.

"We're never going to figure it out from here." I pull my hand from his grip, tuck it in my pocket. "What is wrong with you? Why won't you help me?" I'm not leaning against the wall anymore. My anger is back as suddenly as it left, and my efforts to appear calm and under control don't seem important.

"I'm not helping you kill yourself! It's the same stupid approach that got your grandma killed." I feel his regret instantly. He hangs his head and shakes it. "Adrienne, I'm sorry." I had told Parker everything I knew about Grandma's hitchhiking and the resulting coma the night after her funeral. Now I'm regretting it.

His words are like a punch to the chest. Tears form and fall rapidly, and I stand there mute, angry, broken. Overwhelmed. The one person I thought would understand why I want to do this *doesn't*.

"I'm sorry. I shouldn't have said it like that," he says. "But I'm not wrong, either. We should learn from Effie's mistake instead of imitating it."

"Are you seriously *blaming* my grandmother for her own death?" I've never been angrier than I am at this moment.

"No, I'm saying she took a risk that had little chance of resulting in success. I don't want to see you do the same, Adrienne." He leans over, bringing his face closer to mine. "I'm scared, okay?" He lets out a shaky breath. "I'm scared for you. You being bait . . . it's a risky idea, and I don't think I can sit and watch that."

"Then don't." I say it quietly, my face expressionless. He looks at me in surprise. I feel his relief in one big whooshing wave; he thinks I've acquiesced. Somehow, this makes my anger burn even hotter. I turn on my heel and open the door. "Sawyer, come on. I still need your help," I grit out between clenched teeth.

"Wait, what are you doing?" Parker says, following me out.

"Getting help with this so I don't end up dead," I say tonelessly.

"What kind of help do you think *he* can give you? You don't even know anything about him." He gestures angrily at Sawyer.

"Is that *really* why you don't like me, Parker? Because you don't know me?" Sawyer shoots back.

"Think this through, Adrienne. He's the last person you should be asking for help."

"Why? He's been looking into things with Grandma for years now." I keep walking down the hall toward the exit, Parker on my heels and Sawyer walking as unobtrusively as possible behind him. "He knows more than we do."

"Or is it because you think I'm the reason Effie is dead?" Sawyer says confidently, his question sounding like a statement.

The words stop me from taking another step. I whirl around and look at him. His misery is plain for anyone to see. Why didn't I notice the waves of guilt flowing from him earlier?

"Sawyer," Parker starts, running a hand across his face. He lets his hand drop, shakes his head. "Man, you are not at fault for what happened to Effie. She made her own decision to do something that we just don't know enough about." Sawyer closes his eyes. It's clear he doesn't believe it. "Her death is not your fault, Sawyer." Sawyer looks at him solemnly.

"It is, but I appreciate you putting aside your dislike for me for a minute to try to convince me otherwise," Sawyer says, his eyes narrowed. "Here's a tip for you now: quit arguing and get on board. Also like her grandmother, she's going to do this with or without your help. Trust me when I say you'll feel just as awful if something bad happens whether you helped or not." Sawyer pushes past both me and Parker and out the exit.

"Well?" I ask Parker in the stillness that follows.

"Yeah, fine, I'll help you," Parker answers, the fire gone from him.

"Let's go then. We have a plan to come up with before we recruit more help."

"Are you going to be involving Tom and Thea in this?" Parker's tone is neutral. I can't tell if he wants me to say yes or no.

"There's no way I'm telling them until I'm already there," I say and exhale. I don't want Mom to worry, but I have to do something. "They'll never just let me go on my own."

"On your own? Adrienne—"

"Stop. I don't mean completely alone. But I can't go traipsing back home with an entire entourage of people and expect James to come and knock on my door and kindly ask to speak to me for a moment, especially if he's a murderer."

"What about what your grandmother said about someone controlling her mind?" he asks as we step through the exit and into the early-morning light. I shared her last words with Parker, trying to make sense of it all. "It's possible she was right, and if so, we have way scarier things to worry about than James."

"I think it's possible," I say, hating the thought that it might be true. I can't imagine what that must have felt like to her.

"Then this is an even stupider idea." I've been feeling a steady trickle of fear and anger from Parker, but when he says that, his fear becomes more intense.

"I don't know why James or Marcus would want to control Grandma's mind. It doesn't make sense to me," I continue, unwilling to do nothing just because of fear. "There might be someone else involved in this somehow. That's part of what we need to plan for."

"It's pretty unrealistic to think we can account for every contingency with a bad guy who can use his supervillain mind-control powers whenever he feels like it."

"We don't know that. Maybe he only managed to latch onto Grandma because she visited him first. Besides, we have no idea if Grandma was coherent enough to know what she was saying." The words don't feel right as I say them. My grandmother was strong and smart. "She was clearly sick, and her mental hitchhiking adventure could have really messed with her mind." Even if I don't really believe it, it's true.

"Maybe, but if you're wrong, that's a big risk."

"If I'm wrong, then what's stopping him from coming after any of us no matter where we are?"

"Hey, are you two coming or what?" Sawyer says from a dozen yards away before he gets in the driver's seat of one of the golf carts I usually only see the guards using during patrols.

"Yeah, we need to go meet Megan," I say, already steeling myself for the argument I know is inevitable. She's going to want to come with me, and I can't let that happen.

CHAPTER 28

THEODORA

"Cynthia!" I call to her when she finally exits her car after pulling into a parking space in the infirmary. The air is cooler than usual this morning, and I can see my breath as I speak. "Can I talk with you for a moment?" I fidget with the hem of my T-shirt, crumpling it and uncrumpling it. Today is the first day since Mom's funeral I've bothered to get out of my pajamas and put jeans and a T-shirt on and leave the dormitory. I haven't been able to sleep or sit still for the last few days as I consider Mom's last words, though. I have to know if her attempt to hijack someone's mind resulted in her death, or if someone had been controlling her mind, and if so, were they responsible for her death?

"Sure," Dr. Cynthia Thompson says, fixing a slight smile on her face. "What's up, Thea? If this is about the genetic and rare disease committee, I haven't heard anything back from them yet. It usually takes months to—"

"No, that's not it," I say, interrupting her. "I wanted to ask you about . . . well, it's kind of an unusual question, and I'd rather it stay between the two of us. Can you do that? Can you talk to me like the old high school friends we are?" I give her a tentative smile. I know I can't really call myself a friend at all. Mom's recent care aside, we've hardly spoken since Adrienne's birth twenty years ago. Not because of anything she did. I've had tunnel vision since James's death, seeing only the need to protect Adrienne from any harm. And then Toby too, once he came along. But his safety is less complicated since he's neurotypical. Neurotypical, neurodivergent telepathic. What a strange way to describe the absence or presence of telepathic abilities.

"Thea." Cynthia puts her hand on mine. "I'm here to help. What can I do for you?"

"Have you ever encountered someone with . . ." My heart is beating hard. It goes against everything I've been taught my entire life to expose myself like this. "Give me a minute." I breathe in, hold the breath, and blow it out. I almost let myself do the same thing after Mom's death as I had after James's. Not that James died, apparently. But he was dead to me, that's for certain. I hid from everything and everyone other than my family then, and that's what I've been doing since Mom's passing. But I can't do that this time. That's why I need to get this out, to ask Cynthia what I came here to ask.

"Would you be more comfortable talking in my office?" Cynthia offers. She's sweet, but no, I definitely would not feel better talking about this inside.

"No, no. I'm fine here." I wipe my sweaty palms on my pants. "Have you ever encountered someone with more than the usual telepathic ability?"

"Uh—"

"Specifically, someone with the ability to control others' minds?"

"Whoa," Cynthia says, straightening up. "That's definitely not a question I get very often. Or ever. Why do you want to know?"

"Because," I say, taking another deep breath, "I know this sounds a little out there, but I think someone was controlling or manipulating Mom's mind. I need to know if it's possible and if it's a common ability we just don't talk about because that's our community—we don't talk about anything because it's always a risk." I stop to breathe, afraid and a little regretful at the stream of consciousness I just launched at Cynthia. I clench my T-shirt hem again in my damp palms.

"I can't tell you anything specific about any of my patients, but mind control? That's not something a patient has ever confided to me about. What makes you think Euphemia was being controlled or manipulated?"

"She wasn't herself after she woke up from her coma." I don't want to tell her the real cause of her coma. That's too much of a risk. "She had really bad headaches since then, and she would say things that were out of character for her. Like telling Adrienne about her neurodivergent ability." I shake my head.

"Mood changes and headaches are not uncommon side effects of a traumatic brain injury, and we can assume she had some kind of brain injury to cause her coma. Was there anything else?"

"Yes . . ." I can't say it. The dying words of a woman who hadn't been herself in weeks aren't all that reliable.

"Thea," Cynthia says in a tone I've heard too many times. After James's death—or faked death, I suppose—after Alice, Adrienne's sitter, was taken from my home, and now after Mom's death. A tone that's all empathy and concern. I know it means she's chalking up this entire conversation to grief; she isn't taking this seriously. "Have you been sleeping?"

"She said as she was dying that someone was controlling her mind." I can't leave it alone now that her tone has turned borderline patronizing. "She said, 'He's using my mind,' and 'Mount Hope.'"

"Wait, Mount Hope? She mentioned Mount Hope?"

"Yes, why?" My heart skips a beat.

"Wasn't Mount Hope the first settlement of neurodivergent telepaths in Missouri?" She closes her eyes a moment, tilts her head. "And it was shut down, our people dispersing after they had some trouble with area residents."

"What was the trouble?" I already knew that it was the first settlement in our area, but I hadn't been able to find any information on the reason it was dispersed.

"The verbal history was passed along the generations. It was preserved in a book by . . . I can't remember who. But I know the author was clear that we can't be sure how accurate that verbal history is. It's like that game of telephone we would play in junior high where we would whisper something to someone and by the time it made it through every person in the room, the original message was completely distorted." Cynthia shrugs.

"I'm sure you're right, but I'd like to hear it anyway."

"It's interesting that she mentioned someone using her mind and then Mount Hope. The old lore is that someone was manipulating the minds of the area's neurotypical residents and one of the settlement's residents was almost hanged because of it. There was a confrontation of some kind as a result, and several telepathic settlers were injured and killed. The rest were run off their land by the area farmers and townspeople."

"Why haven't I heard anything about this before?"

"Like I said, we can safely assume parts of it are incorrect. A story like that can't survive intact for more than a century."

"Isn't there a Mount Hope near here?" There's a fuzzy memory I can't grasp.

"No, the original settlement is near Taum Sauk Mountain a few hours away."

"I don't think I mean the original Mount Hope. But I think I've seen those words somewhere."

"You aren't thinking of New Mount Hope Chapel up the hill here, are you?" She points in the general direction of the little chapel across the campus grounds, up the hill from Tom's research lab.

"Yes, actually, I think I am." James wanted us to be the first couple married there once it was done, and we were. It's been two decades now since I've been there. But isn't that where Adrienne collapsed the day Mom died? Cynthia touches my arm and pulls my focus back to her.

"Is there anything I can do for you? If you're not sleeping, please come see me. I can write you a prescription for something that should help."

"Thanks, Cynthia." I keep my most polite smile in place. "I appreciate your help. I don't want to keep you any longer than I already have. Thanks again." I give an awkward half wave and take a step back.

"Not a problem. You come see me if you need anything at all."

My eyes follow her as she walks away, but my mind is on the chapel. We still don't have any idea what happened to Adrienne at that chapel that caused her so much pain that she passed out. Maybe it's time I visit it once again.

CHAPTER 29

ADRIENNE

Stepping into the entryway, I immediately lock the front door of the condo behind me. Reminding myself it was my idea to come back alone, I take a steadying breath, but it doesn't help. For about the fiftieth time now, I wonder if I'm doing the right thing.

The condo looks exactly as it did when we left. It even smells like the essential oil Megan likes to keep in the diffuser in the hall. The fact that it's unchanged feels off somehow, like it should be different here. But it isn't.

The sameness of the condo bothers me because I'm not the same person I was when I was last here. I'm looking for outward signs of the change I feel on the inside, and the world isn't giving me any.

Things have kept on spinning while I've been hiding away, losing my grandmother, learning I'm not who or what I thought I am. Not even my father is who I thought he was. But you wouldn't know it by looking at this place, preserved perfectly in the state we left it.

I pull my new prepaid cell phone out of my back pocket, sending a group text to Sawyer, Parker, and Megan. Sawyer provided both me and Megan with new phones. Although I was surprised he just happened to have two prepaid cell phones with him, I took mine gratefully.

Per the prearranged signal, I send just a smiling emoji to let them know I'm in and everything looks fine so far. I receive two instant replies, answering emojis. Parker's is not smiling.

Part of me didn't expect to make it back here alone. It definitely took a lot of arguing to get Megan to agree. One of the concessions to make this happen was that I would to continue to wear the panic button on my wrist. And that I'd let Sawyer and Parker take turns watching the house. Sawyer's out there somewhere right now, making it look like he just dropped me off. Parker didn't like that part of the plan—my riding with Sawyer, and then Sawyer leaving me completely alone while he covered his tracks before coming back to keep an eye on the condo. But there wasn't much about the plan that Parker *did* like.

I pick up the pile of mail I dropped on the hallway table to lock the door and I adjust my grip on my suitcase. I head for the stairs, thinking for a moment about Calvin's proposal here and my overwhelming nausea when I realized what he was doing. I still feel bad about the way things ended. It feels like a lifetime ago already.

Once I reach my room, I drop my stuff and fall backward in a satisfying trust fall, knowing the softness of my mattress won't let me down. I've missed my own bed, my own space. I could stay like this for hours.

Ding-dong. The doorbell rings, interrupting my plan. I'm instantly tense, not sure who would be ringing my doorbell mere minutes after I arrive home for the first time in weeks. Cautiously but quickly, I head back downstairs. Standing on my tiptoes, I squint through the peephole from a distance, careful not to make it obvious someone is home. I can't make out who it is, though, so I move closer. The form on the other side of the door becomes clearer, and I let out a huff.

"What are you doing?" I say as I open the door. "This isn't part of the plan."

"Yeah, I know," Parker says casually. "And I don't care. Let me in." He pushes past me. I shut the door and hope he didn't just ruin our chances of luring James to us.

"You can't do that," I say, struggling to keep my voice even and calm.

"Do what?"

"Whatever you want. You can't decide things for me."

Parker sighs and heads to the kitchen. He checks the fridge and then the pantry. "We need to get some food in here immediately. I'm starving."

"Parker, you're not staying."

"I am," he says and holds up a hand, stalling my words. "There is absolutely no way you're going to convince me to leave you here alone."

"I don't need to convince you, Parker. This isn't your choice to make."

"Think about this for a minute, Adrienne." He moves to the back door, checks the lock. "It's a little too obvious if you're just sitting here, alone, doing nothing. A fish that can see the hook won't take the bait."

"You're sticking with the fishing metaphor?"

"You started it."

"It's still not okay for you to make decisions for me."

"If I were making decisions for you, I'd kidnap you and take you straight back to the compound where we can slowly, safely figure things out," Parker says without a hint of a smile. "I'm allowed to make decisions for myself, though, right? Because this is my choice—to be bait with you." He runs a hand over his face. "Just put on my grave, 'He knew he was an idiot for going along with this plan, but he did it anyway.'"

"I'm not really up for morbid," I say before turning around and walking away. I'm not. The strangest things trigger more tears, and I've cried enough lately.

"Noted." He follows me to the living room. "But you know I cope with serious situations with terrible jokes, so I can't make any promises that something won't slip out."

"Fine. Why don't you order pizza, and I'll pick something to watch?"

"You should probably go let in Megan and Mike first," Parker says with a straight face.

"You're serious. Did you bring my parents too?" I walk to the front door. "How about Marcus? Is he next?"

"I don't doubt your parents will be here once they figure out you're gone," Parker says with a smile. "But Megan wasn't letting me leave without her." He shrugs. "And I brought Mike as backup. He'll be out there with Sawyer as another set of eyes, just in case."

Sure enough, Megan is standing right outside the door, looking twitchy.

"You have a key. Why didn't you just come in?" I ask as I wave her inside. There's no sign of Mike.

"We didn't want to both come in at the same time because that's unusual for us," Megan says. "And Parker said he'd let me know when the coast was clear. Typical Parker, he didn't follow through, and I got worried waiting in the car. So I've been standing there listening for any signs of trouble, completely terrified, no clue what to do." She takes a deep breath once she's finished. "Mike is coordinating with Sawyer to cover the front and back."

"I'm still starving," Parker interjects.

I stare at both him and Megan, not sure what to do next, wanting to hug them for being here with me and also force them to leave so they won't be in danger. I'll blame myself if anything happens to them, and we don't know who or what we're dealing with. Our big plan consists of nothing much more than sit, wait, and hope to overpower whoever shows up to hurt me. If someone shows up at all. We have so many questions and no answers.

"You guys, I don't know what to say." I blink at the sudden tears welling up, surprised by my own reaction. "I'm so glad and equally terrified that you're both here."

"Don't say another word," Parker says, arms crossed, leaning against the doorway to the living room. "Just take me to dinner."

"You know, I think that's a great idea," Megan says. "Let's go."

CHAPTER 30

THEODORA

The midmorning light streams through the arched windows, illuminating the dust motes dancing and twirling in slow motion. The old wooden pews have been removed and replaced with padded, stackable chairs. It's a "flex space" now, according to Marcus, whatever that means. While it was never used as a traditional chapel with regular services—it was mostly for special events such as weddings, christenings, baptisms—it was a sacred place for our people to gather for milestone moments. Now it seems like fewer people are having traditional weddings and fewer still are having their children christened. Most of the community is hiding in plain sight, so they don't see the need for this chapel any longer.

In light of the interconnected way most live their lives, thanks to the internet and social media, I understand why the next generation isn't using this chapel. It would be odd today to be married in a remote location where you can't invite any outsiders or share any photos. Before, no one carried a wedding album with them in their purse. Now, technology and cell phones have changed that.

I sneeze, disturbing the musty and disused atmosphere. I run a finger across the sill to my left, passing by it on my way around the perimeter, and then rub my thumb over the dust on my index finger. It falls in slow motion to the floor. I move on.

The pine shiplap ceiling is as beautiful as it was the last time I was here. It's reassuring to see its beauty still intact. Looking down, that feeling is wiped away by the state of the stone floor. It needs some attention. There are cracks in the mortar here and there, pieces and chunks missing.

I pause at the window near the platform and let the sun shine through the window on my face. Its warmth is comforting, like an old blanket I can curl up in with my memories of this place. Of course, this brings my thoughts to James. I can practically feel him here beside me, smell his aftershave. My memories of him and this place are so entwined. We were happy here. We were happy together. Weren't we?

If that's true, why did James fake his death? It's a question I've been avoiding. I can't think about it too much, or I start to feel as if I'm drowning. I've grieved him for most of my life. Now, all I can see is wasted time. He was alive. It was all a lie. But why?

"I don't understand it, James," I say to no one. Used to be I could talk to James's ghost, to pretend he could hear me and that I could feel his presence. Now talking to the absence of his ghost leaves me feeling hollow because I know there never was a ghost. He's taken that small comfort from me. Why couldn't he have told me whatever was going on?

A figure leisurely walks by outside the window. I start in surprise. Peering through the next window, I track his presence. He doesn't look like anyone I've seen around before.

Without giving it much thought, I quickly head for the chapel entrance and push my way through the door and around the side of the chapel as quickly as I can. As I round the side of the chapel, I catch a glimpse of the back of his head as he walks along a narrow trail down the hill.

Moving faster, I consider calling out to him, but I don't. I want to see where he's going, what he's doing. It seems odd that someone else is here at the beginning of most people's day. And other than Adrienne, Megan, Toby, and me, the people here in the compound are here because they have a job to do. Tom even goes to the lab here every morning to continue his work for Synergy Labs. I've met or already know almost everyone here too. This man doesn't look familiar.

Stepping carefully down the steep hill at the back of the chapel, I try to keep him in sight and keep an eye on my footing, avoiding leaves and twigs, but the path here is narrow and covered in the typical forest detritus. Walking quietly requires more attention and effort than I expected. Farther down the hill, my view of the mystery person is blocked periodically by trees. My heart skips a beat every time it takes a moment longer than I think it should for him to reappear.

Almost to the bottom of the hill, he goes around a particularly large tree that hides him from my sight. I don't take my eyes off the other side where I know he'll reappear in just a moment if I'm patient. I continue to watch carefully, and I miss a large rock in my path and step on the side of it. I lose my footing and slide on the loose rocks and sticks on the path. My flailing arms fail to grasp onto anything to stop my downward momentum. I fall onto my rear end and slide down the rocky trail. Thankfully, I come to a stop just before the base of a sturdy-looking walnut tree, and I stay where I am to assess the damage. I'm positive the mystery man heard my fall and subsequent skid, but he still hasn't reappeared since he went on the other side of the giant oak ahead.

I get to my knees and then my feet. My rear end feels like it will have a colorful bruise in no time, and my palms are scraped up slightly, but that seems to be the worst of it. Cautiously, I keep going, head swiveling, scanning the trees for anyone. Moving as quickly as I dare, I make it to the big oak and follow the trail around it, knowing I'll see him farther down the trail on the other side, but when I round the tree, he's nowhere in sight.

Concentrating, I feel for any emotions in the area. Everyone feels something at any given moment. I should be able to get a sense of his direction from his emotions. But there's nothing.

I follow the narrow trail as quickly as I can, but I still don't see him. Sticker bushes grab at the legs of my jeans as I veer off the trail to the right, looking for any sign of him. Nothing. He's gone. Maybe I've missed a turn? The trail stops once it reaches the small clearing at the bottom of the hill, and he isn't in the clearing, either.

I walk back to the trail, turn a full circle, and check every direction. I don't see where he could have gone. There are no other trails or paths. I head for the clearing, stopping when I reach the center of it. On the other side of the open field is a stand of evenly spaced trees. The trees look younger and much smaller than those on the other side of the clearing. Through those trees, the faint outline of the side of Camp Little Creek's laboratory is visible. There are no windows or doors on this side of it.

Closing my eyes, I replay the moments just before I fell. If he had veered to the left, I would have seen him. If he veered off to the right, I would have seen him once he was clear of that large oak. The only possible way for him to stay out of sight would be if he had continued down the hill, but I wasn't down from my fall that long. I should have seen him even if he walked this way and crossed the clearing. And he should have heard me when I fell. Surely he would have investigated so much noise behind him.

Something isn't right.

CHAPTER 31

THEODORA

My phone died hours ago, but if I had to guess—and I suppose I do—it looks to be after six o'clock. The sun should be setting soon by the looks of the sky. That means I've been here for too many hours, traipsing through the woods and then sitting as still as possible, waiting, watching. I should go back to the dormitory, take a long hot shower, and go to dinner with my family. They're surely wondering where I am by now.

But no, I'm not going anywhere yet. After searching the entire area, I decided to stake out the vicinity where I last saw the mystery man. He couldn't have simply vanished. So he must be somewhere nearby, and I'm going to be here when he shows himself. As long as he comes before dark, anyway. I don't have the right clothes on to sit out here on the damp earth for very long after the sun sets. No flashlight either since my phone is dead.

I adjust my position, stretching my left leg out slowly, quietly. I've set myself up downhill of the large oak, to the left of the clearing. It gives me the uphill view of where I saw him last. I put a hand on the fallen log in front of me to steady myself as I stretch my right leg now, peering through the brush pile I'm hiding behind. I reposition to give my bruised butt a break. If I have to chase this guy, I'm not so sure I'll be able to move very quickly.

Am I taking this too far? It's possible he was someone I haven't met just out for a hike. Except he disappeared in an area where there's nowhere to disappear to. I didn't make that up. But what if I'm not letting this go because it's easier to obsess about something? It's easier to do anything than to do nothing knowing I'm in a world that no longer includes my mother's beautiful soul. Since I started following that man, I certainly haven't thought about James and the years I wasted being sad he was longer here. So there's that.

I wouldn't have even followed him if I wasn't still trying to puzzle together pieces of information such as Mom talking about Mount Hope in her last moments and Adrienne having a strange empathetic episode here. I'm grasping at anything and everything now, trying to find the pattern, the secret, the answers. I need Mom's words—Mom's death—to mean something.

What a terrible progression of thoughts. I wipe my eyes, suddenly swimming in tears, with the backs of my hands. I should get up now. I should stretch the kinks out of my lower back, walk away, and try to enjoy my evening. I should. With a sigh, I decide I will. I need to spend time with my kids. Their presence is like a balm to my broken heart.

I stand and stretch. Carefully avoiding the skeleton-like limbs from a fallen tree sticking out of the brush pile, I move around the end toward the trail and hill. The sun is starting to set, and the shadows are longer here than they were earlier. As I step around the large oak and follow the trail, movement up the trail makes me pause. There's someone else coming down it. No, there are *three* someones moving down the trail. I step back behind the trail. There's something about the three figures that makes me not want to be seen by them.

I pay attention to the waves of emotion coming from them, and what I feel doesn't make sense. It's a combination of fear, resignation, confidence, and boredom. The three are too close to each other for me to determine who is feeling which emotion, but that's an incongruous mix to say the least.

I peer around the tree once more. It's hard to make out much in the fading light. Is the person in the middle wearing a bag over his face? His hands appear to be bound too. My heart rate accelerates. Can I make it back to my brush pile without being spotted? They're still up high on the trail, moving slowly. I should have time.

There's a snap of a twig directly behind me. My breath catches in my throat. I feel waves of fear and surprise from the direction of the sound. Please be a deer. Please be a deer. I turn slowly, trying not to send the deer flying through the woods. It would surely give me away.

"Stop," a voice—definitely not a deer—says quietly but adamantly. "Do not move, or I will shoot you."

I stop. I'm facing downhill again. Steadily, I raise my hands and pray it's just one of the guards out patrolling the area. "I am Thea Adams, the wife of

Tom Adams. He works just over there in the lab," I say calmly, reassuringly, one finger toward the lab on the other side of the clearing. If it is a guard, I have to get him to shift his focus to those three coming down the hill before they round that tree and spot us. "Adrienne Adams is my daughter. We came here for her. I'm staying here at Camp Little Creek."

The voice curses, then curses again, more colorfully. "We have a situation. I need Walter to meet me in the tunnel." I don't hear the click of a walkie-talkie or any kind of response; I'm not sure who he's just communicated with or how.

"Sir, please, I am Theodora Adams," I say quietly, my whole body trembling. I don't like this guard's responses at all. What tunnel? Who is Walter? "You can take a look at my ID in my pocket if you'd like. It's right here." I indicate my right hip pocket. "But there are three people coming down that hill, one of which seems to be the captive of the other two."

"Stop talking," the guard says.

I dare a look at him, my fear doubling when I take in his plainclothes appearance—he isn't wearing a guard uniform. He curses again.

"Don't look at me! On your knees," he says, taking a hand off his pistol to point at the ground. "Now!"

His voice is loud and angry. I flinch but comply quickly. Feeling the cold, damp ground and the sting of a pointy rock through the knees of my jeans, I pray for this all to be a misunderstanding. He approaches me, reaching behind him for something I can't see. My imagination only comes up with terrifying possibilities. He grabs my right wrist first, the familiar clicking of a zip tie preceding the bite of the hard plastic into the skin of my wrist. He repeats the action with my left, then adds a third zip tie to keep my hands securely together.

"What's this?" a new voice says to my left. It must be one of the men I saw coming down the trail.

"I came out to help, and there she was—watching you three."

"Bring her. What's one more?" the new voice says with a chuckle.

"She's Theodora Adams," my captor says more quietly.

"So what? What difference does that make? Bring her."

"Get up," my captor says, keeping a hand on the zip tie connecting my wrists as I awkwardly get to my feet.

"Do you know Tom?" I ask.

"Walk," my captor instructs, and I do. He steers me to the right to the rock face at the bottom of the hill. He pulls me to a stop directly in front of the wall of rock. "I don't have another bag."

"I think she's already seen too much," the second voice says.

"Here," a third voice interjects.

My captor moves closer, then holds a scarf in front of my face before wrapping it around my head, securing it in a tie that pulls several strands of my hair. He moves around to the front of me, and I get the vague sense he's checking to make sure I can't see anything. I can't.

"That ought to do it," the second voice says. "Now let's get moving. I'm ready to be done with this one."

My captor grabs my upper right arm, and we continue forward. After less than a minute of walking and changing directions a few times, the ground feels free of sticks, rocks, and leaves. It feels more like grass. We stop, and I hear the shuffle of movement followed by the clang of metal. Then there's a mechanical hum, like an electric motor operating.

"Forward," my captor says and gives me a push. I step carefully, and the grass beneath my feet is replaced by something hard and smooth. Concrete? After a moment, there's another mechanical whirring, a sensation of movement, and then we walk forward again.

The air is damp here, musty. Where am I?

My captor reaches into my pockets, pulling out my ID and my dead phone. Footsteps approach us.

"This is Theodora Adams, according to her ID. She was spying on these three. What should I do with her?" my captor asks.

"Put her in her own room for now," a new voice several feet in front of me says.

"Marcus will want to know I'm here," I say, trying the only thing I can think of.

"There are many things Marcus would want to know," says the same voice with a laugh. "You're safe for the moment. Don't do anything to jeopardize that. Do you understand?"

Not really, but I nod anyway. *Safe* is not a word I would use to describe my current situation.

CHAPTER 32

ADRIENNE

"Still no answer?" Parker asks when I pull my phone from my ear and hit the end button.

"Straight to voice mail again," I answer. "At least I can say I tried, right?"

"That has to count for something," he agrees.

I've been trying to call my mom since we left for food earlier, but she hasn't picked up. Her phone isn't even ringing from the sound of it. I'm being sent straight to voice mail. I wonder if she's still hiding out in her room. In the days leading up to Grandma's funeral, she was busy making plans, arranging and coordinating for Grandma's service and burial. But since the day after her funeral, I don't think Mom has come out for anything. Dad and I have been bringing her meals to her room.

"I'll try Dad, I suppose, but I didn't really want him to have to tell Mom," I say. The two of them have been distant since Grandma's death—or more accurately, since Dad found out Mom kept our abilities from him. I can't imagine they've had a chance to talk about it with everything that has happened, either. Mom has been wrapped up in her grief, not that I blame her.

I don't know how I'd respond if I were in her shoes. Mom is such a private person too, so I can understand why she would want to shut the world away right now. And Dad has had to carry on, his work with Synergy Labs making more demands than usual on his time. It's understanding since he's been working out at Camp Little Creek for weeks.

Let me help you. Let me in. That was Dad's plea to me when I woke up after Grandma's death. I am dreading this phone call because I know he's not going to take me leaving Camp Little Creek well. Leaving without telling him first is the opposite of what he wants. I hit the call symbol next to his name on my phone's screen, anyway.

"Hello?" Dad answers in his I'm-a-professional phone voice.

"It's me, Dad," I say and start to wander around; I like to move around while I talk on the phone. I'm wishing for more privacy too, so I wander toward the stairs and my room.

"Adrienne? Whose number is this?"

"It's mine." I swallow, not sure how to explain to him what I'm doing and why. Will he understand? "For now, anyway. It's temporary."

"Where are you?"

"I've been trying to call Mom, but she's not answering." I avoid his question. "Are you with her?"

"I'm . . ." There's a rustling sound on his end of the call and a pause before he continues. "No, I'm not. I'm still in the lab."

"Oh." I'm not sure how to start this conversation.

"Adrienne . . ." More rustling. "Where are you?" He says this more quietly, his voice sounding stressed. I know he hates taking calls while he's in the lab. He says distractibility is the ultimate human flaw. He also says we would have saved the environment, cured cancer, and invented hover cars like Marty McFly saw in *Back to the Future* by now if only we could stay focused. Mom usually corrects him with a smile that it was *Back to the Future Part II* while Toby and I try not to roll our eyes at them both. I hold onto a memory of one of these times as I utter my next sentence.

"I've been trying to call Mom to let her know I left Camp Little Creek. Now, before you—"

"You did what?" There's no mistaking his anger. "Adrienne, you have no idea what you're messing with." The intensity of his tone tells me his face is probably bright red right now. I'm glad he's never been a yeller, though.

"Dad, I'm not alone," I say slowly, hoping my calm will somehow transfer to him. "I have Parker and Megan here with me, and we're being smart about this." He lets out a strangled sound I think must be a laugh. "Sawyer and Mike are outside too. They're keeping an eye on the street, the condo, the entrances, all of it." I hope that sounded better to him than it did to me. Talking to my dad has transformed me from confident in our plan to feeling a little like a kid playing hide-and-seek or capture the flag with zero idea how to strategically do either.

"Adrienne"—his voice is a harsh whisper now—"I cannot protect you from here. You need to come back." He lets out a shaky breath. "Right now."

"I can't do that, Dad." I'm shaking my head even though he can't see me. "I'm staying put and seeing this through. We need answers."

"I can't go to her right now," Dad says. He's quieter, as if he's pulled the phone away from his face. "I can't go there, and she won't come here. No, she shouldn't come here, either." More rustling on the phone. Someone else talking in the background, Dad talking again, but I can't hear what he's saying.

"Dad?"

"I'm thinking," he says breathlessly into the phone. "You . . . you need to . . . Parker. You said Parker is there with you?"

"Yes," I say, drawing the word out a little. Dad can sometimes act like a mad scientist, but this conversation is a new level of strange for him. He sounds terrified, which triggers my bad-daughter guilt, of course. I'm doing this to him.

"Good. Keep Parker close. Do you understand? Don't let anyone in, and don't go anywhere for any reason. I'll be there . . . I don't know when I'll be there, but I'll be there as soon as I can."

Click. My phone dings, alerting me that the call has ended.

"What's going on?" Parker asks right behind me. "He sounded worse than I expected."

"Yeah, that was bizarre." I'm still processing the call.

"Is he on his way here?"

"I'm not sure. He's definitely coming here at some point, but it sounded like he can't leave work right now."

"Does he usually work this late?"

I check the time on my phone, surprised to see it's a few minutes past eight o'clock. "No, not usually. But he has been off and working less since we've been at Camp Little Creek. He probably has to catch up."

"Probably. You should send him a text and ask him to let us know if he's going to show up so Mike and Sawyer don't get too nervous about a new arrival out there."

"Okay. I'll do that right now." As I type out the message and hit send, Parker's phone starts ringing.

"It's Marcus," he says, staring at the screen for a moment before answering. "Hello?"

I wish he'd put it on speaker. Marcus and Parker aren't best pals or anything. Marcus isn't Parker's direct supervisor, either. It's odd for him to be calling. Isn't it? Parker isn't saying a word, just listening.

"Why?" Parker finally says. I start to walk away, to give him more privacy, but Parker puts a hand on my arm, so I stay put. I want to close my eyes so I can concentrate and figure out what he's feeling, but I don't. It feels like I'm reading his diary when I do. Not that I can always shut it out.

I haven't been able to ignore that his emotions have been a steady mix of fear, concern, and something else that looks like anxiety. There's something else in there that's warm and bright sometimes. It feels like playing in a summertime rain when I was a kid.

"I can't make any promises, but I'll try," he replies. "Let us know when you know more." With that, he hits the end button and puts the phone in his pocket.

"What was that?" I ask. Parker's expression is mirthless. Now I can't mistake the fear and sadness he's feeling. It's flowing from him in intense waves. He hesitates. "Parker?"

"Adrienne, your mom is missing. No one can find her anywhere at Camp Little Creek. Your dad has been trying to locate her since around noon today and hasn't been able to reach her."

"What?" This can't be happening. I can't lose Grandma and then Mom. "How?"

"Marcus has asked us to stay here." He avoids looking me in the eye.

"What, Parker?"

"They're concerned about her mental state, and they think she may not want to be found."

"That's why Dad was being so weird," I respond. My voice sounds a million miles away. He didn't want me to know she's missing.

"Marcus has asked us to send Mike back to help with the search," Parker says, but I can't focus on his words.

Mom's hair blowing in the breeze as we walked to the dormitories after we finished a day of training. The crinkles by her eyes as she smiled at me just before we opened the door and learned James Rutherford is still alive.

Her calm resilience as she lovingly stroked Grandma's cheek one last time, listening as she spoke her last words. Then her sullen withdrawal from conversations and each of us in the coming days. Her tear-streaked face as she opened the door to her room in the dormitory, taking the tray I brought her with a polite thank-you and a fake smile.

Would she do this? Would she go off and not tell anyone? With everything that's going on, I wouldn't blame her for wanting to escape, but that's not Mom. She wouldn't leave me in a perilous position to alleviate her own heartache. My relief is instant.

"Mom wouldn't disappear right now," I say confidently. "Parker, you need to tell Marcus that. I know she wouldn't. That's not my mom."

"I agree," Parker says, pausing in his conversation with whomever is on the other end of the phone. "That doesn't sound like something she would do." He doesn't look any less concerned, though.

Now I feel like an idiot. Of course he isn't relieved. My mom would never willingly escape this whole mess. So that can only mean that someone else has done something to cause her disappearance. Which is really why Dad didn't tell me: He doesn't want me to come back to Camp Little Creek. If someone got to Mom there, then someone can get to me too.

"Parker." I feel like my throat is going to seal up. I can't say what I'm thinking.

"I just sent Mike," Parker says, leaning down a bit to look me in the eyes, one hand on my right shoulder, his other hand on my left. His hands are warm. The heat seeps through the cotton of my shirt. "He's going to try to retrace her steps and actually investigate this. He's not going to wait around for signs of foul play."

"Foul play? Are you serious? How can this be happening?" I rub my hands over my face. "We need to go. I need to be there looking for her too. The more people, the better chance we'll have of finding her."

"Adrienne, I just heard," Megan says, bounding down the stairs. "Mike called me on his way out." She wraps me in a tight hug.

"We need to stay here," Parker says. "I hate to say I agree with your plan now, but we've run out of time. We need answers now. So the sooner we get James or whoever to show up, the better."

It feels wrong to stay here and not be there searching for Mom. I pause to consider what she would do, and I'm not sure of the answer. Grandma has always been the risk-taker. If I were missing, I know she would never be able to sit still. But what would she do with that nervous energy? She would problem-solve, figure out how to best use her time and energy.

"You're right," I say with a nod at Parker. "We should stay here and stick to the plan. Has anyone talked to Sawyer to let him know what's happening?"

"No, not yet," Parker answers.

"I'll call him," I offer, glad to have something I can do.

"I'll make some coffee," Megan says with a sympathetic smile and a pat on my arm.

CHAPTER 33

ADRIENNE

I lie in the semidarkness of my room upstairs in the condo well after midnight. I'm trying to stick to a normal routine for appearance's sake, but sleep is far from my mind. Again, I replay my debate with Parker about returning to Camp Little Creek to help search for Mom.

Your presence will take resources away from the search for your mom because Marcus will want to keep a closer eye on you there now, he had said. It was that final argument that stopped me from going. Should I have relented? Did I make a mistake by not going? If Mom has been taken by someone, there's a good chance it has something to do with James's reappearance and Grandma Effie's cryptic last words. Maybe whoever took her would take me too if I were there. Then at least I'd be with her right now. Then I would know if she's okay.

Now all I can do is pray James finds us and makes a move sooner rather than later. I never thought I'd ever be hoping for a possible serial killer to come to my own door.

"Adrienne!" Megan says in an urgent whisper from the doorway of my room.

"Why are you whispering?" My heart thuds in my chest. Something is wrong. I can see the waves of fear coming off her.

"We have to leave. Now!"

"What's happened?" I get up. I went to bed fully dressed, shoes on, just in case of this exact situation. "If he's here, then we planned for this. We're supposed to capture him so we can talk to him." My words are braver than the sinking feeling in my stomach.

"No, it's too late for that." Megan takes a quick look over her shoulder.

"We have to go! Parker said to go out the front and let him and Sawyer get him." She looks over her shoulder again. "Parker said to go now. We have to go!"

I hesitate. This isn't what we discussed. Since Mike is gone, Parker took his car and parked it down the street where he could watch the back of the condo while Sawyer watches the front. If James did show up and make it inside, Megan and I were supposed to stay up here and wait while Sawyer and Parker cornered him, used a taser, and tied him up. If Parker is changing the plan like this, then something must be really wrong.

"Okay. Let's go." I give her a nod.

After two tense minutes of walking as quickly and as quietly as possible down the stairs and out to Megan's car, we get in and lock the doors.

"Are you sure we should go? I don't see Parker or Sawyer anywhere." I glance around from the passenger seat, trying to find Sawyer—in his car, behind the bushes along the street, anywhere—but I don't. "If something is wrong, we should stay and help them."

"Parker said he'll be more distracted and more likely to get killed if he has to worry about you doing something foolish."

It doesn't exactly sound like something Parker would say, but he has been worried about me and afraid of whom or what we're up against. Not knowing is so much scarier. I think. Maybe I'll feel differently when we finally understand why James is stalking me, why he's just confirmed our worst suspicions by coming after me now. What has he done with Mom?

Megan starts up the car, killing the automatic headlights as soon as they turn on. She puts it in reverse and maneuvers out of the spot and the parking lot before taking a left.

"We should stay close so we're nearby no matter what happens," I say, staring out the back window. As we reach the stop sign at the end of the street, a car pulls out down the block and heads our way. I didn't see anyone get in, and I think I would have noticed any movement.

I keep an eye on the car after we continue straight. It takes a right, and I feel like I can breathe again.

"Hey, where are we going?" I ask Megan after she makes a turn, realizing she's headed toward the river and interstate 55.

"We're going to make sure no one is following us, and then we're going to sit tight somewhere until we hear from Parker." She checks the mirror. I look behind us too, but there are no headlights bobbing in pursuit.

A few more turns and several miles later, Megan pulls onto a gravel road that ends in a gravel parking lot. It's the riverfront trail, but the other end we never go to. Thick brush and trees surround the parking lot on all sides except for an eight-foot-wide path that I know leads to the river. The moon is up and bright tonight, and its light glares at me from atop the hood of a small white car parked several spaces away. I glance around, but there's only one other vehicle here in the lot and I can't tell much about it other than it's black and an SUV. The white car turns its lights on and backs out of its space and leaves.

"I thought we would have heard something by now," I say, checking my phone again. That writhing fear in my chest is back—something isn't right.

"Come on," Megan says, opening her door. "Let's stretch our legs. It will help pass the time if we take a walk."

"Uh" is all I say. I look around again. The black SUV hasn't moved. I don't see anyone inside, but it's hard to tell through the darkly tinted windows. "Sure."

"Stay close to me," Megan says as she starts walking across the parking lot in the general direction of the SUV. "Just in case."

A deep breath in, and the sounds of my feet crunching on the dewy gravel ground me and help me to clear away some of my anxiety. The waves of emotion coming off Megan are beautiful cool shades of blue and purple. They feel calm, confident, and a little detached.

"Adrienne!" a voice calls to me from behind us. I turn, and there's a man standing fifty feet away. He's tall and broad across the shoulders. The way his movements are connected, seamless, makes me think I know him. The shape of his nose—the same shape as mine—tells me who he is. I move closer to Megan. "Adrienne, stop!" He picks up his pace, jogging with hands outstretched.

"I think that's James," I say to Megan behind me.

She curses, then tugs on the back of my hoodie. "Come on, quickly!"

I turn to run away from him, but Megan doesn't move.

"Megan?" I call to her, only a few feet away. She doesn't look at me or respond. I reach my hand out for her, urging her silently to take my hand

and run with me. She doesn't.

A loud bang echoes across the parking lot. Megan falls to the ground, her body hitting the gravel as if someone flipped a switch. She doesn't move.

"Megan?" I hurry to her, staying low. My brain knows what just happened before I do. "Megan?" I reach her. Drop to my knees beside her. Shake her. She doesn't respond. I look her over, trying to find the source of her injury, but I don't see anything wrong with her.

"Adrienne?" His voice is quieter now and too near. James is too close.

"Megan?" I shake her again, and it's then when I see the blossoming pool of darkness underneath her. Deep red on white gravel, the moonlight dancing across the glossy surface. I roll her as gently as possible. She has blood all over her left shoulder, her back, the back of her head. Where is it all coming from? I can't find the wound. It's too dark, and her back has been painted with her blood, making it even darker. I don't see it.

"Get away from her, James," another voice—deep, raspy, aged—calls out from the black SUV. The driver door opens, and a man steps out onto the gravel with a crunch.

"Adrienne," James says again, gently. "You have to come away from here with me. You have to leave her, right now. I promise we'll call for help for her, but you have to come with me right now."

I ignore him completely as I continue to search for her wound. Finally, my fingers find a gaping hole in her jacket that shouldn't be there. What do I do now? What am I supposed to do? Pressure. That's what they do on shows, anyway. I push on it, and blood oozes between my fingers. It's hot on my cold fingers. There's so much of it. I push harder, looking away, hoping I'm not hurting her more.

"Adrienne, you have to listen to me," James says. "That is an awful man over there, and I have no doubt he has backup coming here right now. They'll be here any moment, and they won't let me and my gun stop them from coming for you. We can't let them get you. You have to come with me."

"I don't know what's going on here, but if you're in trouble, come with me and I'll help you get away from that man," the stranger says by the SUV, pointing at James, staying by his vehicle.

"Don't pretend you don't know what's happening here. You orchestrated this entire situation!" James yells at him.

The old man laughs. For the first time, I look more closely at him. He's calm and confident, no waves of fear or apprehension. The colors emanating from him matches those of Megan's. Matched. I don't see or sense any emotions from her now. His lined face tells me nothing other than he's lived a long life. His white hair is still thick, and his frame appears sturdy and strong.

Fiery tears flow freely down my face. My phone is in my pocket, but should I reach for it? Will she lose too much blood if I don't use both hands? Will James stop me from using it?

"Adrienne." James's voice is too close. There's a pressure building, expanding in my mind. "Call Sawyer. You'll discover Megan knocked Parker out and sent Sawyer on a wild goose chase."

He's lying. They're both lying. I can't take a hand off Megan's wound. The blood is still bubbling up, making its way around my fingers. How much more quickly will she bleed to death if I let go? I can't lose Megan too.

"He would know because he's really the one who hurt Parker," the stranger says with a laugh. "If you knew your own daughter at all, you'd know she's smarter than that, James. Don't be patronizing."

"Shut up," James says vehemently at the stranger, pointing his gun right at him while he inches my way. "Adrienne, I'm sorry it has to be this way, but you have three seconds to come with me willingly. We must go. Right now." He touches my shoulder.

The pressure in my head explodes in an energy waterfall of release. The colors flowing from me are red and magenta. James falls to the ground, landing hard on his backside, and the man near the SUV staggers back.

"Was that you?" James asks, sitting on the ground near me. He slowly scoots closer, puts a hand on Megan's wrist. I want to tear his hand away from her. Another tidal wave of red explodes from me. He pulls his hand back.

I'm not sure what just happened. I look at my hands to make sure I'm still pressing on Megan's wound. Covered in blood, the panic button on my wrist catches my eye.

"Adrienne, I'm so sorry." Waves of yellow-green emotion flow from him now. "But Megan's gone. She's gone, Adrienne."

The intensity of his stare, the implications of what he's asking me with his eyes to do, to feel—to trust him, to forgive him, to understand, to leave my friend here on the cold gravel and go with him—is too much. It's too much. Megan's blood isn't flowing through my grip any longer. It's stopped.

He killed her. He killed Megan.

A reverberation within my mind. A pop. I take my hands off Megan's back—*he shot her in the back*—gently. I press the button on my wrist, and then I rise, my breathing the only sound in the silence.

"What have you done with Mom? With Thea?" I ask James, my voice accusatory. I don't sound like myself. I don't feel like myself, either.

"What do you mean? What's happened to Thea?" His eyes are saying more, begging me to stop, to trust him.

"Where is my mother?" I take a step toward him. Waves of magenta are flowing freely from my body. He clutches his temples.

The man near the SUV laughs again and begins to clap. "You're so much more impressive than I imagined," he says.

"Adrienne, you're hurting me," James says, crumbling as he continues to clutch his head.

"Stop," I say, leaning down, "stop saying my name." He shrinks back from me. More yellow waves of fear pour from him. He's afraid.

He's afraid of *me*.

What am I doing? How am I hurting him? I don't know, which means I don't know how to stop, either. I don't want to stop.

"Come on, Adrienne," says the man by the SUV. "Come over here with me, and we'll call someone for Megan."

"Who are you?" I stare at him, my rage fueling me. He has to be my grandmother's age. His face is tan and wrinkled, extra flesh dangling slightly from his jowls.

"I'm a friend, and I'm here to help you and to keep James from hurting you. My name is Charles, and I knew your grandmother quite a long time ago."

James lets out a whimper and clutches his head tighter. "He's lying," he says between clenched teeth. "He's the one who has been after you for months. I followed him here. He knew you would be here." He takes a gasping breath. "He is the one who was controlling your grandmother's mind. He was controlling Megan's mind too."

"Leave," I say to Charles. He shakes his head and slowly steps toward me.

"I said *leave*." The sensation of something flowing from my mind hits me. It's pulling from the pressure that had built up in my chest. The red and magenta are no longer steady streams from my body but rather a gushing tidal wave bursting out of me.

Charles staggers back, catching himself on the open door to his SUV. I don't know how this is happening, but I know it's coming from me.

"Go on, before you end up like him." I point at James on the ground.

Tentatively, Charles gets into the driver's seat of his vehicle, shutting the door behind him. The window is down, and he leans an arm on the opening as he starts the SUV. He hesitates.

"I'll go for now, but we need to talk, Adrienne. Soon. You'll want to talk to me." He puts it into drive and takes off.

His taillights bounce as he drives across the parking lot and then down the road. When he's out of sight, I turn to James again.

"I don't know what I'm doing or how I'm doing it, so if you don't want this to get worse, you should answer me." My voice is scratchy, raw. "Where is my mother?"

"If I knew, I would tell you," James replies. He lets out a cry of pain.

Stepping back, I run my hands through my hair. Someone should have been notified as soon as I hit the button on my wrist. Parker said he had managed to add his number and Mike's to the notification list. How long has it been since I hit the button? Minutes? Half an hour? Time has stopped existing for me.

"You have to get a handle on yourself." James's nose is bleeding now. "You're killing me, Adrienne."

"You shot and killed Megan, my best friend—" My voice is bordering on hysterical.

"I didn't shoot her!" he yells, his voice agonized.

"She was shot in the back. You shot her!" I take a breath. "You were the one behind us with the gun!"

"Look at her chest," James says weakly. "She was shot in the chest. Her injury on her back is where the bullet came out." I hesitate. I don't want to touch her now. I don't want to disturb her. But she's not in there anymore. That's just . . . it's just her body.

Hands shaking, I kneel in her blood covering the gravel, soaking into the dirt. I try rolling her toward me, but she's so heavy now. I try again, and this time I succeed.

Reluctantly, I feel around for a bullet hole. There, on the left side of her chest, is a small hole. Much smaller than the one on her back. He's telling the truth. He didn't shoot her. Charles did.

CHAPTER 34

THEODORA

The faint glow of a nightlight is all I have to navigate by as I examine the room. The floor is cold concrete, and there's no window in here. Not that I expected one since we're underground, but I still had hoped. A window could be a way out at least. The walls are rough cement blocks stacked and aligned unevenly.

I've already checked the door at least a dozen times. There's no door handle on this side, but I keep testing the door by pulling at its edges. So far, it hasn't budged. I try one more time. It still doesn't move. So I move back to the bed and sit down. It's little more than a cot.

Goose bumps rise up on my arms. It's cold down here.

There's a click followed by the echo of metal hitting metal. Slowly, the door swings open.

"Come on," says the same voice of the guy who put me in here. He steps into the doorway, his frame outlined by the light of the hallway. "We need you for a minute."

"What's going on?"

"You just do what we ask you to do, and you'll be okay." He moves out of the doorway. He's taller than I am, his frame is bulky. I can't tell through his jacket whether that bulk is muscle or fat, but I don't see a paunch. His movements are graceful despite his size.

"Where are you taking me now?" I ask as I put one foot in front of the other, willing myself to walk forward and be calm. I might get a chance to get away from him. He isn't holding any kind of handcuffs.

"Come on." He walks briskly ahead of me, not waiting for me to make it through the door before taking a left down a hall with several doors on either side. "You'll see," he calls over his shoulder. He reaches the door at the end of the hall and opens it, holding it for me after he goes through.

I swallow and follow him in. This room is brightly lit. In its center is a chair like the ones I've sat in when having my blood taken. There's a rolling cart next to it with a caddy on top—empty vials, tape, and packages of gauze in it. A box of gloves sits next to the caddy.

"Have a seat, please." He stands beside the chair.

"No." My voice is firm, even.

He lets out an exaggerated sigh. "Theodora—do you mind if I call you Thea? Theodora is a bit much." He smiles.

I don't answer.

"Thea, look, I'm just going to take a little blood. We're not drugging you or harming you in any way. Please, sit."

I shake my head ever so slightly. He doesn't seem eager to harm me or for me to fear him. I'm hoping I'm not misreading his emotions. He isn't overly stressed, and he doesn't seem to be deriving satisfaction from his obvious power over me. He's calm. Composed and sure of himself without a hint of cockiness.

"We can start with a cheek swab if you prefer. Completely painless." He reaches over and pulls a package containing a sterile swab from the caddy.

He wants my DNA. Why does he want a DNA sample? "I'd rather keep all my genetic material," I say.

"Well, no one can say I didn't try at least." He smiles again. He's annoyed, though, not that I can tell by looking at him. He is doing a good job of acting otherwise. He touches his collar. "Send him in."

"What are you doing?" A door down the hall opens. The soft scuff of shoe on unfinished cement is followed by quiet footsteps. Not sure what's happening, I face the sound of footsteps, mentally preparing myself for a battle, sure he just called reinforcements to help him get a sample of DNA against my will. But instead of a muscled goon, the person walking my way is familiar with his dad bod made soft by too many hours in a laboratory. "Tom?" I'm relieved. This has all been some kind of misunderstanding.

Tom doesn't look at me. He avoids me entirely, staying out of arm's reach.

"Vincent, give us a moment alone, please," Tom says to the man still by the chair in the room.

"Absolutely. If you need anything, I'll be right outside." He sidesteps past me and down the hall, exiting the room and then the hallway. The jangle of metal on metal tells me the door at the opposite end of the hall is locked once again.

"What's happening, Tom?"

"Thea, please, sit." He still won't look at me. His aura is pale green and red, regret and anger coming off him in waves.

"What is happening here, Tom?"

"For crying out loud, Thea! For once, do as you're told!" he yells at the floor. Waves of gray-green flow from him. Guilt.

"Tom." I move tentatively to him. I put my hands on either side of his face and try to get him to look at me. "Tom, look at me."

He shakes his head. Then he's sobbing, his face in my hair.

"Tom," I whisper quietly in his ear. "What have you done?"

ACKNOWLEDGMENTS

I didn't write this in a bubble, free from responsibilities, without help, finding all the inspiration I needed within myself. Definitely not. I know I'm going to miss thanking someone because writing this book took a village. Thank you to all those who are part of my village.

My husband, Jacob, deserves thanks for always pushing me to take risks and listen to my heart. Thank you, my love, for being my partner and talking books and plots even when you didn't want to.

To my daughter, Emma, thank you for giving the story a critical eye and being you. I'm always proud of you.

Morgan and Josephine, thank you for expanding my world. I love you two.

To the rest of my family, I love you guys. Thank you for being supportive and understanding when I would show up to hide and write at your house (Mom and Dad), or when I wouldn't show up at all because I needed to write.

My gratitude to my beta readers cannot be quantified. Thank you, Abbey Anderson, Abbi Wood, Annie Hurst, Beth Brockling, Casey Roach, Danielle Cordia, Ellen Smith, Em Daniels, Katie Rhyne, Kelly Hayes, Lee Pettijohn, Marisa Porter, Mary Carlich, Nichole Brewer, and Sarita Stevens.

Abbey, thank you for our book talks. I wouldn't have been able to finish this without those talks.

Annie, thank you for a beautiful cover. You are so talented. Thank you for your unwavering faith and endless encouragement.

Kelly Hayes, your photography made Adrienne feel real. Thank you for the cover photo shoot. It was such a big moment for me when being an author felt more real than it ever had.

Lyric, thank you for the manuscript review and proofread. I needed your professional insights and your hilarious commentary.

Shayla, my friend and my editor, your help with this book really started when we met in 2014. Your insights have helped me grow in the right direction. I'm not sure I would have found the confidence to publish this without you.

Thank you to everyone who has clicked follow or like on one of my posts on social media. Thank you to those who have bought the book, talked about it, and written a review. As an indie author, I wouldn't sell a single book without you all.

Most of all, I give thanks to God for making me who I am and guiding my steps.

MINDY SCHOENEMAN

Mindy Schoeneman has worked with horses and people, zeros and ones. She's been an adventurer in the Philippines and across the United States. She's survived a divorce, given birth to three children, and made it through three home purchases without going through a second divorce. She's always had stories to tell, and *Adrienne's Awakening* is her first official leap into telling fictional stories publicly. The novel is set in Missouri, which is where Mindy and her family reside.

Mindy writes sci-fi and supernatural tales infused with real-life experiences, people, and emotions.

Connect with Mindy on:
mindyschoeneman.com
Goodreads.com/authormindyschoeneman
Facebook.com/mindyauthor
Twitter.com/mindyschoeneman
Instagram.com/mindyschoeneman

Did you enjoy this book?
If you did, will you please leave a review on your platform of choice?
Reviews help others find this book and decide if it's right for them.

Do you want to read more from Mindy?
Subscribe to Mindy's email list
so you'll know where to find the next book, *Adrienne's Arising*.
You can sign up at mindyschoeneman.com.

Made in the USA
Columbia, SC
02 March 2020